# Praise for *The Art of Falling*

"Strikes universal chords in all of us who yearn, who love, who fail and fall, and struggle to find our way back home."

> —*Elizabeth Benedict, author of* Almost, Slow Dancing,
> *and* The Practice of Deceit

"Unfolds with grace and truth...refreshingly and piercingly honest."

> —*Kelly Simmons, author of* Standing Still *and* The Bird House

"The *Art of Falling* is a story of friendship and personal growth, and a helluva good read."

> —*Elizabeth Zimmer, dance critic,* Metro New York

"Craft presents her mesmerizing characters with depth, understanding, and ethos."

> —*Lana Kay Rosenberg, artistic director,*
> Miami University Dance Theatre

"Beautifully written and strongly emotional, *The Art of Falling* will move readers deeply. Kathryn Craft has penned a winner!"

> —*Jane Porter, national bestselling author*

"In her engrossing debut, *The Art of Falling*, Kathryn Craft takes her long-damaged heroine on a quest for healing and truth—true self, true family, true friendship. Craft's sharp and refreshing narrative will leave you pining for more."

> —*Julie Kibler, author of* Calling Me Home

RH

"In *The Art of Falling*, Craft weaves an eloquent story about an unhinged dancer, body image, true friendship, and finding the lost moments, which make us whole."

—*Priscille Sibley, author of The Promise of Stardust*

"Craft's debut novel lovingly traces the aesthetics of movement and gently explores the shattering pain of despair... A sensitive study of a woman choreographing her own recovery."

—*Kirkus*

"Craft, a former dancer and choreographer, captures the entanglement of pain and despair and beauty and hope that often knits our lives and, through the character of Penny, illustrates how self-acceptance is one of the greatest gifts you can give yourself."

—*Booklist*

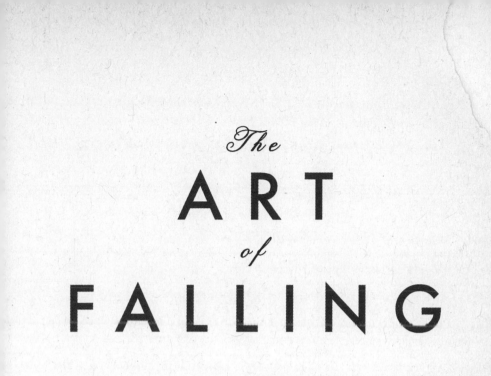

# *The*
# ART
## *of*
# FALLING

## KATHRYN CRAFT

sourcebooks
landmark

The characters and events portrayed in this book are fictitious or are used ficti-
tiously. Any similarity to real persons, living or dead, is purely coincidental and
not intended by the author.

Published by Sourcebooks Landmark, an imprint of Sourcebooks, Inc.
P.O. Box 4410, Naperville, Illinois 60567-4410
(630) 961-3900
Fax: (630) 961-2168
www.sourcebooks.com

Library of Congress Cataloging-in-Publication Data
Craft, Kathryn.
  The art of falling / Kathryn Craft.
      pages cm
  (pbk. : alk. paper)  1.  Women dancers--Fiction. 2.  Accident victims--Fiction
3.  Falls (Accidents)—Fiction.  I. Title.
  PS3603.R338A78 2014
  813'.6—dc23
                                    2013031054

Printed and bound in the United States of America.
VP 10 9 8 7 6 5 4 3 2 1

To Ellen,
who taught me
the meaning of
always

and

To Dave,
whose love
unlocked the stories

# FALL

"The very first thing I discovered was that the body's natural, instantaneous movement—its very first movement—is a falling movement. If you stand perfectly still and do not try to control the movement, you will find that you will begin to fall..."
—Doris Humphrey, modern dance pioneer

# CHAPTER ONE

*M*y muscles still won't respond. It's been hours since they promised a doctor, but no one has come. All I can do is lie on this bed, wishing for some small twinge to tell me exactly what is wrong. My body: a still life, with blankets.

I'd settle for inching my foot back beneath the covers. I command my foot to flex. To point. To burrow beside its mate. It ignores me, as do my hands when I tell them to tend to the situation.

Why has someone covered me so haphazardly? Or—could it be?—that in my dreams, I had somehow moved that foot? I will it to move again—now.

It stays put.

This standoff grows more frightening by the moment. If my focus weakens, I'll fall prey to larger, hungrier questions. Only motion can soothe me; only sweat can wash away my fear.

From somewhere to my right, I hear an old woman's crackling cough. My eyes look toward the sound, but I am denied even this small diversion; a flimsy curtain hides her.

I close my eyes against this new reality: the bed rails, a constant beeping over my shoulder, and the device clamped to my index finger. In my mind, I replace the flimsy curtain with a stretch of burgundy velour and relax into its weight. Sink. Deep. I replay each sweep, rise, and dramatic dip of Dmitri's choreography. My muscles seek aspects of motion: that first impulse. The building momentum. Moments of suspension, then—ah, sweet release. When the curtain rises, I will be born anew.

"Is time. *Merde*." The half-whisper I remember is intimate; Dmitri's breath tickles my ear. With a wet finger, he grazes a tender spot on my neck, for luck, then disappears among the other bodies awaiting him. My skin tingles from his touch.

The work light cuts off, plunging me into darkness. On the other side of the curtain, eleven hundred people, many of them critics and producers, hush. We are about to premiere *Zephyr*, Dmitri's first full-evening work.

I follow small bits of fluorescent tape across the floor to find my place. The curtain whispers as it rises. Audience expectation thickens the air.

Golden light splashes across the stage, and the music begins. Dmitri stalks onstage. I sense him and turn. Our eyes lock. We crouch—slow. Low. Wary. Mirror images, we raise our arms to the side, the downward arc from each shoulder creating powerful wings that hover on an imagined breeze. One: Our blood surges in rhythm. Two: A barely perceptible *plié* to prepare. Three: We soar.

Soon our limbs compress, then tug at the space between us. We

4

never touch but are connected by intent, instinct, and strands of sound from violins. I feel the air he stirs against my skin.

Other dancers enter and exit, but I don't yield; Dmitri designed their movements to augment the tension made by our bodies.

I become the movement. I fling my boundaries to the back of the house; I will be bigger than ever before. I'm a confluence of muscle and sinew and bone made beautiful through my command of the oldest known language. I long to move others through my dancing because then I, too, am moved.

Near the end of the piece, the other four dancers cut a diagonal slash between Dmitri and me. Our shared focus snaps. Dissonance grows as we perform dizzying turns.

The music slows and our arms unfold to reduce spin. Dmitri and I hit our marks and reach toward each other. We have danced beyond the end of the music. In silence, within a waiting pool of light, we stretch until we touch, fingertip to fingertip.

Light fades, but the dance continues; my energy moves through Dmitri, and his pierces me. The years, continents, and oceans that once held us apart could not keep us from this moment of pure connection.

Utter blackness surrounds us, and for one horrible moment I lose it all—Dmitri, the theater, myself.

But when the stage lights come up, Dmitri squeezes my hand. His damp curls glisten.

Applause crescendos and crashes over us. Dmitri winks before accepting the accolades he expects.

I can't recover as quickly.

No matter how gently I ease toward the end of motion, it rips away from me. I feel raw. Euphoria drains from my fingertips, leaving behind this imperfect body.

I struggle to find myself as the others run on from the wings. We join hands in a line, they pull me with them to the lip of the stage—and with these simple movements I am returned to the joyful glow of performance. We raise our hands high and pause to look up to the balcony, an acknowledgment before bowing that feels like prayer. My heart and lungs strain and sweat pushes through my pores and I hope never to recover. I am gloriously alive, and living my dream.

The dance recedes and the applause fades, but I'm not ready. My muscles seek aspects of motion—where's the motion?—I can feel no impulse. Momentum stalls. I am suspended and can find no release.

The curtain falls, the bed rails return, and I am powerless to stop them.

# CHAPTER TWO

*I* sensed someone watching me. How long had I been asleep? I opened my eyes and saw, staring back at me from the foot of my bed, a man dressed in white.

"Finally." The sound of my voice encouraged me, relying as it did upon the coordination of lips and jaw and tongue and vocal cords and diaphragm. Earlier, a woman from the hospital admissions office had only forms and questions; I needed action and answers. "You've got to get these drugs out of my system. My brain—it can't talk to my body. It's freaking me out."

"I'm not a doctor."

Salt-and-pepper hair parted on one side and a large nose slanting away created a question mark on the man's face that mirrored my own confusion.

"Then what's with the whites?"

"You don't recognize me? I'm the baker. From the first floor of your building. Marty Kandelbaum." He held a white box beneath his arm. "I had to come and make sure you were all right."

"Why?"

"I suppose it was the way you said your name," he said. "I heard such anguish. Such defiance. I've thought of little else."

"We spoke?"

"I was there when you…" He raised his eyebrows.

I waited.

"Had your…" The man looked around as if he'd left the rest of the sentence lying somewhere in the room. "You know. Your accident."

An accident—was that why I was here? I tried to remember something. Anything.

He patted my arm and gave me a sweet smile. "You're lucky to be alive."

*Lucky to be alive?* I took another inventory, head to toe—but felt nothing. Oh god. *Oh god.* "Where am I hurt?" Breath fragmenting, nerves sparking, room spinning—

A small woman burst into the room. She wore a navy blue suit and sneakers. Kandelbaum turned and put up his hand; she stopped.

"But I need to know if she's all right," she said.

The woman looked familiar. Important somehow—*think!*—but my brain felt as stagnant as my body. I slowed my breathing to take in more oxygen. My rib cage responded—thank god. Thank god it could move. I would never again take breathing for granted.

I asked Kandelbaum who she was, and he said, "You don't recognize her, either? You might tell your doctor." Behind the curtain, the old woman in the bed beside mine coughed several times, evoking a lifespan marked out with cigarette butts. In a raspy voice, she apologized.

Kandelbaum stepped forward and lowered his voice. "Memory

loss can be a sign of serious brain trauma. How many fingers?" He waved his hand so frantically I couldn't focus.

The woman in the suit pushed past him. She had a pointed nose and chin, and gray hair sprouted from beneath a little red hat. I tried to jump-start my memory by placing her in other settings; nothing about my life looked right from this pillow.

"Penelope Sparrow. It *is* you. I'm so glad you've come 'round."

"You know my name?"

"My dear." Her voice softened. "Of course I do. You are one of the most compelling dancers I've ever seen." Her gaze drifted over my covers, as if seeking some vestige of that dancer within its hilly landscape.

I pictured her face looking up at me from the audience. Wearing that red hat.

The woman reassembled her composure. "Plus, it's my job to know you. I'm—"

"Margaret MacArthur."

She smiled coyly. "I'm flattered."

One of the most powerful dance critics in the Northeast, MacArthur had covered the Philadelphia dance scene for decades. But I'd never met her. To me, Margaret MacArthur was a byline, an incisive opinion, and an aisle seat in Row L.

She held a pair of red gloves, each finger tinged brown with age. Beneath them she'd concealed a small notebook. She flipped open its cover. "How are you feeling?"

I'd somehow scored my first interview with a revered dance critic, and I couldn't answer her opening question. "Why do you want to know?"

Kandelbaum said, "She's writing an article."

"About what?" I said.

"I was filing a late review when your name came across the police scanner," MacArthur said. "My editor let me cover your story. I've been up all night waiting to hear if you're all right."

"Police?"

MacArthur looked at Kandelbaum, then back at me, and flipped rather awkwardly through her notebook. She did not look at ease in the role of reporter. "What do you recall about what happened last night, around one a.m.?"

I'd been here since last night. After some sort of accident. I gave my name to a worried baker. A tired dance critic is covering the story. And all I can think is, what story?

Once again Kandelbaum broke the awkward silence. "I don't think she remembers."

MacArthur nodded. She started to speak, then stopped, as if at a loss as to how to continue. Finally, she dropped the professional demeanor. "Perhaps if we back up to the last day you danced. How were you feeling then, dear?"

*The last day you danced.* The words pierced my heart. I struggled to keep my face neutral and my tone conversational, but my voice sounded watery even to my ears. "You know something about my condition. Have you spoken to my doctor?"

"Of course not."

"I know something about that." My roommate's voice drifted over from her side of the room. "Can we open the curtain?"

When Kandelbaum stepped forward, I said, "Let me."

The curtain hung just inches from my side. I was as determined to perform as I'd been in any audition, on any stage. I would lift my arm and open this curtain. And for a full minute or more, I tried. But the desire that boiled through my veins only succeeded in pushing sweat through my pores. My leaden body lay stiff. Even my hair felt heavy.

MacArthur watched my show of impotence. It was Kandelbaum who saved me from complete humiliation. "Don't worry, Penelope. I'll get it for you."

The charity in his tone unhinged me. *Damn.* I did not want to cry in front of MacArthur.

Ball bearings scraped in a recessed track as he easily swept the curtain aside and my roommate's world spilled into mine.

My first impression of Angela Reed was color. Color so rich and distracting it momentarily lifted my despair. My neck rotated, a small movement that a moment ago seemed beyond hope. Festive prisms dangled from the vivid Tiffany lamp on her bedside table. Sunset pinks, oranges, and purples draped her bed, and a half-moon rug warmed the floor. Even her cell phone had a fuchsia cover. Intricate construction paper flowers decorated the far wall.

MacArthur excitedly pressed pen to paper. "And who might you be?"

Angela spelled out her name. "It's so cool to be bunking with a celebrity," she said.

Only then did I look at her face. Angela wasn't the old woman I'd expected. When she smiled, her freckled nose crinkled. Kinky hair radiated from her head like sunrays. Beneath a nightgown swirled like Van Gogh's starry sky, she had the wisplike figure choreographers covet. A hot pink cast braced her forearm and right elbow.

My roommate's bed hummed as she raised its head. "Your surgeon came by while you were sleeping," Angela said. "He won't be back till tomorrow."

I craved this information—but not with MacArthur in the room.

"Surgeon?" MacArthur said.

"Your arm is broken, up near the shoulder. He pinned it," Angela blurted. "Your incision's about…" The fingers on her good hand estimated its size.

I made a quick calculation from Angela's sign language. Two inches. Maybe it wasn't so bad. But why no feeling—were the nerves damaged? I studied the topography of my blanket. My left arm lay useless across my rib cage.

Kandelbaum proffered the white box he'd been holding. I caught a whiff of danger—the same sweet, greasy scent coming from my hair. Why would that be? After an awkward lag, he opened the box.

"You brought me fastnachts?"

He nodded. "I made them myself."

"Why?"

He seemed wary, as if I'd asked a trick question. "I'm a baker."

"I've been to Independence Sweets," Angela said. "Good éclairs. But what's a fastnacht?"

"Fried dough," Kandelbaum said, with enthusiasm. "Eating fried dough before Lenten fasting is an old German ritual believed to expel the evil spirits that brought the dead of winter. So spring can come. You see, Penelope? Life begins anew."

He displayed the glistening brown lumps like a proud father. I scraped together the energy to say something polite. "They're shiny."

"I glaze them," he said, almost apologetically. "I sell more that way." I asked him to put the box on my bedside table, one short push from the trash can.

"How did we start talking about fried dough?" MacArthur said.

My roommate issued a breathy laugh that outlasted any amusement MacArthur's comment could have possibly prompted. It soon disintegrated into coughing so intense I feared she couldn't breathe.

"Do something!" I said. But Kandelbaum and MacArthur just watched in shock as Angela's face turned an alarming red. I crawled my fingers across the sheet, dragging my useless arm behind, and pushed the call button. "It's Angela," I said, hoping the intercom would pick up my voice. "She can't breathe."

A male nurse burst through the door with a cartful of equipment and yanked the curtain between our beds shut. My heart raced from the emergency and my adrenaline-fueled victory—I had moved my fingers.

Kandelbaum and MacArthur watched the curtain respectfully, as if it took respiratory distress to remind them that hospitals serve the ailing. I heard thumping, skin on skin. Choking sounds. Then, finally, wet coughs.

Angela said, "Put that away."

"But the doctor ordered it."

"Whose body is this, anyway?" she said. "Just write 'treatment refused.'"

The nurse reappeared, his face as red as his hair.

MacArthur put her pen in her purse. "I have to make deadline. I intend to see your story is told, Penelope."

Once MacArthur left, Kandelbaum moved to my side. "What were you doing last night? You could have killed yourself."

Exhaustion weighed down my eyelids, and there, in the darkness, I saw Dmitri. His hungry eyes, the waves in his hair, his taut body springing through space. *If only you would come home, Dmitri. Talk to me. Apologize.* When I opened my eyes, Kandelbaum awaited an answer.

A female voice from the intercom behind me said, "You rang for help, Penelope?"

"I did?" I looked down—I still had the call button clutched in my hand.

"Are you in pain?"

The enormity of my loss seized my heart, squeezing from it the last drops of my lifeblood. I answered, "Yes."

"We can give you more pain meds in another hour."

An hour. A gauntlet during which I could do nothing but let the second hand hack away at me with its razor-sharp edges.

"Here." Kandelbaum dunked a washcloth into a cup of water and pressed it to my forehead. The gesture felt unexpectedly intimate. I closed my eyes and meditated on the cool, the wet, and a man's caring hand against my brow.

"Why, you've spilled some juice on your sleeve," he said, blotting at my shoulder. Then: "Oh dear. Oh dear…"

I opened my eyes. The cloth in Kandelbaum's shaking hand was blood red.

The dance drew me back to the stage. I closed my eyes, and the burgundy velour dropped, and I hardly felt Kandelbaum rip the call button from my hand.

⁂

The second morning, when at last I had the opportunity to get answers from my surgeon, I felt too groggy to form complete questions. "Surgery? Again?"

"It was just a little bleed," he said. "We needed to go in and correct some vascular damage we hadn't picked up at first."

"What else?" I managed. "Besides the shoulder?" When I braced for the news, I was able to curl my fingers.

The doctor held an x-ray up to the light over my bed. "Nothing. Not one rib broken. Amazing." He swapped the film for another. "A smaller pelvis would have shattered."

My big bones. As if I needed x-ray proof. I whispered, "But I can't move."

"Have you tried today?"

What an ass. I aimed to prove my point by straining to lift my head from the pillow. My stiff neck engaged my abdominals, which in turn detonated hidden charges along the length of my spine. I took a breather, my grimace almost a smile. Pain: *Welcome back, you sonofa-bitch.* I tried again, funneling all my energy into isolating head flexors. Neck muscles shuddered, but my chin did move toward my chest.

My head dropped back onto the pillow. Without warning, the doctor pulled my arm from its sling and pushed it up. As if he had flipped a switch, my body screamed to life in excruciating glory. "What the hell?"

He typed a note into his laptop. "Your arm is stable. I pinned it."

After a lifetime of fighting this damned body, it was fighting back. The doctor left me to my private war.

Dance training taught me I could detach from physical pain if I controlled my breathing. In—two—three…out—two—three…in—two—three…out—two—three…. But before I could get a grip on the situation, a man who introduced himself as Dr. Tom walked in.

He asked my name. My answer, on an exhalation, was weak and breathy. He checked my answer against my wristband.

"I understand you're a dancer."

"I was."

"You've retired?"

"Look at me." My body remained hopelessly inert.

"How did you fall?"

This tidbit interrupted the rhythm of my breathing. "I fell?"

"You don't remember your accident? With the car?"

"I don't remember being in a car. Is this brain damage?"

"I'm not a neurologist. I'm a psychiatrist." He opened his laptop and hit a few keys. "It says here you live in the Independence Suites." He paused. "Number 1408." He paused again. "The apartment is rented to…" He scrolled the page.

"Dmitri DeLaval," I said, hoping to speed this up. "Or the University of the Arts, I'm not sure which." Another slow breath helped to both manage pain and allow time to seek other hard facts I might tuck in around my fuzzy memory. "The lease expires soon. Is it February 28 yet?"

"Tomorrow. Who is Mr. DeLaval?"

"He is…he was…the choreographer I worked for."

"Can you tell me how you got to the hospital?"

"Ambulance?"

"You remember?"

"I'm guessing."

He studied my face like a juror seeking signs of guilt. "Do you have a history of depression or suicidal thoughts?"

This brought our little quiz show to a dead halt. "Movement is everything to me."

He typed a note in his laptop and clapped it shut. "Your brain is working well. But the trauma you went through wiped your memory of it clean. That can be a self-protective mechanism, but it may be temporary. When you start to remember, you're going to need support."

Nurses, interns, blood work, bedpans. During a quiet moment later that second day, I asked Angela what was wrong with her. The simplicity of her response surprised me: she had fallen, too.

"But all it took to break my arm was tripping on the curb," she said. "I fell all of two feet. I've been embarrassed to say it, with all you've been through."

A volunteer arrived with dinner trays. Angela dug into her meal as if she hadn't eaten in weeks. Sometimes I wished I could eat with that kind of abandon. Happiness is so accessible for some people; it's as close as their next mouthful of food.

I readied myself for the challenge of picking up the fork. Bend elbow, flex digits, and…yes, yes, I could even raise my arm. I finessed a puckered lima bean toward my mouth.

"Yikes. Please tell me those are tattoos," Angela said.

I twisted my good arm as best I could. Like Angela's side of the room, my bruised skin sported sunset hues—although my purples, reds, and blues approached the edge of darkness. I'd never seen anything like it. "Can't imagine anyone doing that on purpose."

My roommate pulled open her bedside drawer and dipped into some sort of private pharmacy. Her willowy right arm delivered pill after pill to her mouth. I'd seen dancers take pills before eating, but never that many. If those were diet pills, she'd never sleep. If they were painkillers, she'd never wake. No kind of math allows "healthy eating" plus "exercise" to add up to her kind of slim. I'd known dancers who would fill their lungs with smoke, their veins with amphetamines, or the sink with the meal they'd just swallowed rather than gain a pound. They were never honest about what they'd done.

"You get all that for a broken arm?" I said.

"They're enzymes. This hospital doesn't have them on its formulary, so I can self-administer. I need them to digest my food."

That sounded way too technical to be a lie. "This food isn't worth the effort."

She laughed breathily, melodically, before dissolving into coughing. She lifted a tissue to her mouth.

"Sorry to do that during your meal. It's the CF. That's why I've kept the curtain closed—my last roommate asked for a transfer." She chucked the crumpled tissue into the trash.

"Cystic fibrosis?"

"That's one translation. One of my hospital friends used to say it meant Chronically Fucked."

I couldn't imagine a life with hospital friendships. I poked my fork through the salad, then put it down, working up the nerve to ask the question I'd been curious about since the first time I heard her cough; a question I knew better than to ask any woman; a question that if asked of me I'd certainly answer with a lie born of denial. "So how old are you?"

"Five months past the expiration date stamped on my butt." She looked at me with a mischievous smile. "I'm twenty-eight."

Her punch line sobered me. We were the same age. I wouldn't tell her I'd first assumed she was an old woman; there was too much truth in it to laugh about. With what I knew of CF, Angela could be near the end of her life.

She nodded toward the bakery box on my table. "The fastnachts still in there?"

"Dancers and doughnuts don't mix. Knock yourself out." I tried to reach for the box.

"I'll get them," she said. Matchstick legs swung from under her covers. She snatched the tubing from her nose and wielded the IV pole like Mick Jagger's microphone stand.

"Should you do that? Don't croak for a fastnacht."

"I don't need oxygen all the time. And what they don't know won't hurt them." She kicked our door shut, planted herself on the end of my bed, and bit into a doughnut. "So, your boyfriend's kind of cute."

"You know Dmitri?"

"I'm talking about the baker. Marty." She winked.

19

"He's old enough to be my father."

"He's sweet. And that newspaper lady—how famous are you?"

Dmitri had been the one to attract attention, not me. "Let's put it this way: no one's ever asked for my autograph."

"Ooh—can I have it?"

I thought she was joking, but she fetched a marker and held it out to me. "Shall I sign your cast?" I asked.

"No, hot pink's my favorite color. Here, sign this." She ripped off the top of the bakery box.

If only she were holding a program from my choreographic debut instead. But I coaxed my stiff fingers to perform and signed it anyway.

She held up the stained cardboard, admiring my signature. "I've met a few famous people, but this is the first autograph I've ever had that wasn't on a medical chart."

"I'm sorry it wasn't under better circumstances."

"Why be sorry? These *are* the circumstances. Life is life."

She lifted the doughnut again, reconsidered, then hopped off the bed and dumped the box into the trash.

"So were you cranky with the critic because you can't move yet, or did she write bad reviews about you?"

I took a moment to boil down a truthful answer. "The purpose of that woman's life is to judge mine. I can't bear to look at her." My voice cracked, damn it. I slapped away my tray table, satisfied that my palm could feel the sting. "I guess I'm Chronically Fucked, too."

She crossed over to her bedside drawer. "If you want something with more flavor, I'll split this." She unwrapped a Snickers bar, broke it in two, and tossed me half. It landed on my lap, rich chocolate on sterile white cotton.

"I don't eat candy."

"Your body won't heal without nutrients. Snickers have nuts. Protein."

I bit in. Chocolate and caramel bathed my taste buds in a sweetness I had denied myself my whole adult life. I shoved the rest into my mouth when I heard a knock at the door.

Kandelbaum walked into the room, holding a shiny red apple. He apologized for the fastnachts. "This is a better treat for a dancer, right?" he said.

Cheeks full, I looked over at Angela. She politely turned her giggle into a distracting cough. I forced the rest of the candy down. "You came back," I said.

"Given the extraordinary way we met, can you blame me?" Kandelbaum said. "And business has been crazy since Ms. MacArthur's story came out. It's been in all the papers—"

"MacArthur wrote about me, even though I didn't answer her questions yesterday?"

Angela spoke quietly. "It was in the *Sentinel* this morning. Front page. But it was already on their website last night." She held up her smartphone. "Marty and I read it online while you had your second surgery."

"It was also in *USA Today* and the *New York Times*," Kandelbaum said.

"It made *national* news?"

"It's a miracle you're alive," Kandelbaum said. "People celebrate miracles."

"Dmitri DeLaval—did they interview him?" The words flew straight from my heart before my head considered whether I wanted the answer.

He paused. "No. But there were photos of you both."

I closed my eyes to hide threatening tears. It had been almost three weeks since Dmitri stole the dance from my life. No longer able to bear the loneliness, I'd been rambling around our suite Monday night with the minimal movements of the almost-dead, winter biting my face. I shivered, agitating the muscles in my back.

"You're cold. Shall I ask for a heated blanket, Penelope?" I heard Kandelbaum's voice as if from a distance.

"No—I *was* cold. That night." My body told me—I'd been outside.

Kandelbaum returned to my side. "Yes?"

"I was standing on the balcony. There were only a few stars. And it was so dark down on the street."

"You were looking down?" Kandelbaum said. "Why?"

The memory rose from my gut. Its theaters may have been dark at that hour, but the Avenue of the Arts, a half block away, thrummed with the irresistible energy of a siren song. Bustling from studio to performance venue, it had been the beating heart of my world. But alone on that balcony, with fourteen stories of perspective, I'd finally seen how small my artistic footprint had been.

My pride plummeted. "Dr. Tom said I fell…"

Kandelbaum placed his hand on the elbow of my injured arm—supporting it, as if he would usher me across the bridge of memory. Angela got out of bed and grasped the other hand.

Once again they waited for my memory to kick in. Even though their discretion tried my patience, I was in no rush to remember. Once this accident sprang to life in full detail, I'd have to deal with it. But how? If I couldn't move, how would I ever deal with anything ever again?

The harsh truth: without movement, I didn't know who I was.

If I didn't find out soon, I'd lose my nerve. I blurted, "Tell me now or I'll get a volunteer to read me the damned newspaper."

They looked at each other, eyebrows raised.

"There were no eyewitnesses," Angela began.

Kandelbaum said, "But you landed on my car."

# CHAPTER THREE

*A* woman arrived to clear our dinner trays. Kandelbaum paced. When she left, he closed the door behind her.

"What I can contribute starts around two a.m.," he began. "I had gotten to work early, because of Fastnacht Day, and I parked in the alley. I never park in the alley—it's a no parking zone—but I would only be a minute, so I chanced it."

"I love that part," Angela said.

Kandelbaum smiled at her. How touching—they had already bonded over my misery.

"I cleared my counters of the fastnachts I'd boxed the day before and carried them out to the car. I set the tray on the roof and—"

"And?" I said.

"Bam! You landed right on top."

"Mind-boggling," Angela said.

This man had no reason to lie to me. And my body had obviously suffered severe trauma. Still, I couldn't believe I would star in such an outlandish tale without knowing it.

"I was afraid you were dead. But once I recovered from the shock—it was probably only a few seconds—I called 911. You were so still. But when the ambulance crew climbed on top of my car, you moaned. A paramedic called out, 'She's alive!'" Kandelbaum paused before adding, "I…I choke up now to think of it. Alive, Penelope! You scared me half to death when you spoke, though."

"What did I say?"

He tilted his chin slightly upward. "I am Penelope Sparrow."

He said each word distinctly; I tried to make sense of this implied drama. "I don't remember any of this."

"The photograph in the paper showed the dented roof of my car, along with some squashed fastnachts. You can see the sign on my window behind it."

"And MacArthur assumes I fell fourteen stories?" I said.

"Her article stuck to what facts she knew," Kandelbaum said.

Angela added, "She called it 'Fall of a Sparrow.'"

Fourteen stories. Unbelievable as that was, it had to be so—I didn't know anyone else in the building. What was my body made of, to survive that kind of fall? My fortitude impressed me. Kandelbaum seemed so emotional that I couldn't bear to tell him that if I could never move again, this miracle was wasted.

"Thanks," I said. "For telling me. And for getting me to the hospital."

"Meeting you has been a blessing for me. Today I sold more baked goods than any other day in the twenty-one-year history of my shop. If God wills it, maybe I can be a blessing for you."

For a minute he got me wondering. While this late-night drama played out on the great stage of life, had some unknown force indeed positioned Kandelbaum's car to save me? I couldn't buy it—in my experience, such machinations were the work of well-paid union stagehands, and no one would spend that kind of money on me. Anyway, a god with that much power could have put me on a European stage, dancing. With Dmitri. Far away from that fateful balcony.

Yet how else could I explain my survival?

Moments later, Margaret MacArthur again breezed into the room. Her diminutive size and pointy features made me think of a mosquito, and her attention was just as welcome. As Kandelbaum and Angela backed away from my bed, I whisked away the emotions Kandelbaum's revelation must have left on my face. The shock. The horror. The not knowing. If I stuffed much more inside my skin I'd explode.

"May I speak to you alone?" MacArthur said to me.

"This isn't a good time."

MacArthur pulled a chair to my bed. "You caught my attention the first time I saw Dance DeLaval. You stood out."

How sweet of her to remind me I'd never really fit in. MacArthur lowered her voice. "Trust me. I'm no investigative journalist, but I fought hard for this story. Now that we have national interest—"

"We? It would seem you don't need my input at all. I hear your article made quite the splash."

"We both know there's more to what happened here." She lowered her voice. "With your help, my exposé will make a difference. I'm the one to write it. I just need some facts."

"What exposé would this be?"

She glanced up—Kandelbaum did not try to hide the fact that he was monitoring the conversation. She leaned even closer. "You aren't the first dancer who's been pushed to the brink of despair over body type."

I couldn't breathe. Couldn't speak. Kandelbaum stepped forward. "You promised if I shared what I knew you wouldn't needle her."

MacArthur kept her eyes on me. "My readers want to know why this happened. Forgive me if this causes discomfort, Penelope, but you were dancing less—why would Dmitri cut your stage time?"

*Discomfort?* I felt like she'd slapped every one of my bruises. And if she knew anything about dancers at all, wouldn't she sense how deeply I ached for the movement the others in the company still enjoyed? We'd functioned as such a unit that I still couldn't imagine them replacing me. I imagined Dmitri's body inhabiting my former space on the stage, then slipping beneath my skin to engulf my inner space as well. I tried to harness his muscles to move my limbs—but Dmitri was never one to share his power. I remained motionless but for the quiver of my lip.

MacArthur added, "Sometimes talking about our problems helps."

"Talking to a therapist or a friend, maybe, but not the media," Kandelbaum said.

"Is it true you have no comment whatsoever, Penelope? When speaking out might help others? Please. This is personal."

"Damn right," I whispered.

MacArthur stood. Grabbed her handbag. Clapped her hand to

my bedrail and gripped it until her knuckles turned white. And all I could think about was how she took all of those small movements for granted.

"Why are you dancers so stubborn? Women need to know what can happen when they turn on their own bodies."

I shot Kandelbaum a pleading look, and he took MacArthur's arm. "It's time for you to go."

MacArthur took a deep breath. When she spoke again, her voice was saccharine. "I've been trying to locate Dmitri for comment. Do you know how to reach him?"

I managed only two words: "Get out."

"So you are angry with him?"

"Get out!"

MacArthur moved toward the door but stepped aside when a volunteer walked in, her face hidden behind a flower arrangement.

"Wow," Angela said. "Someone knows how to cheer a girl up."

The bouquet cut a fragrant path through the bleach, rubbing alcohol, and anxiety in the air. My skin tingled at the thought that the flowers might be from Dmitri. But wait—what did he think—or know—of what happened? I feared his words. I asked Kandelbaum to read me the card.

He plucked the envelope from the bouquet and opened it. "It says, 'From your friends at Dance DeLaval.'"

*Friends?*

I turned on the closest known irritant. "That woman in the doorway is from the media," I said to the volunteer. "Her name is Margaret MacArthur. I want her barred from my room."

Later that evening, a ringing phone woke me. Angela spoke through the pulled curtain. "Do you need me to get that for you?"

"I can do it." I labored through each painful twist and flexion until I got the handset to my ear.

"Penny, is that you? Penny?"

Despite the hysterics and the intervening years, I recognized my greatest cheerleader and harshest critic. "Mom?"

She picked up as if we'd left off yesterday. "Thank god—what a runaround. They didn't want to put me through. They said I *couldn't* be Penelope Sparrow's mother because their *computer* says her parents are deceased. I asked them, do I sound dead?"

"Sorry." It had seemed easier, when I was so out of it yesterday, to lie about those next-of-kin questions.

"Then they tried to make me leave a message. Why didn't they call me, I want to know?" I pictured her pacing the kitchen floor, strangling her fingers with the twisted phone cord. "I shouldn't have to find out something like this by reading the paper."

"Okay, calm down."

When she spoke again, her voice had lost its bluster. "Are you okay, honey?"

"That's what they say."

"Your beautiful body…I'll be right down."

"Maybe wait a bit."

"If I had thought for a moment you weren't happy…" Her voice sharpened. "I'll take off work tomorrow and be down first thing."

After I hung up, Angela spoke through the curtain. "That's

29

cool that she's coming. My mom works in Maryland and can't always break away when I'm in the hospital. A fact of my life—I'm here a lot."

"I've got to be well enough to walk out of here by morning," I said.

"Don't push yourself. Your mother will understand. These things take time."

"It will kill her to see me like this."

"Point of protocol: they don't let you leave while you're still using a bedpan."

I slept little that night, disturbed by images of my mother scraping my broken body from the sidewalk. She didn't know what to do with the pieces.

Near morning, I tried to summon the energy to rise. Motion denied.

*You look like you're dead!* I heard Bebe Browning's fingers snap to gain my attention, and recalled her voice as clearly as if I were fourteen and incurring her wrath in the dance studio. She fluttered over with caftan and frizzy hair billowing. *You are pausing as a courtesy, for the audience to appreciate your shape, but you can't stop dancing while you're doing it.*

Miss Browning, as I called her then, taught me of the power hidden within stillness. Could I harness that now?

I heard a door latch click—Angela had gone into the bathroom. When she was done, I'd take my turn.

I had to stop thinking of my body as a mannequin. Hadn't it already suggested I had movement yet to recover? I closed my eyes. Even across the dark backdrop of my eyelids, small particles knocked around in a crazed dance. I sent my awareness deep within my unresponsive muscles. It only took a few moments for my perspective to change: everywhere I looked I saw motion. Blood lazed through arteries. Fluids meant to push through membranes swirled, waiting instead for an invitation. Faint electrical charges pulsed a spastic rhythm. My body was functioning like a dance company on break; it was time to marshal efforts. I imagined again the snap of Miss Browning's fingers and urged everyone back to work. My physiology may have been pausing as a courtesy, so my traumatized anatomy could rest, but now it was time to move.

Leaning hard on the pain, I rolled to my side. Then, summoning every muscle that still had the grace to report for duty, I fought to sit up.

Such effort for this small reward.

My legs dangled over the edge of the bed. The floor may have only been an inch away, but its distance was dizzying. Fear of falling might have stopped me if my body hadn't already been slipping over the edge.

I transferred my weight slowly, tentatively, onto my feet. My quads quivered and complained, but at long last, I stood.

I inched forward, my sights fixed on the bathroom door. A trickle of sweat crept like a spider between my breasts.

The bathroom door opened. "Penelope!" The sudden light and Angela's startled cry dislodged my equilibrium. I started to fall, but

Angela rushed toward me. We stood propped against one another until I regained my balance. "You okay now?" came her muffled voice. "I can't breathe."

"Move away slowly."

It was a trip to the bathroom, not a debut at the Met, but I wore the sheen of sweat on my brow like a crown of triumph. My pain took its rightful place on the extreme end of a familiar spectrum. I no longer feared my brokenness. If I could move, I could heal. If I could heal, I could dance. I would probably remember, too, which scared me a little, but I could handle anything if I could dance.

When I emerged, Angela applauded, bless her, but the redheaded nurse didn't join in. He had the overhead lights on and was placing my clothes in a plastic bag. "Well, look at you," he said.

"So the doctors think I'm ready to leave?" I tried to look casual as I coaxed my trunklike limbs to life.

"Not leave. Move," the nurse said. "You can have a seat right here."

I stood before the wheelchair he held, but my legs refused to bend. "I can't."

Angela whipped back the curtain. She wore brightly striped socks and held scissors and construction paper. Behind her, on the wall among the handcrafted roses and tulips, hung the cardboard with my autograph.

I swayed with dizziness.

The nurse slipped his beefy arms around my rib cage. "Release your knees. I've got you."

"Where are you taking her?" Angela said.

"Psych."

Why did they think I needed psych now, when for the first time, I was starting to sense the power within me? I had fallen fourteen stories, rested a few days, and then walked to the bathroom! I didn't need psych any more than I needed to be shut out of our company's European tour. I needed to move.

"Then I'll sign myself out," I said. "I don't want treatment."

The nurse wheeled me toward the door smoothly, inexorably.

"Rest up while you can, Angela. You don't want a setback," he said. "We're transferring you to the CF Center at Presbyterian tomorrow. As for you, Penelope, this is not optional."

Angela grabbed her IV pole, peeled something from the wall, and crossed the room to lay it in my hand. A construction-paper tulip. I didn't know whether to laugh or cry.

"I'll come see you," Angela said. The nurse placed the huge flower arrangement from Dance DeLaval on my lap.

"Nope. Only family," he said. "And psych is locked."

Out in the cold, uncaring corridor, I shrank into anonymity, unable to find one sliver of identity to which I might cling.

Voices clashed at the nurse's station ahead. The arguing grew louder. I peeked between the flowers and saw the broad backside of the woman causing the ruckus. "Just try to stop me," she shouted.

Hundreds of pounds stormed in my direction. No one stopped her; I wouldn't have wanted to try, either. I ducked my head, wincing at the pain this caused my shoulder, and told the nurse to take me away.

Too late. My broken shoulder hit the quilting of the oncoming jacket. As unwelcome as the collision was, I drank in the scent of fresh winter air clinging to that jacket before the nurse backed up.

"Wait," the woman said. She leaned over and parted the flowers, revealing ruddy cheeks framed by dark curls newly tinged with gray. Her green eyes mirrored mine.

"Penny?"

Mom.

# CHAPTER FOUR

*M*y mother reached through the bouquet and caressed my cheek so tenderly I rested my head against her hand.

"They're moving me," I said.

"I know."

In bold defiance of visiting hours, my mother accompanied me the rest of the way.

Once the door to the psych wing locked behind us, we passed a cast of unwelcoming characters. Their eyes frightened me—some diverted, some masked by a strobe of mad blinking, some altogether devoid of animation. I tried to keep mine focused forward.

The nurse dropped my belongings, my flowers, and my mother at the office and wheeled me into a room. My new roommate hummed—at least I'd been paired with a musician. She didn't answer when I said hello. Or alter pitch. Or turn around—all I could see was the back of her torso and her unkempt hair. She sat cross-legged on her bed, staring at the wall, that same sound one long monotonous tone. I felt acutely the loss of my mother's presence.

The nurse moved me to a chair, removed my sling, and replaced it with a new gadget. Everything now attached with Velcro: the band circling my chest, and the cuffs attaching my wrist and upper arm to it.

"This is called an immobilizer." What a word—I felt claustrophobic already.

The sling I'd previously worn had a strap—did they think I was at greater risk to harm myself now, as opposed to the past two days? Or did they know something I didn't about the effects of a psychiatric unit?

When the nurse turned to leave, I suddenly feared his abandonment. His gaze drifted to my new companion. "Good luck to you."

I would have felt better if he'd said, "Break a leg." My roommate's monotone sliced the air with a desperate edge. "Wait."

The nurse turned.

"Could I have a piece of tape?"

"You're not going to eat it, are you?"

I opened my hand. On my palm, the unfolding flower Angela gave me slowly blossomed.

The nurse looped a piece of paper tape from the roll in his pocket, stuck it to the back of the flower. "You'll see your friends again. Don't worry," he said, and tacked the flower to the wall by my bed. Kind of crooked. Perfect.

A few minutes later, my mother scuttled into the room, carrying my sweatpants and sneakers.

"So I take it you weren't able to spring me?" I said.

"Maybe you should take advantage of this. Work through

some stuff. If I had thought things had gotten so bad you'd want to jump—"

"I did not jump."

"Really? Or you just don't want to tell me?"

"You're being melodramatic."

"This is serious, Penny. They wouldn't let you have your shoes back until I pulled out the laces. And mother of god, these bruises." She touched my arm, tentatively, then reached for me. The immobilizer made me feel like I was in the middle of a quick costume change gone awry, but the awkwardness didn't seem to faze her. She wrapped me in her soft flesh, as if to cushion me should I fall again.

When she pulled away, she said, "What on earth is going on with you?"

The let's-get-down-to-business voice, the look on her face—I felt like I was sixteen again and fighting off that last spasm of doubt before entering CAPA, Philadelphia's High School for Creative and Performing Arts. She'd said, "This cannot possibly be a mistake, Penny." She then invoked the mantra we'd repeated to all the public school teachers who felt dance was not a reliable occupation for a bright girl like me. "Who are the only people who need a fallback plan?" She waited a beat for me, and as always, I'd joined in: "Those who plan to fall."

As my mother pulled up a chair, it struck me that it had taken two years and the locked doors of a psych ward for my mother and me to have a conversation.

"I just wish you'd called me," she said.

"Me too." Right then, feeling protected by her love, I meant it.

"This looks bad right now," she said. "You've got to promise me you'll fight, Penny. Fight like a shark."

"You want me to eat my way out?"

My mother looked at me for a beat before we both cracked up. She bared her teeth and made chomping noises against my hand as if I were once again a toddler wanting raspberry kisses. Once she got her bouncy chuckle cranked up, I laughed even harder and had to breathe deeper. I felt like Pinocchio—part wood, part real—and here's Geppetto trying to make me dance, yanking on strings that had now become nerves. I closed my eyes and tried to take shallow breaths as my back spasmed something fierce, my mother still thinking we were having a grand old time. I sank my nails into her flesh until she ran for help.

Pain upon pain upon pain. I had to wait while a nurse made my bed and then tolerate the move into it before she rolled me onto my side. Soon I receded into a safe, sleepy place, where lamb's-wool walls insulated me from my mother's expectations, my roommate's hum, and the pinch of the hypodermic needle in my ample behind.

I felt my mother kiss my cheek and heard her parting whisper: "Sharks have to keep moving to stay alive."

Later that afternoon a nurse arrived to take me to group therapy, my head still muffled from the drugs and my back stiff as the shank of a new pointe shoe. I heard pounding on the locked door to the wing. I looked up—Angela and Kandelbaum were waiting at the door, their faces a vibrant totem pole through the narrow window. The nurse wheeled me past so quickly my smile didn't have a chance to rise to my face.

Dr. Tom opened the session by urging us to put our feelings into words. "It's freeing," he said. "Our words can build a bridge to other people so we feel less alone."

I was screwed. Dance: the great wordless medium.

Yet I had never known a purer form of expression. To open the heart with wide-flung arms; to melt as regret spirals through neck and shoulder and down through the spine; to rise again with feet planted defiantly upon the floor. When I was a child, that movement was powered by my own feelings. In my career, I moved because Dmitri told me to, in the way he told me to, summoning whatever emotion would spark the movement to life. This was both my job and my great joy. Until he left, and the movement died. I closed my eyes. For a moment I could almost feel my damp leotard clinging to my torso. Oh, how I missed it.

"Penelope, how about you?"

I opened my eyes and crash-landed back in the psych ward. "Excuse me?"

"You just survived what should have been a deadly fall. Then you woke up. How do you feel about that?"

I wanted to answer well, as I sensed that my release from psych hung in the balance, but all I felt was empty. From the drugs, the surreal circumstances, the trauma, the odd company, who knew—but no words came. Yet I wasn't so sure silence was my ticket out of here.

As I considered my response, the fingers on my right hand twitched against my thigh.

"I think I'm irritated," I finally said.

"Interesting," he said, nodding slowly. "Why do you think that is?"

"I need to move."

Dr. Tom took his time before speaking. "Do you want to move away from something, or toward something?"

Didn't he get it? I needed the movement so I could feel. In answer to my confused silence, he said, "Sit with that."

But I was done sitting.

When the session ended, I refused a ride and steadied myself on the hall railing for the long walk back to my room. Although my feet flopped like swim fins, I was grateful for their willingness to give it a go. A nurse pushed the wheelchair slowly beside me. For when I surrendered, I supposed.

Halfway down the hall, my legs started to shake, and I stopped as if interested in a framed poster hanging on the wall. It turned out to be a Patient Bill of Rights explaining the limitations of voluntary and involuntary commitment. I figured the nurse couldn't keep me from reading it, so I propped myself against the rail to rest. I skipped the first part since nothing about my trip to the psych ward was voluntary. I also skipped the part about the involuntary commitment of violent criminals—no one had mentioned I'd gone down shooting. I wasn't eager to give voice to the notion, but I knew why I was here. I scanned for the relevant words. It said that unless someone witnessed me trying to "commit the act" or "threatening to repeat the act," I couldn't be held beyond one hundred twenty hours.

"What's one hundred twenty divided by twenty-four?"

"Five days," the nurse said. Her turbo math impressed me until I realized this must be the most often-asked question around here. Reassured that my stay would not be indefinite, I found the strength to make it back to my room.

But the trip used me up. When I got back in bed, my whole body cried out. Only a syringe full of the aggressive, awareness-robbing pain therapy embraced in the psych ward finally lulled me to sleep.

I woke, disoriented. Time was difficult to parse in psych, where our room offered no window to the rhythms of the natural world. The walls were painted the bleak gray of boredom. My roommate sat cross-legged on her bed, humming. With nothing else to do, I listened.

The sound was like a bagpipe drone to which no one had added the pleasure of a melody. After several minutes, I could hear that its tone was far from monotonous; it surged and ebbed. Resisting the amplitudes of hope and despair, it cycled instead within a narrow band of highs and lows, fighting its way through the middle.

I did not know the woman whose heartache inspired this lament, but my pain aligned with hers, so minimally yet perfectly expressed.

In time the hum wavered, sputtered…stopped. My roommate's

head bobbed toward her chest; my heart beat faster. She had abandoned me for sleep, leaving nothing to distract me from the introspection I'd been so carefully avoiding.

As frightful, intolerable silence stretched on, I sought calm within the emptiness I'd felt the day before. But my inner being had since taken on the gloom and chill of midnight, and from its blackness arose the unwanted question: *What was I capable of?*

My sore body tensed against the answer. Was I battle ready, or poised to flee?

I brushed a tear from my cheek. Words pushed their way into the room.

"Was it"—muscles clenched, even my gut contracted—"was it suicide?"

My roommate gently snorted. I waited out the silence. She awoke and resumed her hum.

I welcomed the return of its soothing presence. My muscles unwound. My heart slowed. I sensed that I belonged, in this room, in this moment, and was disturbed now by only one sensation…

The way the word "suicide" had tasted sweet on my tongue.

After a few days of prescribed chit-chat, I decided my healing wouldn't come in the realm of talk therapy. Just because I suffered traumatic memory loss didn't mean I was out of my mind. If anything, I was out of my body. The conversation I needed to re-establish was neuromuscular. So I claimed my legal right to sign myself out of the psych ward.

I would not escape without a private audience with Dr. Tom.

"Your chart indicates you haven't been eating much. Is that normal for you?"

"I eat enough."

"It makes me wonder if perhaps, when you were out on that balcony, you may have fainted."

I smiled. To seem agreeable, so I could leave. "Your guess is as good as mine. But I've never fainted in my life. I'm strong as a moose. You've got to be, to withstand six hours of exercise a day."

"Six hours? That's excessive."

For crying out loud. This guy had "outsider" scrawled all over his forehead. "You don't earn a professional dance career by lying on a couch and eating bonbons. The effort may seem excessive to you, but it's necessary."

"Do you ever vomit after meals?"

"Oh lord. Please don't be so cagey. The very thought of bulimia makes me want to puke."

"Your chart says you weigh one-twenty. That's underweight for five foot ten."

"Keep in mind I'm a dancer *and* a woman. I lied."

"Then what is it, really?"

I paused. While I carefully tracked its daily fluctuations, I had never uttered aloud my real weight. I fiddled with a new calculation that would put me close enough to "healthy" to get him to back down without crippling my pride.

He lost patience. "Of course I could bring a scale in here—"

"Okay, okay. It's one hundred thirty-two."

He gave me another one of those x-ray stares, as if checking out my contours beneath the supersized sweatshirt my mother had lent me.

"Can we get the paperwork wrapped up? My mom will be here soon."

Dr. Tom released me grudgingly, and only after "prescribing" three well-balanced meals a day and handing me a vial of antidepressants. The orthopedist had to sign off, too. He wrote something on a prescription pad and signed it. I tried to decipher the words as he scrawled—Vicodin? Oxycontin?

No, when he handed me the slip of paper, I saw two words: "physical therapy." He would allow my body to heal me. Tears of relief sprang to my eyes.

Both doctors told me I could recuperate "at home," a term which had lost all meaning. With no other options, I had called my mother, who now huffed along beside my wheelchair.

I tried to tell myself everything would work out fine. My mother had always taken great care of me. She loved dance as much as I did, although that was both a blessing and a curse. For a woman of her bulk, the rigors of dance training were a physical impossibility, and weight loss was a mountain she couldn't scale. So she threw all her energy into supporting my career.

I feared she might be thinking that I had blown my big chance. A chance she'd never had. So when she acted as if all along it had been our big plan that I come home for Easter, the pretense ate at me. When she offered to drive me back to the Philadelphia hospital for rehab—more than an hour's drive each way—her generosity whittled away at what was left of my self-esteem.

I stuffed the feelings down. The independence I had fought so hard to earn had vanished. I hated to admit it, but I needed her.

When she opened the car door for me at the hospital curb, she reminded me how resourceful she could be: in her back seat sat my trunk. She'd gone over to the Independence Suites and somehow talked the super into fetching my stuff.

I would never again have to return to the apartment and face the concrete evidence of Dmitri's absence. The corner that had smelled of salt and musk, where he'd pile the contents of his dance bag each night—now odorless. The frame of the bedroom mirror, where he had tucked the picture of his parents—emptied. The couch that had chafed me for weeks because I could no longer get any rest in the bed we had shared—abandoned.

I would never again have to face the door to the balcony.

As my mother turned onto the Northeast Extension of the turnpike, she spoke loud enough to be heard over the talk radio station. "Did you know Miss Judith died?"

"No." The news shocked me—Miss Judith, my first and last ballet teacher, had the kind of life force you couldn't squelch if you wanted to. And I'd wanted to. In my adolescence, I'd fantasized her death in a multitude of settings. My favorite: Miss Judith flailing around in the ocean, finally drowning because she had no body fat to help her float or fight the chill. Even now, fourteen years since I'd seen her and with her body gone to dust, her words remained sharp enough to cut me down.

# CHAPTER FIVE

*I* was fourteen when my body first betrayed me.

I'll never forget when Miss Judith asked my mother and me to step into her office. I was mortified—this was where Miss Judith took people to chew them out. The thought of having to go in immediately put me on the defensive. I was a model student who picked up sequences of steps quickly. I could reverse them to the left without extra practice, a feat Miss Judith often asked me to demonstrate for the rest of the class. I ran through the studio rules—arrive on time, black leotard/pink tights/pink shoes, hair in bun, no gum—but could think of none I had violated.

Miss Judith stood behind her desk and asked us to have a seat. Her office was no more than a nook off one side of the waiting room, so I took the chair in the tight corner near the wall. My mother angled herself near the door, her dimpled thighs spilling over the sides of the folding chair.

"Listen, this is difficult to talk about, so I'll get right to the point," Miss Judith said. "Your daughter's body is changing. We often see it at this age. Breasts develop, hips spread, you know what I mean."

I wondered who she meant by "we"—Miss Judith was the only teacher I'd had for the past eight years. I wondered why she kept talking to my mother and not me. I wondered why she mentioned breasts—my training bra still had wrinkled cups. But I had to admit I wasn't blind to my increased inventory in the hips department. I had shared my concern with my mother while we were doing the dishes together that very week. She explained that muscles develop different ways in different people. My hips were perfect for the mambo, for instance, and my thighs were sturdy. Then she would put on Tito Puente, and we'd snapped our damp tea towels and boogied away my worries.

Miss Judith continued. "Penny is a very hard worker, and will no doubt be a success in life. She aims high. She says she'd like to attend the scholarship audition for the School of American Ballet's summer program." My mother looked at me and we both smiled. She was the one who had taught me to work hard and aim high, with constant references to dancers who achieved fame in like fashion. I worked harder than anyone else in the class, and everybody knew it. Miss Judith looked at my mother. "In order to avoid undue heartbreak, we need to steer her in a different direction, don't you think?"

Heartbreak? Different direction—what?

"I thought you were going to get to the point," my mother said.

"Pursuing a career in ballet will be a mistake. Penny has the wrong body type. Ballet choreographers want a long, lean leg to achieve certain aesthetic results—"

"She's five foot eight, how much longer do you want her legs to get?"

47

"—and to develop a corps de ballet with a cohesive look. Due to recent changes…" Miss Judith lowered her eyes and looked at some papers on her desk, as if to check facts. "Specifically, her hips, your daughter will not fit in. She's too big."

"My daughter is not fat." My mother nudged me. I stood but stared at the floor, a slab of meat without a voice. "Her belly is as flat as your chest."

Tiny Miss Judith flashed a smug smile, secure in the fact that for a dancer, neither large breasts nor curvy hips were a relevant standard of beauty. "Ballet is a cruel, unforgiving profession. I'd change it if I could, but…" Her gaze drifted to me.

"Perhaps she might try African," Miss Judith offered. "Or study choreography."

"My daughter is a beautiful dancer. The best you have here. I don't get this. I've paid you plenty, and always on time—"

*Stop, Mom. Everyone can hear.* I wanted to melt from my chair, slip under the door, and reform—with smaller hips—somewhere on the other side of town.

"Hope is not available for purchase at this studio," Miss Judith said. "Penny aspires to be a professional ballerina, and I cannot endorse her choice. Unless she would like to pick up baton, I suggest we remove her from the roster."

Until then I'd hoped my situation was still salvageable. But my mother wasn't quite through. "I shouldn't be surprised, a little thing like you can't have much heft to her brain," she said. "*You* were lucky to have *her*. You should have counted your blessings while you had the chance. Come on, Penny."

I'm sure my mother wanted to make a dramatic exit, but tension fizzled when the chair released her with a humiliating groan, and the vinyl door came off its track as she tried to sweep it open.

How had this happened? Any choreographer would have been pleased with the prepubescent version of Penelope Sparrow—narrow hips, flat chest, and long, strong legs. None of the womanly lumps and bumps that would detract from a clean line. That day I needed to go home and see my father's face light up when he saw the girl I still thought of as me. To hear him call me his "mysterious little artist," his smile promising that my identity would not be tainted by the inappropriate blossoming of my body. I wanted to bury myself in his arms until I felt reassured, from a source I trusted more than my overly invested mother, that I was still beautiful and worthy.

But my father never came home that night.

And by the next morning, he was dead.

For a month we moped around the house, my father's customary absence now concrete, my future in dance an unspoken question between us. My mother and I poured our displaced creativity into the embellishment of Jell-O. It seemed the perfect choice: it is one of the few foods that can sustain movement. One day, while eating lime with cottage cheese and pineapple, we read in the paper that Muhlenberg College was bringing Bebe Browning in from Philadelphia to teach evening modern dance classes. The possibility of a fresh start inspired me to phone for more information.

Because I was too young for continuing ed classes, I had to

meet with Miss Browning for a private audition. My mother was asked to wait outside. Miss Browning demonstrated steps, which I repeated. Her movement called, I responded. She pulled things from me and I pushed my limits—and soon we'd lapsed into one of the most exciting conversations of my life, held entirely without words.

I fell hopelessly in love, both with my new teacher and with modern dance. Fall and recovery, contraction and release—this language spoke of the effort it takes to create meaning in life. My body had loved the exacting standards of ballet, but modern dance claimed my imagination as well. Engaged in co-creating every movement—adapting it to my body, interpreting Miss Browning's ideas, seeking a story within each dance that made sense to me—my mind was too busy to cave in to new anxieties about my shape.

During my junior year, I drew the first boundary between my mother and me, and moved into the small apartment above Miss Browning's studio to finish high school at CAPA. Leaving my mother was hard, but necessary if I were to dance my dream instead of hers. Once I pressed my bare feet to Bebe's floor, I never wore a pair of pointe shoes again.

Or ate Jell-O. Having a wiggle in your middle may have been perfectly acceptable to my mother, who ran the candy factory she'd inherited, but I was determined to succeed at weight maintenance where she could not. For this I would credit Miss Judith.

Now that I'd returned to dance, I vowed to do everything in my power to never again inspire such humiliation.

"It was breast cancer," my mother was saying. "Miss Judith was only forty-eight. I guess the school is closing." She paid the toll and pulled through the booth. "Hey, you could reopen it. Wouldn't that be a headline full of poetic justice? 'Rejected Ballerina Returns after Successful Professional Career.'"

"I can hardly walk."

"Martha Graham choreographed from a chair for years—"

"She was almost a hundred years old." I didn't bother asking her to stop making such comparisons, though. My mother had always seen me on par with the world's legendary dancers, living or dead. When I was young, it thrilled me to hear I was as quick as Kirkland or as quirky as Tharp. But I was starting to wonder if, when she looked at me, she really saw *me*.

"We'll have plenty of time to check out the want ads. I have the new issue of *Dance Magazine* at home and I already circled a bunch. I know the director of the arts council, too. He might have some leads."

"You don't even know what I've been through—"

"And whose fault is that?" she snapped.

She let the question dig at me while we passed the Cape Cods and ranch homes of the neighborhood. Our corner lot created the illusion of property expanse in an area where most of the houses butted up one against the other. But still, the brick ranch looked smaller than I remembered. The ivy my mother had planted at the end of the house after my father died now swallowed the whole wall and crept along the rain gutters above the garage door.

"Listen," I said. "You'll have to be patient. I can only take this one step at a time. Literally."

My mother parked the car in the driveway. If the garage weren't full of junk, she could have put me three short steps from the family room. "I'm willing to help you, Penny, but you have to promise me you aren't going to try this again. If I'm going to wake up one morning and trip over your body on the way to the coffeemaker—"

I gazed out the passenger window at the impossibly long trip to the front door. "Come on Mom, think about it. If I jumped off a building without dying, what could I possibly try next?"

When the car rocked gently, I turned. My mother was sobbing. How could I comfort her, when her imagination was more real than any memory I had of the event? But her grief did pain me: my own mother thought me capable of self-destruction. I'd left the notion behind—I had to. What energy I could muster had to go toward healing.

My more immediate struggle with the car door brought her around. Once she'd helped me into the recliner in the family room, she scurried around the house ablaze with energy. She fetched me some water, then bustled back to the kitchen to make dinner, all the while muttering that everything would be fine now that I was home.

I quickly fell asleep. Sometime later, the smell of fennel and the sizzling of sausage woke me. I had a pain in my side—the bag with the pill bottle Dr. Tom had given me was wedged between my hip and the arm of the chair. I pulled it out and studied the leaflet. The antidepressants had a longer list of side effects than benefits. Among them: memory loss, inability to concentrate, and—the pièce de résistance—weight gain. I ripped up the leaflet.

My mother kindly set aside her disappointment when I said I wouldn't join her for dinner. It took a few minutes and most of my remaining energy to free myself from the recliner's embrace before heading to my room.

As I labored down the hall, I was surprised to find the collection of framed dance posters lining the wall had grown. Especially since I hadn't considered my mother's house my home for twelve years, and hadn't been back to visit since leaving for New York City six years ago. During my youth, she had bought one each year to commemorate my birthday.

Within one of those frames, hanging at the end of the hall, the contours of a body I knew only too well confronted me. He crouched low, arms spread, voracious eyes stalking me in a pose from a solo work I had helped him develop. It was a poster for Dance DeLaval's debut at the Kennedy Center, and my mother had hung it right next to the door to my room.

I braced myself against the doorframe and looked back at my mother padding down the carpeted hallway behind me, folded sheets in hand.

"Why is this here?" I said.

"You deserve a place on this wall." The conviction in her voice made every single cell in my body ache. My circumstances were hard enough to face without adding what I may or may not "deserve" into the equation. "Those performances were the highlight of your career." Fingerprints already smudged the glass where she now placed her hand. "This one's *Puma*, right?"

Maybe I should have taken comfort in this display of maternal pride. But seeing Dmitri on the prowl right next to the room where I had dreamed as a little girl rattled me. "I told you I didn't need help."

"And I heard you, Penny. But how are you going to get these sheets on the bed with only one arm?"

How was I going to live without the career Dmitri yanked from under me? I grabbed the linens from her and whipped around fast enough that my good elbow hit Dmitri with a satisfactory snap. I was so bruised already it was like using mincemeat as a weapon, but the poster crashed to the floor.

My mother stared down at the web of broken glass over Dmitri's face, her mouth agape. I shook with a torrent of emotion: pain and rage mixed with an equally disturbing desire to laugh.

"Oops," I finally said, and let myself into my room.

# CHAPTER SIX

*D*mitri DeLaval. Dmitri DeLaval.

I used to love hearing him say his name. A quick two-syllable climb up a mountain and a three-syllable slide back down. I never would have met him if Bebe Browning had accepted me into her company, as was my hope. But years of studying with her and teaching for her never resulted in an invitation. Finally, after graduating from the University of the Arts, I worked up the nerve to broach the subject.

"Is that what you're hanging out here for?" Bebe, as Miss Browning now insisted I call her, had finished fitting her company members for new costumes and was rolling her measuring tape. "You wouldn't fit in. Performers like you command the stage. You're solo material."

"Then why can't you give me solos?"

"You wouldn't be happy here. Not for long. You're a creative, darling. Your name will be in lights. My girls are just dancers."

I couldn't believe it. Another teacher was cutting me loose. And this time—because I was too good?

"Come on, Bebe."

She reached up to grab me by the shoulders—I was taller by a head—and nailed me with her pale blue eyes. When she spoke, I caught glimpses of the discolored front tooth she tried so hard to conceal. "You need to move to New York."

"But I work here—"

"You're fired." She picked up her clipboard, ripped off a piece of paper, and scrawled a phone number onto it. "I have a friend who juggles sublets. She should be able to hook you up with another dancer for housing."

"You can't do this to me."

The green caftan she wore over her dance clothes swept the floor behind her as she moved to the door. "Consider this sparrow pushed from the nest. You have a brilliant career ahead of you. Go. Dance."

I showed up for work the next day—at least I peeked through the window, still unsure of whether or not she was joking—but someone else was preparing to teach my advanced modern class.

Once I got settled in New York, I learned just how inconsequential my college degree in dance would be. I combed websites and trade publications for opportunities and tackled auditions. I managed to score a few special projects as a pickup dancer, but nothing with a contract. I watched my first roommate come and go as she won a position with a modern dance company in the Midwest.

Frequent callbacks provided enough hope to try again. I was so close. But hope couldn't pay the rent: I needed a dependable job to support my career. Even after replacing my departed roommate as sales associate at the Capezio dancewear store, I couldn't afford to live alone.

I again contacted Bebe's friend. This time she sent me Suzanna Franke, who dreamed of Broadway by day and waited tables by night. She never worked as an actress the entire time we lived together, but she lived the life of an actor wannabe and that was enough for her.

I wanted more.

During one of our Sunday evening phone calls, I admitted to my mother that I could no longer afford to take classes. I'd been signing up for any free audition I could, just to stay in shape.

"Are you eating?"

"Enough." I'd had two plums for dinner.

The phone was quiet for a few moments. "Mom? Are you still there?"

"I was figuring. I can do it. I'll pay for your classes."

"I'm twenty-two years old. I don't want a handout."

"Call it philanthropy, then. Listen, Nureyev wasn't much older than you when he defected to Paris with all of ten bucks in his pocket. Others helped, and he turned out to be a worthy investment. And it won't be for long. At this point, it's a numbers game. Your turn's coming soon."

But audition after audition, month after month, year after year, I'd make it through callbacks, then stand before my jury. Sweat would ooze from my pores as if my entire body were crying while one artistic director after another looked me over, head to toe, then shook his head.

Time and again I drew inspiration from Bebe's enduring belief in me and my mother's cheerleading: Tomorrow was another day. If they don't want you, then you don't want them. Something better was waiting around the corner.

By the time I was twenty-six, my mother's interest in philan-thropy had worn as thin as her platitudes. She said, "If the candy factory ate money like this, we would have shut it down years ago. You're going to have to move back home."

I hung up the phone determined not to speak to her again until I could make a go of my life in dance.

Later, while I was icing my knee, my roommate Suzanna begged a favor that would change my life. She pinched her dark eyebrows, flicked at her pale hair, and said, "Tina is coming into the city next weekend. She heard about some Russian guy coming to audition dancers for an out-of-town company. It's her first audition. Could you go along and show her the ropes?"

"Sure," I said. "Who's Tina?"

As if I needed one more reminder that my career possibili-ties were pinched by a looming expiration date, she answered, "My daughter."

*Give me a break.* Yet by the time I next received an incoming call with my mother's name attached to it—one I did not pick up—I'd already left New York City for a new life.

In the bedroom of my childhood, I woke to the sound of my mother pounding on my door. "Penny! It's almost time to leave for your physical therapy appointment. Are you okay?"

My eyes snapped open, frantically seeking my ballerina alarm clock. Her painted arms sloped gracefully down the clock face, as always, but she held her legs above her head in an impossible V.

Eleven o'clock? I'd missed class. I leapt from the bed—or tried to, anyway—before slamming back into my current reality.

I struggled out of bed, shuffled to the door, and opened it. "Why didn't you come in and wake me?"

"I was afraid."

"To come in? It's your house."

"I didn't know what I'd find. You've been quiet so long—I thought maybe you'd taken pills or something…"

Which did she fear more: that she'd find me dead, or alive? Defeated and defenseless, I had to turn away.

"You don't believe it happens? Patrick Bissell was one of American Ballet Theatre's shining stars when he overdosed."

"He was also an addict."

Shouldering my own fears was hard enough; adding hers squashed my spirit flat. Should I have flushed those pills? I felt so low I doubted whether an overdose of antidepressants could have released me from it. Most of the night I'd relived a past as frustrating as my present, save one thing: back then, even when hope was in short supply, I had danced.

I aimed my body toward the closet. Put it in motion, as dancers do. Each step forward an agonizing effort. I had assumed correctly that my mother had put some of my clothes away while I napped the day before.

She picked up the sheets from the floor to make my bed. She was right—I'd been unable to do it myself, so I'd slept on the mattress pad. She opened the fitted sheet with a snap and let it float down to the surface, muttering. "I shouldn't have stayed out of your life. I knew you were dancing so I thought everything was fine. But I should have kept calling. Or insisted on seeing you. Or had Bebe check up on you. Or—"

"I wasn't trying to hurt you!"

She stood with a pillow in her hand, stunned into silence. As if she had forgotten I was even in the room.

I looked at the clothes I held, wondering how to get them from my hand onto my body.

The phone rang.

"We have to leave in ten minutes," she said quietly, then went to the kitchen to answer the phone.

Through trial and error, I found my way into a short-sleeved button-down blouse. Its frilly collar would look ridiculous with the black sweat pants I planned to wear, but it was the easiest top to get into.

My mother returned. "It's for you."

"Who is it?" I couldn't imagine anyone knowing—or caring—that I was at my mother's house.

"I didn't ask." She handed me a portable handset, which I set on the bed. "Mom, first…" I pointed to the sweatpants lying at my feet, an impossible distance away. "Could you?"

She labored onto her knees and slid the pants up my legs, politely refraining from exclaiming about their color. I'd checked them in the full-length mirror—now nine days since my fall, my bruises had turned a deep blue-black. After she helped reattach the immobilizer, I thanked her and picked up the handset.

"Penelope, please don't hang up. This is Margaret MacArthur from the *Philadelphia Sentinel*."

I steadied myself with as deep a breath as my back muscles would allow.

"Penelope?"

"How did you get this number?"

"I called all the Sparrows in the Lehigh Valley phone book. There are only eight."

"Why are you calling?"

"Our readers want a follow-up. Are you doing better?"

"Let's see. I can shuffle a few steps farther. Good luck turning that into a Pulitzer. I'm not half as interesting as you think."

"I disagree. I followed Dance DeLaval to New York, once, for your debut at the Joyce. I wrote about it. I believe it was right after Dmitri appointed you rehearsal assistant—"

"I have to go." It was then I noticed the frame on my desk. Why was it out? Years ago I'd tucked it away. In its picture, I was seven, waiting in the wings for my first recital. My entrance was imminent, but my mother had called my name from the wings and taken the photo when I turned to her. My face was flushed from warming up and a bit too much rouge. My mother had slicked my hair into a bun and added a glittering tiara; the whole ensemble was lacquered into place with hairspray. Huge front teeth crowded baby teeth on either side, but I couldn't deny the way she had captured the beauty of anticipation: I would soon dance.

I folded the frame and put it back in the drawer.

"Do you still have my number?" MacArthur was saying.

"I won't need it."

"I'm not the enemy, you know. My recommendation helped

Dmitri get the residency at the University of the Arts. I've known him his whole life."

I madly re-sorted the facts of Dmitri's life as I knew them.

"Are you still there, Penelope?"

"He never mentioned you that way."

"Of course not. He feared if people found out, it would undermine the authority of my reviews of his work. But I studied ballet with Ekaterina Ivanovna in Paris. She emigrated from Russia the summer after he was born."

"His mother."

"I've kept my eye on his career."

My mother—the self-appointed guardian of my career—waved to me from the hall.

"I have to go."

My finger was poised to disconnect the call when MacArthur added, "I found out where he is."

He. Even the personal pronoun had the power to choke me up. Then choke me. Gag me. I couldn't speak, couldn't hang up.

"His tour has dipped into northern Africa."

"I don't care." I shouldn't care. So why did my pulse race at this morsel of news? We were still connected, Dmitri and I, whether pushing together or pulling apart, because what art had joined no man could put asunder. He was still accelerating toward his goal; I, reaching back for what I'd lost, had created my own terminal velocity. Now Dmitri had custody of work that shared our creative DNA. MacArthur's unwitting implication dawned on me: I had not been left behind after all. Not completely. Dance DeLaval was performing choreography built on my body, shaped with my movement, for an international audience. With a gnawing hunger, I craved what MacArthur knew of Dmitri, of the others, of how African audiences received it.

My mother reappeared at my door, this time with her purse over her arm and the car keys in hand. I dropped the handset as if it were hot. As if my mother had caught me, once again, hurting myself while reaching for dreams she'd stored too high.

"So who was it?" she said.

"Margaret MacArthur."

She picked up the handset, almost as if she might flick it back on to see if MacArthur were still holding. "The *Sentinel* critic? You didn't even say good-bye."

"New priorities, Mom. If she can't help my body heal, then she isn't all that important."

"But the influence she could have on your career—"

"Please." I waddled through the doorway and into the hall. My mother had cleaned up the broken glass and removed the poster. "I'm not going to worry about what critics think as I relearn to walk."

"I'm just saying it wouldn't hurt to be polite. Someone like Margaret MacArthur could be a powerful ally."

"She bugs the shit out of me."

"Penny."

"Just keeping it real." As we passed the kitchen, I grabbed an orange from a bowl on the counter, then continued chugging toward the front door. "If you're all hell-bent on being my agent, you talk to her next time."

"Exactly my point. You hung up on her. There might not be a next time."

63

# CHAPTER SEVEN

*M*y therapist unfastened the Velcro on my immobilizer and slipped it from around my chest. It had been a while since a man's hands had so tenderly removed an article of my clothing. Without it, I felt vulnerable and impetuous and infinitely more alive, right down to the fine hairs now exposed on my arm.

"You won't need this in here," he said. "We'll help your body heal itself through movement, not rest."

He spoke my language so beautifully I almost giggled. I could tell he had personal experience with the benefits of muscular contraction by the way his knit shirt draped across the rolling landscape of his shoulders and chest. He was about my height, with dark shiny hair. His nametag said "Mauricio T."

"So, Penelope Sparrow," he said, reading the name from my chart, "why are you here?"

The very question I'd been asking myself since waking up in University Hospital nine days ago. I pointed to the thick chart in his hands. "Don't you guys ever read those things?"

He smiled. Handsomely. "I've never met a woman whose

fourteen-story flying experiment resulted in an unexpected new chapter of life. I guess I want to hear it straight from you."

"I move like I'm ninety years old. I want to turn the clock back a bit."

"I imagine we can accomplish that, as long as you're ready to work. Physical therapy isn't easy."

"I'm used to hard work. In fact, I miss it."

"Is that why you dressed up for the occasion?" He fingered the lace at the collar of my blouse. "Nice touch."

I tried on a smile for size. "The muscle spasms are the worst. It's hard to breathe, sleep, walk…did I mention breathe?"

"Have you been using ice?"

"I'd have to stuff myself in a chest freezer to get ice on everything that's sore." Mauricio laughed. "I've put it on the shoulder, though."

He had me lie face down on a cushioned massage table and propped my bad arm on a low stool to one side. Already I was more comfortable than I'd been in recent memory. He affixed sticky electrode pads to my upper and lower back, explaining that they would stimulate the muscles along the length of my spine to relax them. On top, he placed a moist heat pack.

The stimulation therapy felt weird. When it came to my muscles, I was used to being in control. But when he dialed up the machine, they became independent, playful caterpillars, climbing over one another under my skin. The heat relaxed me. The caterpillars started to spin a cocoon and I felt…so…so…

"You look so cozy I hate to wake you up." A dimple in his left cheek punctuated Mauricio's crooked smile. He peeled the sticky pads off my back, apologizing all the while for tugging at my bruises. "Time to roll onto your back."

I tried to tuck my good wing under and roll, but halfway through this bravura movement, I slammed into an invisible wall of pain and got stuck. My body, trained over the course of a lifetime to push past the pain, now ignored me.

I didn't appreciate the way Mauricio studied me as I struggled. "Could I get some help here?"

"I was wondering when you'd ask," he said. Instead of a hand, he offered verbal prompts. Following them, I climbed off the table, turned around, sat. Holding on to a rail with my good arm, I eased myself to a reclining position. I could grasp the concept of moving within limitations—we all have them—but the smallest effort was now a freaking production number. I felt like an idiot. Tears pooled in the corners of my eyes.

"You okay?"

I took a deep breath and nodded.

"We're going to bend your knees up to your chest—that's it— I'll hold them. Are you sure you're okay?"

I wanted to move so badly that even if I weren't okay I wouldn't have told him. "Yes."

The stretch hurt in that good kind of way. Like I knew it was doing something positive. Such a small accomplishment, and yet I felt encouraged.

"Now the hamstrings. Relax your right leg. Give me all its weight and let me do the work. We'll stop when you tell me it hurts."

He raised my leg until it pointed straight up at the ceiling. "You're already within normal range. You still with me?"

"Yes," I said. Or maybe grunted. Normal? Please. "Keep going."

He pushed another forty-five degrees. "How's that feeling?"

"I'm good." It had started to pluck my taut back muscles something wicked, but I didn't want him to stop. When body motion stops, body judgment begins, and I did not want Mauricio's opinion of my potential swayed by the size of my thighs. And it was only my back complaining. My leg felt great.

He kept pushing; I kept testing myself.

In another few moments, my back was screaming for mercy and a tear had spilled down my cheek—but my leg was lying on my torso.

"You a dancer or something?"

I was hoping I'd impress him. Extraordinary effort would invite the extraordinary attention I'd need for the results I sought.

Half-inch by half-inch, Mauricio lowered my leg toward the table, allowing my back muscles time to readjust. His pen scratched across the paper as he wrote a lengthy note in my chart, then he looked up at me with an accusing glare.

"The muscles in your back are balled up in knots so big I can see them. What I just did to you must have hurt like the devil. Why didn't you tell me to stop?"

Pain had never before seemed relevant. In fact, I'd partnered with it. In order to stay in top form, I'd pushed muscles and joints to their limits, and learned to live with a gnawing hunger I'd never fully sated. One time, I broke my big toe during a performance—actually heard it snap—when another dancer blew his entrance and we collided. But what could I do? I taped it up and headed back onstage. Breathed deep to fight the nausea.

All I knew was a whole different kind of pain would result if I left therapy with my sides uneven. So I said, "Can you stretch the other leg, too?"

Mauricio laid down the law: pain must be our guide. I needed to tell him when it hurt. Only I could draw the line, he said, between what might help and what might cause lasting damage.

Later, at home on the living room floor, my mother's underused exercise mat crackled beneath me as I exchanged the equivalent of a doctorate in movement for Kindergym. I intended to practice gauging my pain response, I really did, but my raised leg was so stiff I once again found myself pushing through the pain. Once it loosened up, I added a syncopated rhythm, lowering the leg slower than I'd raised it. Lift up—two and down—two—three. Up—two and down—two—three.

Two beats up a mountain and a three-beat slide back down.

The day of my audition for Dmitri's company in New York City, Suzanna's daughter, Tina, and I arrived early enough to register before anyone else. I grabbed number "1" and pinned the "2" above her perky, petite breast. I had to hand it to her: at nineteen she kept her body fat so low I wondered if she'd yet started to menstruate.

While we were warming up in the studio, Tina told me what she knew about Dmitri. I found it easier to listen when not looking at her; the blue she'd streaked into one side of her blond hair distracted me. It seemed the buzz surrounding Dmitri was in his genes: his mother, Ekaterina Ivanovna, was the prima ballerina from the Bolshoi who defected to France in the early 1970s. "The media was all over it," Tina said. I nodded; I'd read about Ivanovna. Her husband was a French diplomat.

"So what's he done?" I said.

"Nothing, yet. He wants to set up a big modern dance school in Russia and start a company."

"Then why's he here in the States?"

"Word is he wants to brush up his choreography before he puts it on the world stage."

Modern dance was all about the pioneers of expression, and in Russia, a country still wriggling free from the constraints the Communist government placed on artistic content, Dmitri had identified a new frontier. Outside of cultural centers like Moscow and Leningrad, the form had barely been encountered. Fetching the banner of artistic freedom and planting it in Russia was an endeavor I immediately latched on to. Any dance job would have affirmed my mother's tireless faith in me, but this was more than a job—it was a cause. This would be the sort of achievement my father would be proud of.

Caught up in my own thoughts, I didn't give Tina any coaching at all before Dmitri entered. He instantly dominated the room. He was tall, over six feet, with the kind of lean, tapered torso that before I met Dmitri I had always called a "swimmer's body." Even his hair moved well, with the light skipping off brown, shoulder-length curls. Instead of a pianist, an ensemble had set up an unusual array of instruments.

The sum total of my advice to Suzanna's daughter consisted of five whispered words: "It begins now. Absorb everything."

Dmitri tied his hair into a ponytail as a *djembe* player slapped out a seductive beat. A-one-AND-two-AND-three, four. Dmitri faced the mirror and swayed side to side as if to absorb the rhythm, accenting with elbow, shoulder, or head on the upbeats, stroking long through the air with arm or leg on the downbeats. I recognized the same sinuous, earthy movement Bebe had introduced me to; my body couldn't help but follow along. In the mirror I saw dancers behind me stop their chattering to watch, no doubt fearful they had somehow missed the official start of the audition.

Dmitri signaled for the drummer to pause and turned around.

"Now, please." He gestured to us with his hands, palms up. "You do." He turned to the drummer. With a downward stroke of Dmitri's hand, the drummer once again picked up the beat. Dmitri crossed his arms and waited for us to begin. Several of the dancers watched him back, no doubt hoping he'd turn back to the mirror and repeat the sequence. But I began shifting my weight from one foot to the other, and closed my eyes to let the beat seep through my pores.

When I opened my eyes, I unreeled the memory of Dmitri's movement like a film in the mirror, matching my body to his, elbow to elbow, stroke to stroke, riding the arc in the beat. His movement fit my low center of gravity like custom-made jeans, accommodating my body and comforting my soul. I was no longer a stack of imperfect bones, but a series of levers coordinating a thrill ride of twists and torques. Others watched, and eventually followed. I set aside both my prior obligation to Tina and any nervousness over the audition's outcome: it was just mind, heart, muscle, and the unbridled joy of moving my body through space.

By the time I stilled, Dmitri was standing next to me, smiling. "Yes, yes."

At Dmitri's prompt, a didgeridoo energized the room by adding an energizing buzz beneath the drumbeat. Dmitri had everyone's attention now. He crouched low, a dance animal sculpted for strength, flexibility, and speed. I crouched behind him; others followed. By the time the guitarist joined in, he had dozens of dancers following him in waves.

And I was up front, helping to power the tide.

There would be no break. No callbacks. No agonizing wait. Dmitri picked up the sign-in sheet, checked names against numbers, and looked up.

"This is the last United States audition and I am only taking two dancers. I want Penelope Sparrow and Tina Franke." By way of dismissing the others, but looking right at me, he added, "Thank you very much."

And with that it was over. Dmitri was a man who knew what he wanted. And he wanted me. *Me!*

And Tina, of course. I turned to give my protégé-cum-colleague a quick congratulatory hug, my breast flushed with warmth. In brightening my career with its first rays of hope, Dmitri had won my unwavering support. My body longed to sing his praises. Fresh ideas coiled within my muscles; I could have danced hours more.

After so many years of subsisting on a meager diet of perseverance, I wasn't yet ready to feast from the full banquet of life. I didn't call my mother. I would wait until all felt secure.

Right then I wanted to savor the notion that dreams really could come true.

# CHAPTER EIGHT

*A* draft of cold air; the front door had opened. So deeply relaxed after my home therapy my eyelids didn't flinch. The floor creaked as my mother approached. She stopped—good lord, was she checking to see if I was breathing?—then moved away. Her leather purse plopped onto the hall table; she made room for her coat in the closet with a metallic scrape. She passed by again, pants swishing. The legs of the piano bench whispered across the carpet.

The moody adagio from Beethoven's "Moonlight Sonata" rose from the piano. I felt her fingers crawl over the keys to seek out the yearning that, beneath everything, had always bound us together. I relaxed more deeply and images swirled: Dmitri. His body. The music. The dance. Tina.

Memory pricked me, and I noted the pain.

Then the doorbell rang.

My mother lifted her hands from the keys and spoke gaily when she answered the door, snapping right out of the trance her music induced. I couldn't. She'd interrupted the sonata before the second movement could lighten the mood, before the urgent third movement could re-invigorate and goad me back to life. So much was unresolved.

With only half my heart in the process, I went through the effortful and awkward actions now required to stand.

"There she is," a female voice said.

She sounded familiar, but it had been so long since I'd lived in the area I was surprised anyone would know me. I had to move so damned slowly. But as soon as I'd straightened, I recognized them at once: two fresh-faced, exuberant Philadelphians I'd last seen in the hospital.

I stayed where I had risen. "This is a surprise."

"Penny, your manners. I'm Evelyn Sparrow, Penelope's mother." With more animation than I could have possibly mustered, my mother smiled and extended her hand. "And you are?"

"Angela Reed. An absolute pleasure to meet you." Still in a cast, Angela awkwardly shook hands with my mother. She turned to introduce Marty Kandelbaum, then said, "I was your daughter's hospital roommate."

"What are you guys doing here?"

"Penny." My mother threw me a sharp look before turning back to our guests. "She's not herself yet." She took their coats, stowed the mat I'd been using in the closet, and pulled the coffee table back into position.

"I apologize for not calling first," Kandelbaum said. "Angela stopped in the bakery while I was closing, and driving up to look for you was sort of a spur-of-the-moment adventure. Did you know there are eight Sparrows in the Lehigh Valley phone book?"

"I'm thrilled you're here," my mother said. "It's been so gloomy."

"What do you expect from me, Mother?" I snapped. "I'm trying as hard as I can."

"I meant the winter weather, Penny." She kept her voice light, as if we teased each other this way all the time.

"We'll try to be the sunshine Mother Nature has denied you," Kandelbaum said.

"Go on in and sit down," my mother said. "I'll get some snacks."

Angela, surveying the room, spied the dance posters in the hallway beyond. "Oh my gosh, this is like a museum. Look, Marty."

When Kandelbaum and I joined her, the flawless ballet bodies of Edward Villella, Mikhail Baryshnikov, Fernando Bujones, and Julio Bocca invited us down the hall. A museum—she was right. Each dancer on display, frozen in time, limited by frame, trapped behind glass. Each taunting the viewer with photographic perfection from a distant, untouchable place. Not one moment of messy, glorious, immediate movement to be experienced. It was the opposite of dance.

"Were these all your partners?" Kandelbaum said.

I chuckled. "In my mother's fantasies, I suppose."

"Now, Penny," my mother called, "they could have been, if they weren't too old for you."

"Or too short," I called back.

It suddenly occurred to me—even after my exile from ballet, when my mother switched to buying the modern dance posters that hung in the next leg of the hallway, she only chose male choreographers: Paul Taylor, Mark Morris, Merce Cunningham. Why had she done this, in a discipline where females far out-number the males? Where was Martha Graham, I wondered? Trisha Brown? Twyla Tharp?

Neither Angela nor Kandelbaum mentioned the empty hook and the ghostly impression the missing poster had left on the wall near my bedroom door, but it haunted me.

"This one's different," Angela said on the return trip, referencing the poster closest to the living room. "It really grips you."

"Rudolf Nureyev. In *Petrushka*. It's my favorite as well. See the yellow marks here?" I pointed through the glass. "My mother rescued it from the door of my closet, where I'd taped him."

"His face is so expressive."

The role absorbed him: his lips parted and brows raised, hands bent at odd angles, and feet turned inward, he was a tragic doll whose soul struggles to emerge. "It's like the photographer caught him in a moment of great potential—about to do something—and I never tire of trying to figure out what."

"Yes, that's it," Angela said. "I knew this place would be artsy before we rang the doorbell. We heard the piano—your playing was so moving. Heartbreaking, really."

I explained that my mother was the piano player.

"Such talent in the family," Kandelbaum said.

My mother reappeared with a pitcher of grape juice, a plate of sugar cookies, and a glass bowl of cheddar Goldfish. She placed the tray on the coffee table. "Penny's father bought me that piano the first year his sporting goods store turned a profit."

"And you never told me?"

She shrugged, as if it were unimportant. She had to know I craved details about my father—and now she was coughing them up for people she'd just met? Even thirty years ago, a baby grand was a considerable investment, and one more clue to my father's character.

Angela and Kandelbaum took the overstuffed love seat beneath the front window. Kandelbaum popped a whole cookie into his mouth and grabbed a handful of crackers.

It was hard to watch anyone endorse my mother's nutritional sensibilities. I'd rejected her practices in my teens, knowing they would destroy my health and career options. It was Bebe who taught me how to optimize nutrition within minimal calorie guidelines, and Bebe who introduced me to that slight euphoria that undereating, just a little, could produce—and I loved her for it. By taking me from this home of excesses and into her studio and its apartment, where austerity was a way of life as well as a diet, I could create the body I sought. She made me believe that with religious adherence to the right program of exercise and nutrition, I could capitalize on my father's half of my gene pool and fend off obesity.

Despite the crumbs on his shirt, Kandelbaum and Angela did look cute sitting across the coffee table from me, their cheeks rosy from the March cold and eyes twinkling like snowflakes in a streetlight. From a cold ladder-back, I watched as their arms and hips touched in a comfortable familiarity that full-body pain, if not life itself, seemed determined to deny me.

Angela said, "Would you play for us, Mrs. Sparrow?"

"I haven't played much since Penny left home…"

"Please?" Angela said.

"I'm really rusty."

"Go ahead, Mom," I said. "It would be nice."

She played one song, then another, then another, her fingers loosening and finding their way. Through grace notes, arpeggios, and thunderous chords, the spirit of music moved through us, reminding me of a time when camaraderie and human touch were part of my daily existence.

The music ended, and the debut of Dance DeLaval was behind us. Applause still reverberated through our bodies. The six of us awaited the early morning review in the *Philadelphia Sentinel* while piled on Dmitri's couches at his Independence Suites apartment. My hands, Mitch's head, Karly's feet, Tina's torso—these body parts were the instruments with which we had built the performance, and we valued them in a spirit of joint ownership. We fell asleep against one another, stage makeup still on, well before the *Sentinel*'s review hit the stands.

The next morning, Dmitri ran out to get the paper while the rest of us took turns in the shower. Lars cooked breakfast; Dmitri scanned the review. The others ate ravenously. I dissected my eggs, whisking the yolks away and laying the whites on top of dry toast, taking small bites to make it last. I listened for the critic's judgment with keen interest. It had been two months since I joined the company, and I still hadn't worked up the nerve to tell my mother. She wanted my success so badly—I couldn't let her down again. And I couldn't bear to hear her say I'd made the wrong decision in casting my fate with the untried Dance DeLaval.

Dmitri tried to read aloud to us, but his English was so choppy Karly yanked the paper from his hands and took over.

"First of all, Dmitri, you have to start with the headline. 'Dance DeLaval refreshing addition to Philly dance scene.' How about that?"

We whooped and clapped.

"Get on with it," Lars said. His Scandinavian lilt always sounded boozy, even when he was sober.

"Okay, here we go: 'In a city the size of Philadelphia, dance companies come and go with some regularity. Making predictions about such a changeable scene can be foolish. But I will venture a guess that when Dance DeLaval leaves Philadelphia at the end of its three-year residency at the University of the Arts, our audiences will not want to see the company go.'"

"You can't ask for much better," Tina said.

Karly scanned down the page. "Then she goes on to give Dmitri's background...looks like it's straight from the program notes...then it jumps to an inside page."

"Just read the underlined parts. The good stuff," Dmitri said.

Karly opened the paper and refolded it to the right spot. "I can't believe it—you did underline, you control freak."

"This is how you do advertising in America, no?"

"Okay, let's see. *Smoldering athleticism*...she's talking about you, Dmitri. She must want you bad—"

Mitch and Lars howled; Dmitri flushed.

"...*style which fingers the edges of human kinetic potential*—"

Dmitri and I caught each other's eyes and smiled. That one meant a lot to him.

"...*a broad range of subject matter...a disparate group of bodies*—"

"Desperate bodies? This is good, no? Shows hunger for

movement?" Dmitri said. His wordplay raised a hearty laugh from the group.

I set down my toast. I had already started to feel queasy when I heard the word "broad." For the most part, Dmitri had chosen his dancers for their *lack* of disparity. The men were tall and thin, the women a few inches shorter and thin—except Tina, who was very short and thin. Thin, thin, thin, the dance world mandate. The American ideal.

Then there was me. Dmitri's movement inspired a fierce confidence in my body—from the inside looking out, I felt equal to any challenge—but critical evaluation of my performance brought back all my fears. Mine was the desperate body. I didn't want to have food in my mouth if I was about to hear MacArthur say my chunky bottom was responsible for creating her sense of the company's disparateness.

Although she hardly seemed finished, Karly folded the paper and dropped it onto the couch. "It's all good news. So, who's using the phone?"

Mitch reached it first and called Evan. While the others waited their turn, I snuck off to the kitchen for a private audience with the article. I scanned down to where Dmitri had underlined "a disparate group of bodies." The critic wrote:

> *Mr. DeLaval uses his long torso to great advantage;*
> *opposing forces of expansion and contraction that might*
> *seem minimal within another body become a bold state-*
> *ment on his. Others in the company are similarly lithe and*
> *strong, but two are so different that the viewer searches*

*for meaning. Without an emotional context, one can't tell if Mr. DeLaval is making a statement with his casting. My eye was drawn to the larger girl in the second piece, for instance—her Amazonian strength, her mercurial fluidity. Was the petite blond meant to be her daughter? Her incomplete self? Only time will tell whether Mr. DeLaval can continue to generate the kind of material that will make this ensemble shine.*

I let out my breath. It wasn't pretty, but it wasn't as bad as it could have been. When I looked up, Dmitri was leaning against the doorway of the kitchen. Even at home, in this casual pose, he looked like a god. By extension—because he had chosen me—I could imagine a bit of goddess in me. He nodded toward the paper and said, "Amazon mother is good image. We will show her."

Those last three words juiced me up enough to make a call of my own. When the phone was free, my Amazon fingers flew across the keypad.

"Hello?" Her voice sounded muffled, like she was speaking into a pillow. I glanced at the clock. It was only six a.m. On a Sunday.

"Mom, it's me." Pride—mine and my mom's, all tangled together—swelled within my breast until it pushed the words from my mouth in a tumble. "I can't wait to tell you any longer—I made it into a company! Dance DeLaval. We're based down in Philadelphia, at the University of the Arts."

"Well, I know that much."

"You do?"

"Bebe told me."

Of course she had. I had moved back into the little room above her studio on South Tenth. Bebe had let me have it back on one condition: I swear an oath not to give up on my performing career. "I've made it this time, Bebe," I'd said, the words so significant their conveyance required no more than a whisper. I told her all about meeting Dmitri, the audition, and his three-year residency right here in Philadelphia.

It was a moment I should have shared with both my mothers.

"I thought you'd be more excited."

"Bebe called weeks ago. The blush has worn off." I heard her thump some pillows as she repositioned herself. "We've wanted this for so long. I just wish you had told me."

"Believe me—I wanted to climb to the top of a New York high-rise and shout to you. But my success felt too fragile. As if it still might disappear. But guess what?"

"What?"

"Last night was our opening night and—"

"Damn it, Penny! I don't suppose it occurred to you that I only live sixty miles away. I would have driven three times as far to see your debut with a major company. After all the crappy recitals I sat through—"

"Crappy? You loved them—"

"I'm just saying. The stairs look rickety when you look back on them from the top."

The top—she'd said it. While I'd never dared to give them credence, I'd always secretly enjoyed my mother's lofty expectations. They gave me the confidence needed to try and try and try again. Someone would one day recognize my brilliance! But as the wait grew long and my youth grew stale, my dreams lost focus. I was no longer sure that if I reached the top, I'd recognize it. And if I reached the top and fell down the mountain, what would my mother have to show for Penelope Sparrow, her lifelong project? She'd have to measure her success in conveyors full of perfectly glossed chocolates. And if she were so proud of that accomplishment, she wouldn't have pushed me so hard to have a different life. I'd needed time to hang out with the company on my own, and get a new sense of my potential here, before raising her hopes.

"So are you going to tell me how the performance was or not?" my mother said.

"Pick up a copy of today's *Sentinel* and you can read all about it."

"I will. But tell me—how did it feel?"

"Dmitri was proud of us. He said if our next performance goes as well—"

"I want to know about you, Penny. Are you happy?"

"Oh, Mom." I was literally beside myself, watching Penelope Sparrow tell her mother she was living their dream. The feeling it and the watching it and hearing her affirm it overwhelmed me and I couldn't say anything more.

My mother said, "Are you nodding, or what?"

Laughter cracked the gridlock in my vocal cords. "Dmitri's movement is like a song rising from my bones—as if it's always been a part of me. The company has international potential. I'm in exactly the right place."

My mother drew her song to a close with a long, unresolved chord, quietly dropping in the final note. Angela was the one who finally broke the spell.

"On the way up here, Marty and I heard a commercial about this pianist who's going to perform with the Philadelphia Orchestra next week. We should all go."

An auditorium full of artsy types who might recognize me. Who might have read about me in the paper. My heart started to agitate. The dark house, the spotlights, my mother suggesting I go backstage to commission a score…. "I couldn't afford it."

"I could drive you down, and treat you," my mother said. "It would be good for you. After all, Balanchine listened to music all the time."

"Balanchine?" Kandelbaum said.

"George Balanchine, the founding director of the New York City Ballet," I said. "One of the greatest ballet choreographers of all time." One of the great incomparables meant to goad me into international prominence. Even now, while my career lay splat on a Philadelphia sidewalk and every movement still pained me. "She knows all about him because he came to dinner last night."

My mother emitted such a sigh it increased the pressure in the room. "You know damned well he's been dead for twenty years. But the man knew something about success, Penny. You could give it a try."

Rage reared within me, but I bit down on it—any friendship still possible with our unfortunate witnesses would not survive its expression. I let two words leak out: "Stop pushing."

Angela came over to me. Face to face, our injuries mirrored

one another. She caressed my good elbow with her good hand, as gently as if it were a leaf she feared might drop from a February poinsettia. As if she knew that tenderness was the only weapon that could take down the beast inside me. She spoke softly. "I'm sure none of us knows the right thing to do. But we care. Right, Marty?" He offered a sad smile. "I'll write down my number, and you call me when you want to get together."

A trail of orange specks littered the pale carpet where they had fallen from Kandelbaum's lap. Hansel and Gretel had not only survived their trip to the tangled forest my mother and I shared, they'd left a trail of breadcrumbs so I could come find them when I was ready.

As I lay on my bed that night, I tried to re-create the wordless communion I'd shared with Angela and Kandelbaum while my mother played. When, for a moment, I had not felt so profoundly alone.

Then finally slept, at peace, all through the night.

# CHAPTER NINE

*T*he words shocked my ears; I hadn't planned to ask. But while my bruises faded to splotches of yellow and green over the next several weeks, physical therapy had developed muscle fibers and nerve pathways that, stitch-by-stitch, reattached body and mind. All my senses were reawakening— when Mauricio leaned over me to adjust the tension on the pulley stretching my shoulder, I could smell the soap he used on his hands.

I suddenly found myself asking, "Will I dance again?"

Mauricio's lopsided smile tightened. He paused a little too long.

"I don't want to discourage you—the human body never fails to amaze. But at this point, I'm only hoping to restore normal function of the shoulder and spine."

"Oh." I suddenly felt dizzy.

Mauricio pressed the back of his hand to my cheek. "You're clammy. Maybe you overdid it. Sit tight—I'll get you some water."

My hands clenched the edge of the bench I sat upon. I had never let go of my former life. Not completely. I remained dangling from it, holding on with all my might. And now Mauricio, the man charged with my healing, added to the jeers: *You might as well let go. You won't have the strength to hold on anyway.*

He came back and handed me the water. "I want you to start taking daily walks. Just fifteen minutes or so, don't go nuts, but the alternating contractions will help your back."

Walks. Ha. How could a connoisseur of fine movement ever be satisfied with baby food? I hungered for more intriguing textures—a cup of swing, a spoonful of salsa, a dash of syncopation. My muscles twitched at the ready, begging for more.

Two weeks later, after returning from a forty-minute walk, I heard my mother at the piano. I slipped off my damp shoes, left them by the door, and paused to listen. Splayed fingers exploring full octave chords over most of the keyboard, my mother rocked back and forth on the bench, her eyes only sometimes open. I wasn't sure she knew I'd come in.

She was playing "When I Grow Too Old to Dream," a waltz she used to sing to me when I was little, after I changed into my nightgown. She'd intended it to be a lullaby, I suppose, never realizing the music's opposite effect. My dad knew, though. He'd put out his hand and say, "One more dance, Penny?" I'd put my hand in his, hold my skirt out to the side, and curtsy. Without skipping a note, my mother would chastise him, but with a big smile on her face. She couldn't resist the performance to come. My father couldn't dance. She'd laugh as he took me in his arms to trip around the room, with me squealing as I hugged his waist and tried to keep my bare feet on top of his moccasins.

Today the notes conjured my father once more. I felt him here, in the room, inviting me to dance. My muscles, warm and eager to respond, lifted me into a gentle triplet step—down, up, up; down, up, up. Just a slight flexion of knee and ankle. Jerky, at first, like my father. But soon I'd traversed the living room, made a half-turn at the piano in the corner, and continued my ellipse moving backward. My toes found dents in the carpet from the legs of the coffee table my mother had moved to make room for my exercise mat. My arms swayed in breathy swirls. I cocked my head and…yes, there it was…that stirring against my cheek, an acknowledgment from the air in the room that is always as sweet as a lover's kiss.

A wisp of memory, a trace of the movement I had loved, that imagined kiss: something hibernating in the darkness within me awoke and reached tentatively for the sun. The fierce beauty of it stilled my step. Tears streamed down my face.

My mother stopped playing, her lips parted in a hopeful smile. "Penny." She left the bench and reached for me, but accepting her touch felt dangerous. The frond unfurling within me was too tender; I didn't want her to smother it. I turned and walked away.

It was a few months after Dance DeLaval's Philadelphia debut when Dmitri first singled me out to work with him in the studio. Dmitri had promised us a few days off to recoup after our tour of the Northeast, so when Mitch parked our used van by the Terra

Building at ten p.m., we grabbed our luggage from the back and prepared for the first time in a month to go our separate ways.

Dmitri was antsy, though. While we unpacked the van, he paced the sidewalk beside it. I could almost see the new ideas surging beneath the surface of his skin. Still, when he called to me, I was surprised.

"Penny." He always said my name as though the "y" were leading to something more.

All of us turned as one.

"Just Penny. Could I see you? Inside?"

This singling out inspired a sudden stillness around the van. "Sure." I turned to the others. "Guess I'll see you guys in a few days."

After we climbed the stairs, he paused before entering the studio. "You are probably tired, but…"

"It's okay. I'll be out in a minute." I went into the bathroom, splashed some cold water on my face, and changed into the ripe-smelling leotard and knit pants I'd balled together in my dance bag. I'd been sure their next stop would be a sink with some warm soapy water.

I re-entered the studio. Dmitri wandered the room, marking a floor pattern. He was already in a zone, and I kept an eye on him as I slipped on a pair of leg warmers and coaxed gentle movement from joints confined for hours to a van whose heater was broken. At one point Dmitri sank into a deep, twisted lunge and lifted his dark eyes to the mirror before him. I knew that look: time to begin. I mimicked his position.

"Watch," he said. "I go…" He unwound as he rose, so that in the next move he could leap high into the air, turning on an angle as would a parasol over a woman's shoulder. "I stay…" He landed again in a crouched pose and glared at the mirror. "I go like…" He raised his arms to the sides, his fingers talons that had dropped their prey. "Then, pop, pop, pop." He said each word as he leapt around the edge of a small circle.

"Do together now, we?" Or maybe it was "Do together now, *oui*?" It was hard to tell with Dmitri. But to me it didn't matter; his intention unfolded in the movement. On the tour I'd begun functioning as an interpreter. He'd try to explain something, fail to find words, then say, "Penny?" I'd ask something like, "Is it like a huge ball of energy that moves upstage on the diagonal, hitting one, then another, until we're all affected?" He'd relax and smile. "Yes."

Now we ran through the movement again side by side. Untwist, spring, parasol, talons, pop‑pop‑pop. "Now what?" he said.

"Solo? Duet? Group?" I fired back in similar shorthand.

"Ah, duet." I held my position, waiting. Eventually he turned to me and said, "Run in a circle. Around me. I stay here and turn, turn…"

I tried. But the day's earlier inactivity had taken its toll, and I'd been holding my crouched position for too long. When I tried to do his bidding, my right foot was asleep. My run took on a syncopated gimp.

"Yes, Penny, better!" he said. "Wounded, yes."

The studio lights blazed long into the night, and Dmitri's signature work, *Puma*, was born. The whole experience was exhilarating, but fatigue claimed us by four a.m.

He locked up the studio and said, "It is late. Where is your place?"

"Over on South Tenth."

"Too far. Crash with me." Inappropriate as it seemed, the offer tempted. His penthouse was luxurious compared to my little room at Bebe's, where you could simultaneously sit on the toilet and spit in the sink. It was all I could afford, but I didn't elaborate on that with Dmitri.

"It's only seven blocks."

"You were a help to me. *S'il te plaît. Pozhalusta.* Please."

It was his eyes. They seemed to see beyond the glow I absorbed from him, and recognize a light source of my own. They seemed to say thank you and please and I value you and you're safe. Okay, it was his ponytail, too, and the way it revealed soft dark hairs that curled against the back of his neck. As he led the way down the stairs, it was all I could do not to touch them. Once out on the street, I tamed my thoughts by bringing up a subject I hadn't had enough time alone with him to broach during our jam-packed tour.

"Dmitri—you know that review of our first performance, where the critic was trying to find meaning in the size difference between Tina and me?"

He must have tensed; there was a slight hesitation in the rhythm of his footfalls. "Why?"

"Before the tour, I was talking to my mother about the review. She thought it might be interesting to experiment with a role reversal the next time we perform it here—I'd dance Tina's part and she could dance mine."

"You talked to your mother about this?"

"It's more like she talked to me about it, but yes. I thought it would be a neat idea. MacArthur could see for herself whether she still felt the need to create meaning from the size difference. Her perspective would change—"

"You never told me your mother is choreographer."

"Oh, she's not. But don't you think it might be interesting to try?"

"Just a dancer, then."

*Just* a dancer? The put-down felt personal. "Who?"

"Your mother."

"No, no—she works in a candy factory," I said. "And she's a pianist."

"And a dance critic."

"Not officially." I chuckled. "But I think she has a pretty keen artistic sensibility. I was wondering if we might try it."

"Penny." He turned to me. His expression, once blurred by shadow but now etched by the streetlamp, told me I had overstepped a previously unmarked boundary. "I trained for dance my whole life. All around the world, from the best teachers and artists. And you want me to take career advice from candy factory worker?"

"Well, she's not a 'worker.' She runs the place."

"My mother was the most famous ballerina, and she cannot tell me how to be an artist. Critics cannot tell me how to be an artist. Ideas must come from here." He put his fingertips low on his chest. "True artists must listen for the voice inside, not for the words of others."

"I-I'm sorry." We walked on for a bit before I spoke again. "But you and I were working together—you do believe in collaboration?"

"Among artists, yes. You have an artist inside, too. I see this. Let her grow without your mother or a critic to tell her what to do."

He offered me the couch, but I couldn't sleep. My stomach felt uncomfortably full, as if I'd overfed on bad advice. I'd always thought my mother nurtured my artistry. Bebe may have instilled the discipline that kept me on the path, but without my mother, I wouldn't have had a path. I wouldn't have known what artistry was, or why it was worth striving for. But maybe Dmitri was on to something. At this new level of professionalism, my mother did not have the experience to serve as my adviser.

When we gathered again to rehearse a few days later, Dmitri conducted a quick business meeting. "I am building onto my new solo, *Puma*, to give roles to other dancers." He looked to me. "Penny, you describe."

So he wasn't angry with me—I was so relieved. And by choosing me to communicate on his behalf, wasn't he seeking my continued collaboration? Honoring my inner artist? I stood and marked through the material he and I had come up with, allowing the movement to inspire my description of the predator and prey themes it evoked. As the music played along in my head, once again I lost myself in the dance. I snapped back to the present when my body came to rest. I heard Dmitri saying something about hiring an assistant.

In the mirror I saw the stupefied expressions of the other company members behind me. Certain I'd missed something important, I said, "Excuse me?"

Dmitri looked at me and smiled. "You are already so busy you do not hear. I promote you to rehearsal assistant."

I clutched my hands to my heart and turned to the others. Their faces gave away little. Perhaps they were as stunned as I was.

Or maybe they were waiting for me to say something. But I was not accustomed to speechmaking, and although I gave my voice a chance to burble up from within me, no particular inspiration arose. "Thank you," I said, at last, and gave Dmitri a quick hug. As he pulled away, he kissed me once on each cheek.

I ran into Dmitri's office, shut the door, and called my mother.

"Rehearsal assistant already? Penny, that's great."

I kept my voice low so the dancers on the other side of the door wouldn't hear. "I'm still trying to work through his reasoning myself. Of course Tina and Karly are much younger. Lars has this big, powerful body and he's as affable as a big floppy dog, but half the time I think he comes to rehearsals hungover. Mitch, though, is closer to my age. And he's responsible, as well." Had Mitch been overlooked because he stood up to Dmitri over wearing his wedding ring onstage? I'd have to watch my step.

"Penny, stop. I know why you got it. Because you deserved it."

"Thanks, Mom." Buoyed by my mother's pride, I dared to think it may have been more than a numbers game that landed me in Dmitri's company. Maybe the Great Artist had a reason for carving my soul in the shape of a dancer—even if his chisel slipped when shaping my body. "Mitch has a family to support, is all. He could have used the raise."

"That kind of thinking is why you'll make a great leader. But wait—do you think you'll be able to support yourself with your dancing now?"

"Looks like you're finally off the hook."

"Oh, Penny, congratulations! And I was never on the hook. Most artists need help somewhere along the way."

Even my mother was now calling me an artist. "I've appreciated your support. I know it's been a long countdown, but our project succeeded: Penelope Sparrow has finally launched. So let's talk about you for once. How are things at the candy factory?"

"Don't you change the subject on me. Now that you've won Dmitri's trust, we should figure out how to leverage it."

"This promotion wasn't a prize I won for entering some contest. I didn't even apply for the job. As you said, I earned it. And you don't have to plot and plan. I can chart my own course, you know."

"Of course you can. But we've always talked about this kind of stuff together. Hey, did you ever ask Dmitri about switching yours and Tina's roles around to see what MacArthur writes? I've been thinking more about how it would call meaning into question—"

"Dmitri knows what he's doing, you know. He doesn't need creative input from you."

The line went silent for a moment. "Oh."

"Dmitri says an artist needs to listen to the voice that arises from the soul."

"I have a soul."

"But you aren't a member of the company."

"Didn't you think I had a good idea?"

"That's beside the point. This residency is an opportunity for Dmitri to grow as an artist. He says it can be an opportunity for me, too, if I listen for that inner voice—"

"Well of course—"

"My voice. As opposed to yours."

"Pfft. He may know artistry, but what does he know about

mothers and daughters? We're a team. Where was he all those years I drove you to dance lessons?"

"In France, learning dance from one of the most famous ballerinas in the world."

"You trusted me with your career back then."

"An eight-year-old *has* to depend on a parent, Mom. I couldn't drive myself to lessons any more than I could pay for them. But I'm at a whole new level now. Dmitri is my artistic director. I have to put my faith in him."

A frosty silence crystallized between us. "Mom, are you still there?"

"You."

"I'm done talking about this, but I don't want to hang up if you're mad at me. Tell me how things are going at the candy factory."

"You don't care about the damned factory and never have. You've never even come to see the new facility. Our whole relationship is based on dance—what else have we ever talked about?"

The despair I heard in her voice was exactly the reason we'd never before had this conversation. But it was now clear: I needed to create this boundary, and enforce it. "I just need some space."

"We're breaking up?"

My mother always could make me laugh. "It won't be forever."

"But this isn't fair. We've worked so long for this, and I've suffered with you through every setback—don't I get to share the good part, too?"

"Let me call you. When I'm ready. Give me a chance to try my wings, okay? I love you."

I heard a knock on the door. Dmitri stuck his head in. "We are going out to eat. You coming?"

I put up a finger and said into the phone, "Sorry, I've got to go."

Dmitri mouthed, *Your mother?*

I nodded, and rolled my eyes for effect.

"Penny. I need this. You don't know what it's like for me to worry about you from afar."

"Gotta go."

"Don't shut me out. Something could still go wrong."

"I called with good news, remember?"

"Say you'll call me if you need me. Otherwise I'll be a wreck."

"If I need anything, I'll figure it out. That's what this is all about. Bye."

"Penny, don't hang up—"

I hung up, grabbed my jacket, and turned toward my future.

# CHAPTER TEN

*I* hid out in my bedroom all afternoon after my little trip around the living room, too embarrassed to face my mother. I felt like a dancer who hadn't heard her number dismissed and showed up, unwanted, for the second stage of the audition—and my mother had witnessed the whole thing. And if she said one thing about Graham or Balanchine or Patrick Bissell, I would lose it.

Dancing again was too much to ask. Mauricio had said so. And circumnavigating the living room was nothing like the controlled abandon of real dancing. And what if that was all I'd ever have— just enough movement to keep the shadows inside me all churned up, but not enough to set them free?

The doorbell rang. I waited for my mother to get it, but a sharp rap on the door soon followed. When I opened the front door, I found Margaret MacArthur, decked out in her red pillbox hat and red leather gloves. I looked past her to the driveway. My mother's car was gone.

MacArthur seemed content to wait for me to speak first. "I don't buy Girl Scout cookies," I said.

"Wit returns. A good sign. How are you doing?"

"You are one nosy—"

"I was simply being polite. Even critics possess social grace, Penelope."

"Oh." I stood between the door and its frame, holding both MacArthur and the cold April air at bay, wondering whether to believe this. "And how are you?"

"Right, let's skip the niceties. Ignore me all you want, but you will not stop me from writing an exposé on the harsh treatment of women in the dance world. I'm here to tell you why. May I come in?"

When I stood back, MacArthur walked into the living room and planted her tiny frame in the middle of the plaid love seat. I took it as a good sign when she didn't remove her coat, or produce a notepad. But I was determined not to let down my guard. I perched on the edge of the ladder-back.

"You opened and shut the door with fluidity, you walked into the room with a steady rhythm, and now you are balanced well, if somewhat recklessly, on the edge of your chair."

"If I knew you were reviewing, I would have thrown in a head roll."

MacArthur removed her gloves and twisted them; without note-taking it appeared she didn't know what else to do with her hands. "I want to tell you about my sister Laura. She and I both danced. I was a scrawny little thing, but she was tall and stalwart. She was the one with the talent. Watching her inspired more kin-esthetic sensation within me than my own movement ever did."

I thought I heard MacArthur's voice catch, but she covered with a quick cough.

"Laura's movements began in a more spiritual realm. Her body didn't rise up as a function of foot pressing against floor as did mine; she harnessed unseen powers from beneath the floor. Her love of the space alone held her aloft. I could only approximate the effect, but I somehow won a scholarship to a summer program in France, so when she graduated I went, thinking the change might inspire me. That's where I studied with Ekaterina Ivanovna, Dmitri's mother. By the time I left, Laura had stopped dancing."

Dmitri. I envied her casual use of the name that still clutched my heart, her inference that the man who'd been at the center of my world could be peripheral to any story. I cleared my throat. "She sounds extraordinary. Why did she stop?"

"While I was in Paris, a London company hired Laura as an apprentice." MacArthur smoothed the coat over her lap, as if it were possible to press flat its nubby surface. "Under the condition she lose weight. By the time I found out why she had left the company and where she'd gone, she had developed anorexia that had spiraled out of control. One day she was found passed out beside her oven. It was a miracle the place hadn't exploded."

I could think of only one reason MacArthur had driven all the way up here to tell me this: she assumed my story was like her sister's. I had enough self-control not to argue with a woman with the power to memorialize words I might want to take back. "And you're hoping I'll help you get the scoop? 'Big, Disenfranchised Dancers Speak Out'?"

"Do you want this to happen to anyone else? We have a chance to influence change. To open people's eyes to their prejudices about ideal size."

"Yet you're the one who called me an Amazon in the paper."

"I beg your pardon?"

"In your first review of Dance DeLaval. An Amazon is hardly a flattering image for a dancer."

MacArthur sighed. "I wrote that review on a deadline, you know. In about forty minutes. And I was watching Dmitri's work for the first time. Trying to orient myself, seek meaning. That you were larger than the rest was simple fact, not accusation. But your own assumption proves my point. That's why I want to do this interview."

I was larger. *Simple fact.* I slid my hand over my stomach and fingered the comforting edges of my rib cage. I tried to respect her candor about my size, because in many ways I'd needed to have this conversation with someone my whole life. Someone who saw me and recognized the challenges of my shape instead of treating me like the elephant in the room no one dared mention.

But the conversation wouldn't happen here, and not with MacArthur. Why would I share with the press what I couldn't face sharing with those I wanted to be close to? Plus, my mother would be back soon, and I really didn't want her and MacArthur to meet. I stood up to signal an end to the conversation, but the move wasn't as bold as I would have hoped. My joints, already stiffening from my earlier walk and attempt at dance and now wrung out from MacArthur's audacity, shook with the effort.

I steadied my large self on the ladder-back. "Here's my advice on this whole interview thing: give up. You're the word warrior, not me. I speak through movement. If I can't open the audience's eyes through my work, I'm of no use."

MacArthur stood as well. "Then open your own eyes and get back to work."

"That's not fair—"

"Spare me. You can move, my sister can't. The brain damage she sustained has rendered her virtually inert. It's permanent. Your injury, on the other hand, is healing."

"You haven't spoken to my physical therapist."

"Taking yourself out of the dance won't solve a thing."

"Why do you care?"

MacArthur wriggled into her blood-red gloves as her voice took on a surgical precision. "For decades I'd been scanning the stages to find a performer who excited me as much as my sister did. Then one day I recognized her way of moving again. It was while I was in the wings at the Joyce interviewing Dmitri after a show. His rehearsal mistress was onstage, demonstrating something for the company. They had been moving arms and legs through his choreography, but she was showing them how to move heart and soul. It was as if I'd found my sister again—in you."

She went to the door, opened it, and spoke once more before crossing the threshold. Her voice sounded smaller, facing away from me as she now was, casting her words to the winds of spring. "I was the one who found my sister, Penelope. Thankfully she hadn't thrown the deadbolt. I was able to get into her flat and drag her to safety. I will not witness an implosion of such talent again. It diminishes us all."

Without a word of good-bye, MacArthur walked to her car. I watched until she pulled out of the driveway—some small acknowledgment, perhaps, that I had heard her.

And when I shut the door, I stopped short of flipping the deadbolt.

In the dining room, my mother served up a platter of fatty beef slices. Why did she insist on sharing these evening meals? We had little to talk about. Between my elusive memory and her reckless optimism, my fall stretched between us. We twirled around it, shimmied under it, and leaped over it in awkward silence.

I raked my fork through my potatoes and thought about the way MacArthur had gouged me. How dare she come here and ask so much of me? As if my injuries and rehabilitation were all about her and her sister and the rest of the goddamned dance world. If I could pull the pain from my body, I'd gladly share it so they could all have a taste. And how nice of her to point out my lack of contribution. Like that was so easy to figure out in the shape I was in! Couldn't she see how my muscles had atrophied? My stomach had been churning ever since she left.

What exactly was I holding on to here? My nonexistent dance career? Hell, I might as well eat.

I raised the beef to my lips. A caramelized onion, still glistening from its butter bath, fell to my lap. Meanwhile, my mother dredged her meat through her potatoes and shoveled forkful after forkful into her mouth.

My fork froze for a moment longer—then fell to my plate. I couldn't do it. Denying myself food was the one small element I could control in a life dictated by everything I couldn't. Like body type. Talent. Luck. Oversized mothers, and bulldog critics. The only way I knew to reach my potential was to exercise hard and deny myself the foods that had led to my mother's obesity. Restricting was the closest feeling I'd ever had to self-love, and I would not abandon it.

Anyway, this was my mother's food. What I put into my body should be mine. I got up from the table and sliced a banana into a bowl of yogurt.

"While you're up, would you get the butter?" she said.

"You don't need any more butter."

"Why the hell do you care if I want butter on my potatoes?"

"Because YOU—ARE—FAT!" I wanted to smack her with this proclamation and all of its implications: that I no longer could witness this long slow death. That she should care more about herself. That she'd been a crappy role model and an embarrassment. That I hated my body because I feared its similarity to hers.

Maybe her layers of fat protected her from all this subtext. She folded her napkin and placed it beside her plate. "Not all dancers are so allergic to food, you know. Jock Soto loves to cook. This recipe is from his book."

"Really. Jock Soto suggested dripping onions? The gravy? The jelly? That stack of white bread waiting to sop up your plate?"

Her chair scraped across the wood floor. "No, Penny, this is Soto's skirt steak marinade. But you've got to fill up on something. If handing me the butter is too much to ask, I'll get it myself."

Could I say anything to pierce that fatty armor and make the woman hidden inside hear me? She waddled over to the refrigerator; I feared never being able to eat again.

Her voice came to me from inside the fridge: "You know, Jock had an earlier cookbook with Heather Watts. Of course she had retired from the New York City Ballet by that point, but what a career she had—"

"Shut up. Now!"

My mother turned, butter in hand. "What's gotten into you?"

I stood, shaking with rage. "If you compare my life to one more famous person, I will scream."

I left the table and marched toward my room but could not get past those damned posters. Judging me from the security of their international fame and airbrushed perfection. Holding positions they'd practiced for so many years they'd better damn well have them perfect. Behind their glass, as untouchable as my mother. I would never be able to compete with these silent, more perfect children. *I don't fit in here. I am alive, Mother, and changing, and life is messy. I have skin and organs and I feel things deeply and I'm scared that I've lost more than my career, maybe my entire self, because all I loved is gone and you can't fix that.* What did my mother know of risk? She stayed at home behind the bulletproof glass of her inherited career and steady paycheck, with no clue of what it felt like for me to again and again expose myself to another artistic firing squad. *Mother, I am riddled with bullets.*

I pulled down Baryshnikov. Not for one minute more would he stay stuck to our wall—the man was made to leap through the air. I sent the poster flying, and damned if he didn't look good doing it before he crashed to the dining room floor.

"What was that?" my mother called from the kitchen. "Penny?"

Jacques d'Amboise: I imagined the trademark fluttering of his *entrechat huit* as he followed Baryshnikov's arc.

My mother appeared. Frozen in the frame between dining room and kitchen. "Oh my god, Penny. What are you doing?"

"Just making room, Mom." I gripped a trio of ballet dancers, took a few running steps, and heaved. Was that my mother shouting, or the roaring "Brava!" of the dancers? *Friends, you need hold these positions no longer!* Granitelike glutes relaxed so they might contract again; calves uncramped from relentless *relevé*. Setting these dancers free to move again felt like one of the truest things I'd ever done.

When I hit the wall of moderns, I found the rhythm and form and purpose that had deserted me. Taylor—*Smash!* Morris—*Smash!* Cunningham—I gave him a flip across a longer trajectory—*Smash!* My mother's voice was laced with hysteria. "Stop, Penny, please, my posters. They were our dream. You can't throw it all away."

"Only now you hear me? Because I'm threatening your posters?" I had never before inspired such emotion in my mother. She took advantage of the lull to rush forward and pry Edward Villella from my hands. *Worth a try, Mom—Smash!*

My mother was racked with such big heaving sobs that I held the last few posters over my head until the quiet caught her attention. She looked up at me. *Do you see me now, Mother? I am Penelope Sparrow.* I smashed the posters onto the pile.

Only one poster remained: Nureyev as Petrushka. My adrenaline ebbed in empathy for that soul struggling to emerge, from a puppet whose awkward appendages recall their strings. I placed my hand on his chest and waited for a heartbeat. An inhalation. Warmth. Something. Finally I took him down. I'd return him to my room where he belonged; he was all the inspiration I'd ever needed.

My mother skirted the mess and walked toward me, her sobs now soft hiccups. The three of us—she, Petrushka, and I—surveyed the empty hallway.

"You've erased our life," she said.

"No, Mom." I didn't touch her or attempt to comfort her. It felt too good to stand beside her, separate, feeling stronger than I had in a long time. "I've cleared some space so we can start over."

She stepped back and studied my face. "I don't know who you are."

This simple truth pleased me. "You know what? That makes two of us."

I sent my mother off for a bath while I cleaned up the mess. I rolled up the few posters that had survived the mayhem and stuck them at the back of her bedroom closet. A small peace offering. Baryshnikov was a goner, though—I'd sent a glass shard right through his Achilles.

By the time I was done sweeping up the glass and vacuuming, I was physically spent, but in that invigorating way only dancers and athletes can appreciate. I turned off the lights behind me and lingered in the hallway. The walls were pale blue—funny how I'd never noticed. It looked so much bigger now. I ran my hand along the wall. Despite the lasting images of the missing rectangles, it felt relieved. Like my heart.

Back in my bedroom, I released Petrushka from his solitary glass confinement and once again taped him to my closet door.

There.

I tried to rest, but the house's energy was haywire from sudden change. The open spaces in my heart begged to be filled with more positive energy.

I pulled out my cell phone and placed a call. While I couldn't connect, the recording cheered me.

"Angela Reed here. Not! Leave a message."

# RECOVERY

"In its structural sense, movement is 'the arc between two deaths.' On the one hand is the death of negation, motionless; on the other hand is the death of destruction, the yielding to unbalance. All movement can be considered to be a series of falls and recoveries; that is, a deliberate unbalance in order to progress, and a restoration of equilibrium for self-protection."

—John Martin, dance critic

# CHAPTER ELEVEN

*I*f Mauricio said fifteen reps, I did thirty. When he said rest, I took but a single breath. I'd show him what I was made of, and I'd find my way back to the life I'd always known to be my destiny.

I was pumping the shoulder press like a madwoman when a female voice broke my focus. "Hey, girl. Don't break that equipment. I need it, too."

I opened my eyes. Before me stood a thin woman with friendly brown eyes and a splash of freckles across her nose.

"Angela?"

She clapped her hands and gave a little jump. Her breathy laugh bounced up and down the musical scale before a cough chased it away.

"I left a message on your machine last night."

"I know, I was so glad to hear from you! My first physical therapy appointment wasn't until next week, but I called and told them I had a conflict." She winked. "They said they could squeeze me in today."

"How's your arm?"

"Shrunken." She held it up to show me. "I had complications,

so my cast was on for more than two months. It felt like forever."
She threw what was left of her delicate arms around me. "We
wonder about you all the time, but we didn't want to bug you."

"We?"

"Marty and I."

"So are you two dating?"

She waved away the notion. "We're more like buddies. So tell
me what's new. Are you dancing again?"

"Soon, I guess." The words leapt from my mouth of their own
accord. Mauricio wouldn't call me on it; he was finishing up with
an old woman learning to use a walker.

"Marty will be thrilled. Hey, let's go over and see him when
we're done here."

Mauricio walked over. "Angela Reed?"

"Yes, I am. How do you do?" She shook his hand and turned her
head back over her shoulder to mouth a word in my direction—*Cute*.

"I'll get you started in a minute. Penelope, you still need a massage, but I'm down one therapist and I had to squeeze in an extra
appointment. Can you come back tomorrow?"

With that, a new plan fell together. I'd stay the night with Angela,
and my mother would return to get me the next day. I was happy for
the separation; the air in the car on the ride down was so charged I
was surprised it didn't interfere with the car's electrical systems. I sat
down to wait for Angela in the same seat my mother was vacating.
She tossed me the magazine she'd brought along with her.

I smiled and shook my head as I opened the cover. At least she
was consistent.

*Dance Magazine.*

After Angela finished her PT, we walked south on Eleventh. "So how've you been?" I asked.

"Okay, I guess. I lost another roommate, though. A CF friend. That's always tough."

"Did you have a fight, or what?" I couldn't quite imagine anyone having a poster knockdown with Angela.

She shook her head. "She died. Only twenty-two. She just couldn't hang on any longer."

The language struck me. Was death—or life—really a choice?

"Did she die…at your place?" I could not imagine the horror of it.

"No, she went back to her parents'. It's weird, all you think about when you're young is gaining your independence, but when those final hours come, people want to go home."

We lapsed into silence. Death was a tough act to follow.

The city's bustle soon distracted me. People propped open shop doors, strolled baby carriages, walked dogs. Thrumming engines energized the streets. Car horns traded pitches; a distant siren trilled. Snips from overheard conversations created random poetry. On Locust, the Philadelphia Muses—giant dancers and musicians painted on a five-story brick wall—blew stimulating breezes at our backs. In the midst of it all, once again finding their balance and rhythm, were my footfalls.

Thirteenth. Spruce.

Then I saw it.

Up ahead, over the other buildings, the top of the Independence

Suites. For a while the happiest home I'd ever known, it now stared me down, determined to bring me to my knees. Why? I tried to convince myself that if I had no memory, I had no problem. But my heart raced. Palms dampened. Couldn't catch my breath. I looked over at Angela. Had she sensed the sudden thickness in the air? The rattling of her lungs offered a convincing answer.

"You've been speeding up," she said. "Could we knock back the pace a bit?"

I lost momentum; had to concentrate to place one foot in front of the other. The distance stretched, the sidewalk pitched, I had to train my focus at street level for balance. Doors propped babies strolled dogs walked that pink neon blinking "Independence Sweets"—did no one sense the danger?

Horns blared—*Now! Now!* The penthouse lured and my gaze responded. Five, six, seven, eight…I squinted against the brightness of the sky even as darkness chilled my core. Too close to the edge of the eighth-floor balcony, a lone scarlet flower swayed in the breeze.

Angela followed my line of vision. "Oh no—I just wanted to say hi to Marty. I didn't think. I'm so sorry."

Eleven, twelve…fourteen. There it was, so very far above me.

I shivered. My knees gave way; I braced myself against the building beside me.

"Penelope? Are you remembering something?"

Fingertips on concrete, icy-numb, grazing the balcony's edge. A clacking, like bones. I looked down. Below me, a great tremor opened a crevice in the sidewalk. The void sucked me down. A fierce wind flattened my cheeks and whipped my hair and wicked the moisture from my eyes, my mouth, my throat.

"The wind…" I reached for Angela—little Angela—to keep from falling.

"What wind?" She pushed her shoulder into my armpit to brace me. "Are you all right?"

With Angela's touch, the forces calmed. The sidewalk healed. The only shaking was my knees, the only crevice a scar on my soul. The space raging around me was once again, simply, space.

My throat was still dry from the wind and the falling and my words gelled—I had to squeeze them out. "I fell so far. How can I ever climb that high again?"

"Who said you had to build a high-rise? Not everyone likes them, you know."

Angela looped her atrophied right arm through my mending left—a move that would have been unimaginably painful when we met—and gave it a squeeze. "Before you go razing the Independence Suites, let's explore ground level. It's pretty sweet." Then, imitating Mauricio, she said, "You ready? Are you with me?"

I nodded, and together we crossed Spruce to enter the bakery.

# CHAPTER TWELVE

*I*t felt odd to be standing, for the first time, in this space at the very foundation of the building in which I'd lived for two years. Apparently, not everyone chose to pass it by.

It was so busy that Angela and I had to stand in line. I didn't want to stare at the two women in front of us, but couldn't help it—like rising dough, their flesh bulged beyond the confines of their colorful saris. Angela nodded toward them and mouthed the word "beautiful." I waited for a giggle that didn't come. Hmm. What did she see—their voluptuous health? Perhaps the red and gold and turquoise in the material struck her as an expression of vibrancy. Or flawless skin as brown and smooth as an acorn, or black hair so glossy it reflected the daylight. The delicate movements the one in turquoise made with her hands as she spoke.

Whatever Angela had meant, it gave me the courage to free my hips from the black sweater I'd tied around them to legitimize their bulk. I slipped it over my arm. In this place I would not be criticized for my size.

"Oh look, there he is," Angela said, as if she had spotted Bruce Springsteen, not a Jewish baker. She pulled me from line by the sleeve, towed me past some tables, and knocked on a window separating the store's back wall from the kitchen. Kandelbaum looked up from his work. Angela smiled, waved, and pointed to me as if I were some sort of trophy.

Angela threw her arms around him when he joined us. He kissed her on the cheek. When she pulled back, we laughed at the flour that had transferred from the belly of his apron onto her navy sweatshirt.

"No hug for you, then, Penelope. You are off the hook for today."

"You guys can call me Penny." A delighted look passed between them, as if I'd shared a secret handshake.

The two Indian women waved to Kandelbaum before leaving the bakery. "May Lord Ganesha smooth your path as he has mine," he called to them, and they blew him kisses. Already inspired by a fit of well-being, I tossed them a wave as well.

Kandelbaum pulled out chairs, and we sat at one of the tables. "So what brings you downtown, Penelope?"

"Wait a minute. Ganesha?" Angela said. "That's a new one."

"No, that's an ancient one. Ganesha is the Hindu elephant god, the remover of obstacles. And here's Penny—it seemed appropriate."

Angela told him about how she'd rescheduled her therapy appointment to coincide with mine.

"And so, are you stronger already? Let's see." He set his elbow on the table, and Angela accepted the challenge. He pretended to wrestle for a moment before laying his arm down in defeat. "I can see I'd better start working out."

Musical laugh, punishing cough.

"So, Penny," he said. "How are you doing? You look wonderful."

"It's great to be here." I wondered at the enthusiasm in my voice. Last night I'd suffered a meltdown with my mother, and moments ago, an odd wind rush due to trauma I couldn't recall. Just two months ago, on the other side of the front wall and feet from where I sat, movement had deserted me. The perilous scents of flour and shortening told me I was surrounded by foods I wouldn't be caught dead eating. But this unexplored pocket of my former life held a surprising sweetness, and I wanted to dust my soul with it.

"Are you still in pain?" he said.

"I feel a hell of a lot better than the last time I dropped into the neighborhood." After a beat, we all laughed. "I feel bad about your car, though."

"Has your memory returned?"

"No, still going on your testimony." I wished I could offer to help replace Kandelbaum's car, but my microscopic savings account and the twenty in my pocket wouldn't go too far. "So, how have you been getting to work?"

"I drive a van now," Kandelbaum said. "The insurance covered it. I should have gotten it long ago. My wife's car was never really appropriate for the bakery."

"You're married?" I said. Angela warned me off with a subtle shake of her head.

"Stories about me can be told another time," he said. "Tell me about you."

"Penny's been at her mom's in Allentown. She's staying the night at my place. Why don't you come over? We'll get pizza."

"If you make it Vito's so I can get the salad bar," I said.

116

"I'll treat. Shall I meet you at Angela's after I lock up?" Kandelbaum stood.

I raised my eyebrows and looked at Angela. Even I didn't know where she lived, and I'd be staying overnight.

Angela stood and nudged Kandelbaum's arm. "Aren't you going to…? You know."

"I almost forgot." He offered an elbow. "Miss Penelope Sparrow, may I please show you to my product case? Perhaps you and Miss Reed would like to pick out something to take along."

Perhaps not. To be polite, though, I took a look. Petits fours, baklava, rugelach, scones—they may hail from different countries, but they all spoke the same language to my thighs. In a corner of the case, though, down on the bottom shelf, was a hand-lettered sign: "Try our low-fat health breads."

"It's because of you I did this, Penny." He gestured toward his new products.

"How so?"

"Your disdain for the fastnachts I brought—"

"Disdain?"

He looked at me, raised his eyebrows, and smiled. He'd read me correctly—I hadn't had a doughnut since eighth grade.

"This made me question the nutrition in my baked goods. For the first time, really. The foods I bake have a long history of comforting people. Feeding the soul is what was important to me—I'd never thought the body might suffer from doing so. So I made up some new recipes."

I squatted down to read the labels. They listed ingredients like whole grain flour and egg whites, dried cranberries and applesauce, spinach and carrots, honey and maple syrup. Listed prominently were calories, fat grams, fiber content—information no baker in his right mind would attach to a rack of fastnachts.

"I used to work at this dance supply store in New York," I said. "For years I tried to tell the designer it was pointless to make a toe shoe so hard if the first thing its new owner did would be to soak it in alcohol, rap it with a hammer, and slam it in a door to soften the glue. He never listened to me. Now I refuse some doughnuts and look what happens." I rose. "Any interest so far?"

"Like any change, people are slow to accept it. We try to mention it to all of the customers, and we put out free samples. But people like you are, as we say in the trade, a tough cookie. I'd value your feedback."

I really hoped he hadn't gone to all this effort just for me. My heart stuttered as if viewing the calories had already thickened my blood. Angela saved the day by ordering some maple oat bran muffins and something he called Harvest Loaf. "You're going to love it," she said. I slipped my hands into my pockets and nestled my palms against my hip bones. Around this much sweetness, I'd have to work hard to maintain my edge.

Angela and I took our time on the walk to her apartment. We actually strolled. The waxed bakery bag in my hand was evidence: I had crossed into a more malleable world, one that just might respond to my needs. If this were true, I'd have to watch what I asked for.

# CHAPTER THIRTEEN

*A*ngela lived in a row home on an ancient cobblestone street. Hers had been divided into a first and second floor apartment. When we stepped inside her building, the woman on the first floor stuck her head into the hall to greet us.

"Hello, Mrs. Pope," said Angela. "Penelope Sparrow, meet my landlady."

Mrs. Pope was a squat woman with no neck, like a jack-in-the-box lowered into its container. A *Sentinel* lay on her doormat, rolled and rubber-banded. I waited for a look of recognition—MacArthur had, after all, splashed my name and picture across the front page of this woman's newspaper—but the woman flashed a wide smile that was at once comical and endearing.

"Listen, Angela, I'll be at my son's for a week, starting on Tuesday. Could you stop in and feed Shakespeare?"

"Cat-sitting?" I said, after they'd made their arrangements.

"Shakespeare is a parrot. She taught him to say, 'To be or not to be.' And then—"

"Let me guess. 'A rose by any other name'?"

"No—"

"'To thine own self be true'?"

"Believe me, you won't be able to guess. His other phrase is, 'Spread 'em, baby.'"

I laughed. "Former owner?"

She flashed a pixie smile. "Something like that. We're heading up this way."

We stood on a landing at the top of the stairs while Angela unlocked her door. She entered; I remained in the doorway to take it all in. Wrapped around two walls of the apartment, a mural in an earthy palette suggested a dune-filled desert. The effect added expanse to the efficiency, whose interior had been transformed into an oasis of self-expression. Amber track lighting illuminated two platform beds installed at different heights against the wall and accessed by a set of shared stairs. The first bed, about waist high, was along the left wall and had built-in dresser drawers beneath it. The other was a few feet higher and angled across the corner, creating a spiral effect toward the high ceiling. Within the cubby beneath it Angela had nestled a desk.

"Eight more steps and you're done with the tour—the kitchen and bathroom are back here," she said, pointing around the corner of the back wall.

"This is amazing. It's so—you."

Practicality and whimsy lived here in happy relationship. A rug of woven pine and turquoise fabric warmed the center of the room like a heated pool. Gauzy curtains framed a shelving unit to my right. A stereo and miniature television broke up its rows of colorful books. Large velvety pillows in greens and blues, with tassels evocative of an Arabian harem, were piled on the floor near a low glass table, filling in for pricier and less fanciful furniture. I felt giddy, as if experiencing a world more fertile than any I'd ever known.

"You can see how difficult it is to find the right roommate. Shared bedroom, constant coughing, quirky décor..." With a butane lighter from the bookshelf, she lit several votives floating in a bowl on the table. The room filled with the scent of eucalyptus. "I hope you don't mind. It helps clear my sinuses."

Angela disappeared around the corner while I explored an oddity in the front corner: freestanding pipes that would otherwise be an eyesore were painted like bark in striations of brown and gray. Thick copper wire wound up the pipes, then separated overhead into corkscrew branches, from which dangled feathers and a variety of other ornaments—including the piece of cardboard I had signed in the hospital. She had threaded a length of yarn through a hole in order to hang it. Grease stains surrounded my signature.

"My Tree of Life," she said, stepping back into the room.

"Where did you get these feathers?"

"The yellow came from Shakespeare's cage. I found the grays around the city. They're probably all from pigeons."

My breath set the feathers in motion, revealing an unexpected shimmer of purples and greens. I touched a white baby shoe, not much longer than my thumb. "Was this yours?"

She shook her head. "My sister's. She died young to CF. My mom has its mate."

"I'm sorry."

"I keep it to remind myself how lucky I am."

I turned around to take in the room again. It felt positive, creative, and complete—like Angela. "I don't know if I'd have enough perseverance for a project like this."

"I work like a tortoise."

She pulled the piled pillows away from the wall. Beneath a thin coat of primer on the exposed patch, I could see the greens and blacks of a former design. "This used to be a rainforest. I've been working on the desert for two years." I found the disguised incompletion endearing.

"If I'd worked for so long on something like that jungle, I don't think I could cover it up and start over," I said.

She shrugged. "You would if you wanted to keep painting." She finished restacking the pillows and her buzzer rang. Opening the door tossed the feathers on her Tree of Life.

"Anyone hungry?" Kandelbaum said.

"What's in the bag?" Angela pointed to the package balanced on top of the pizza box.

It was not my requested salad. "Wine. I didn't know, white or red, so I got both." He set the bottles on the table, went into the kitchen, and reappeared with a wine opener and three jelly glasses.

When we laughed at his choice, he said, "You only have two wine glasses. I thought it better that our glasses match. White or red?"

He poured white for Angela, but I put my hand over the mouth of my glass.

"Oh come on, Penny," Angela said. "This is a celebration."

"It's nothing personal, it's math. Dancers only have so many calories to work with, so the ones I take in have to count for something. I never saw the point in drinking."

Kandelbaum looked at me calmly, with a smile I couldn't discern. "You are quite hard on yourself." He uncorked the red and poured it into his glass.

I tried a lighter approach. "And pizza? My hips threaten to swell at the mere mention of it. Everything that goes into my mouth rushes through my stomach and gets dumped in the landfill of my thighs."

He raised his hand with quiet command. My best material, and he sat through it like some sort of Zen master. "You falsely assume the calories are empty. Wine is an important part of many transformative rituals. It carries our wishes for success, and good health."

"No matter what you say, I won't believe wine is a significant source of vitamin C."

Finally, he laughed. Angela and I took pillows off the pile and sat down on them next to the low glass table. Kandelbaum stacked two—he'd clearly done this before.

Oh, what the hell. It's not like I was off to an audition in the morning. "I'll try the white." The liquid was cool on my tongue, yet almost immediately heated the center of my body. Pretty magical alchemy. Angela opened the pizza box and put a slice on a paper plate for me. When the dance company used to go out for pizza, I'd suck on mentholated cough drops so I couldn't smell it. The gentler scent from Angela's candles couldn't mask Italian spices. My salivary glands responded.

"I only want half a slice," I said.

"Then only eat half," she said.

"A toast." Kandelbaum raised his glass. "*L'chaim*. Where there is life, my friends, there is hope."

"*L'chaim*," we repeated, and sipped from our jelly glasses.

"Now me." Angela raised her glass and called out, "*Tusherekee pamoja!*"

I froze with my glass halfway to my lips. "What the hell was that?"

"It's Swahili," she said, and took a bite of pizza. "I think."

Everyone cracked up. "You had me there for a minute," Kandelbaum said, his words bouncing along on his chuckles.

Angela coughed a few times and said, "No, really, it means 'Let's celebrate together.'"

"How would you know?" I said.

We looked at her expectantly. "I can't remember!" We melted into giggles once again.

The wine, the jelly jars, the mouthwatering oregano, the forbidden cheese, the way the mushrooms curled their lips atop the pie, the fact that I was touching something called pie, the sudden rush of alcohol and simple carbs and fats into a bloodstream unaccustomed to them sending my hormones into a frenzy, the fact that we were sitting on the floor like dancers but with pillows to keep us comfy, the smiles, the foreign wordplay—it was all freakishly intoxicating.

I looked down at my plate. Somehow I had eaten the entire slice. I drank straight from the bottle of white to wash away my sins.

"Whoa, you forgot to toast!" Angela said.

"*Putyourtushinmycheeky!*"

"No, seriously. You have to give a toast of your own." She smiled and waited, a sheen of sweat on her upper lip.

"Then how about this." I sat straighter and held up the bottle.

"*Cent'Anni*, Angela. One hundred years." I took a swig and passed the bottle to Kandelbaum.

"*Salud!*" He drank and passed off to Angela.

"Um, um…Clinkies!" We laughed until Angela no longer had breath enough to cough.

The next morning, a warm glow invited me to open my eyes and gaze out across the desert. When I turned over to look down at the other bed, Angela was looking back at me.

"The lights are on timers," she said. "I wake to a sunrise every day, even on days as rainy as this one."

"Thith plathe ith tho cool." The inside of my lips were sticking to my teeth. When I tried to sit up, an entire corps de ballet pounded boxed toes into my brain.

"When you decide to do something, you really go for it," Angela said. "So, which did you like better, the red or the white?"

"Unfortunately, I don't remember," I said.

"You'll feel better after a muffin and some coffee."

My stomach lurched as I sat up. I couldn't quite imagine eating for, say, another week. "I can't believe I ate pizza."

"I love Vito's. Yum."

I rested my hand against the front of the tee shirt I'd borrowed from Angela. "I can still feel it sitting in there. All in a lump."

"But the lump is in your stomach, not the landfill of your thighs?"

"Cute."

After a shower, I started to feel better once I found I could still pull my sweatpants up over my hips. As I flipped my hair forward to work Angela's comb through its wet, tangled strands, a memory formed. Not in my head, but in my abdominal muscles: laughter. Angela's bright eyes and freckles leaning toward me, her tapping my knee to make a point, the warmth of Kandelbaum's arm against mine as we rocked back and forth.

I hadn't had so much fun since my early days with Dance DeLaval. Back then, it felt like we were all traveling coach into the same storm of possibility—enjoying the jar and jostle, together in dance and life. Until Dmitri bumped me to first class by promoting me to rehearsal assistant. Perhaps it appeared to the others that riding up front by Dmitri's side gave me an unfair advantage. An added layer of job security. And it was a more comfortable ride, while it lasted. But didn't they know the survivors in a plane wreck are usually found near the tail?

# CHAPTER FOURTEEN

*I* stared at the rehearsal schedule, sure for at least a few heartbeats he'd made a mistake. Our first post-tour performance, at the Arts Bank in Philadelphia, and Dmitri had cast me in only one piece. Why would he do that? Dancers improve with use. They thrive on it. I needed to dance like I needed to breathe. He knew this, didn't he? As rehearsal assistant, I deserved more. Or did I deserve any of this? I was so grateful to finally have a job. Oh no. What if my size had finally become a factor? Our kinesthetic synergy wouldn't mean a thing if he no longer knew what to do with me. This wasn't a partnership, after all. Dance DeLaval was his company; the rest of us were expendable.

Tina popped in front of me to see the schedule. "Shit."

"What?" I struggled to escape the suction of my emotional mire.

"I'm in every single piece." She threw her dance bag over her shoulder and sighed. "It's going to be a tough couple of weeks."

I watched her grow ever smaller as her figure receded down the long hallway.

A few minutes later, I regained enough control over my voice to drop by Dmitri's office to oh-so-casually question his casting. He waved me in. Before him, a laptop played a DVD of material he and I had developed in rehearsal. I watched over his shoulder for a minute. Dmitri gently ran a finger down the computer screen. "I love your dancing, Penny. You are my muse."

Had I heard right? This stunning dancer, born of ballet royalty, saw me as inspiration? Penelope Sparrow was to Dmitri DeLaval what Nijinsky was to Diaghilev, what Suzanne Farrell was to Balanchine? As a child, fancying my future on the stage, I never dreamed I'd be so utterly appreciated.

The conversation had taken such an astounding turn I struggled to remember my reason for opening it. "Then let me inspire you by doing what I do best. Let me perform."

Small movements of Dmitri's eyes followed every nuance of my body—on the recording. "You are the one to dance if others get injured."

I spun his chair around. "An understudy?"

"This makes sense, *oui*? You know all roles. You will dance much, I promise."

Fear began to obscure my view from the top. I worried about the knee starting to bother me. That I'd lost so many years finding this company, I might not have many left. All dancers fear aging, even Dmitri. The subject was too volatile to broach.

Besides, he wouldn't realize the immediacy in my case. I'd shaved three years off my age on my performance résumé.

"So this constant reduction of my performance time." I sensed my career teetering on a fulcrum, but had to know. "It has had nothing to do with my body?"

"Of course," he said. He actually looked confused. "It is always about the body."

Unused to being discussed openly, my body almost contorted with tension. I said, "Use more words."

"Your body brings to life my movement and adds many ideas."

He stopped, as if seeking vocabulary. I waited. This time he could damn well come up with the words himself.

"You are beautiful."

He stood, cradled my face, and kissed each cheek. "I depend on you much now. In Washington, when we open at the Kennedy, you will perform *Puma* with me."

"Really? Promise?"

He closed out of the DVD player and opened a file with his proposed Kennedy Center cast list. And there it was. *Duet: Dmitri DeLaval and Penelope Sparrow.*

"I'll make you proud, Dmitri."

"You do every day." He touched his finger to the end of my nose. "I was wise to choose you."

I did get my opening at the Kennedy Center. The stage was larger than the space in which the piece had been first set, requiring we make constant readjustments to pull it off. I loved that kind of sharp challenge, and appreciated the opportunity to meet it. Right up until my entrance, when I smelled the Jameson on Lars's breath. I shook off my concern, hoping he'd simply taken a quick shot to quell his nerves.

In the middle of the piece, after the duet I performed with Dmitri, a series of turns took me offstage—for the audience, the effect is that the dancer continues to turn into the wings and beyond, in perpetuity. Since the stage was broad, I had to perform additional turns, which rendered me a little dizzy as I neared the blinding sidelights known as "shin busters." In the dress rehearsal, Lars and I went over and over the timing: he would enter early and slightly downstage so I would have a clear shot into the wings.

His buzz apparently trumped all that painstaking negotiation. Because as I spotted those turns into the wings, I also spotted Lars, again and again, blocking my way. By the time I realized he had no intention of moving, I had no time to decelerate and I hit the base of the shin buster. I knew by the crack that I'd broken my big toe, but without a moment's hesitation, I stood in the wings and taped it to the toe beside it, masked the tape with a few dabs of makeup, and re-entered without missing my cue. Adrenaline saw me through because I was not Penelope Sparrow, I was part of the dance, and the dance needed me. The next night, the dance would need Karly.

I hobbled into the star-studded opening night reception, late, in a $260 dress accessorized with a pair of flip-flops and a cane from the local ER.

When we got back to Philadelphia, my mood was as black as my toe.

"You need to fire Lars," I told Dmitri. "His drinking is a liability I should not have to pay for."

"I'll talk to him," Dmitri promised. I don't know what he said. Maybe they shared some sort of guy-to-guy backslapping. Because the next night Lars was back in the studio—and everyone was swinging wide. Fine by me. My foot was swollen and sore, and I didn't want anyone stepping on it.

For the next several weeks, while my toe was taped, I spent more and more time alone with Dmitri developing new work in the studio. Finally, weeks after my toe healed completely, he gave me a small role in his largest group piece, *Arena*. My relationships with the other dancers, however, never truly healed. Even Tina, who had thought of me as a sort of mentor ever since we auditioned together, made an unwarranted comment about me shacking up with the boss.

I had traded friendship for leadership, and was no longer one of them. I missed the camaraderie, but creative time with Dmitri fed my spirit in a way that kept me coming back for more.

At the time, it seemed worth it.

"That smell—I'm in heaven," I said.

Angela looked up from the low table, where she had been simultaneously reading the paper and squirting whipped cream from a can onto her oatmeal. "Nice hair." She pointed to my chest, where hairs from the right and left sides of my head were knotted together.

"I didn't want to break your comb. You're out of conditioner."

"Why don't you wear your hair short, like me? It's so easy to take care of. It would look cute on you."

"I can't. Dmitri wants it long enough to pull back."

Angela waited for my brain to catch up to reality. "You miss him, don't you?"

I nodded. I missed everything he had brought to my life. He

had connected with my purest form—my energy—and honored the way it moved through my body and the company and his life. How had I lost that?

My heart ached from emptiness. And my stomach growled—it was probably still wrestling that pizza. I pointed to her oatmeal sundae. "That stuff will clog your arteries, you know."

"That is a long-range consideration. Off my radar."

I pulled up a pillow and sat down across from her. "Is that why you're dating a married man? Because you're running short on time? I'm not judging, you and Kandelbaum are adorable together. I'm trying to understand."

"You're misreading his interest." Angela stood up. "I'd better get my pills."

"Don't you need a roommate?" I asked when she returned. "You know, for the thumping?"

"You mean the chest PT? It helps, for sure, but I can do it myself if I have to. Over at Presbyterian they have this vibrating vest that can do it, but my insurance company has given me crap about it and I can't afford it on my own. I put a 'Roommate Wanted' sign up over at Presby. The right person will come along eventually."

"Maybe I'm the right person," I blurted.

She said, "I meant someone with CF."

"Are you prejudiced or something?"

"But…you're living at your mother's."

"I don't know about the living part—I'm staying there." I thought of the rectangular impressions lining the emptied hallway. "The house is haunted by the ghosts of dancers past."

"Dance was an important part of your life." She looked over at the unfinished section of mural, exposed again now that we were sprawled on the cushions that had been stacked in front of it. "You can paint over it, but it's still there, underneath."

"I don't think I have a choice. It's time to start fresh." Angela's apartment made going home to my mother's a drab alternative. This place was alive with art. I wanted more time here. To smell it, to taste it, let it soak into my skin. Although it was too small to allow for much movement, I felt freed here—as if I were one of my mother's dancers, broken from its glass cage. A daughter freed from her mother's comparisons, a dancer liberated from the studio mirror. This room invited me to just…be in it. I'd made such a long trip across my own creative desert. I was thirsty for what creativity Angela nurtured here.

The phone rang. Angela said, "It's probably Marty, wondering whether you lived through the night."

It was her night he cared more about, I was sure of it. Angela had desecrated what was left of the oatmeal, so I sipped the coffee and sliced off a piece of Kandelbaum's bread. Its orange and green flecks assured me of vegetable content.

Angela put her hand over the mouthpiece. "It's my manager at the Bibliophile. She wants me to cover an extra shift. Noon to six. I'd say no, but I could use the money."

"We'll still have the morning." I pinched off a bite of bread and tasted it.

"So what do you think?" she asked, after she hung up.

"Crusty outside, moist inside." I took another bite and pushed the plate away. "He did good. That was delicious."

"You didn't like it?"

"Did I not use the word 'delicious'?"

"You only ate a third of a slice. It's health bread, for goodness' sakes."

"Healthy or not, unneeded calories are still unneeded. And I have last night to make up for, thank you."

"Dang. Eating is serious business with you, isn't it? How can you stay healthy?"

"It takes some planning," I said, reveling in one of my few remaining strengths.

"If I ate that little, I'd be dead. CF complicates nutrient absorption. Doesn't eating so little—you know, mess with your head?"

"Believe me, I know what anorexia looks like—the skeleton showing through, the fainting, the amenorrhea. I just have to stay on the right side of that line. And I have—I've always gotten my period, I have plenty of muscle—"

"I can't argue about your bone strength, that's for sure."

"It's all about self-control."

"But a slice of health bread won't—"

"You saw my mother. Genes are not on my side. She eats like—well, like you do."

"Okay, okay."

I hadn't meant to hurl the words quite as hard as I had, and I apologized. But the damage was done—Angela took one last look at her calorie-enhanced oatmeal and dumped it.

While I cleaned up the breakfast dishes, she asked if I wanted to come to the gym with her. "You can burn some calories as my guest. I have a pass right here." She lifted the pass from the Tree of Life, where it had hung behind my autograph.

I thought of her arm, her lungs. "Don't hurt yourself on my account."

"I've been doing a modified workout all along, even with my cast."

"But you're sick—"

"Not now," she said. "CF applies certain parameters to my life, but I'm not always sick. I need to stay strong as much as the next person." She flexed her bicep and a cute little walnut popped up.

The gym was only a block away. The Adonis who scanned Angela's card at the front desk greeted her by name; she called him Joey. We warmed up with a beginner aerobics class, during which our bombshell instructor offered specific encouragement to Angela. I sampled the machines at the same low weight settings Angela used. While others asked her how she was doing now that the cast was off, I quietly tested the limits of my strength. The workout wasn't so different from physical therapy, except one thing: here, I wasn't a patient. Working out alongside Angela and these other women increased my physical confidence.

By the time we got to the butt blaster, Angela looked ready to drop.

"Why do you do this to yourself?" I said. "Wouldn't it make more sense to conserve your energy?"

"You wouldn't say that to a dancer, would you? My spirit needs a strong house or else it leaks out all over the place. Whirlpool?"

"Seriously?"

A half hour later, Angela and I parted out on the street. My spirit felt lighter, as if I'd whitewashed the dark jungle of my past. Feeling more myself, I recalled that I, too, once frequented a place where people knew me and treated me with warm regard. A lifetime ago, yet only a few blocks away. I had some time to kill before my therapy appointment, so decided to stop in.

# CHAPTER FIFTEEN

The familiar scent of dry-cleaning fluid wafted over from Chen's Laundry and Herbal Supplements on the first floor, the source of a running joke that dance at the Bebe Browning School of Dance was "good clean fun." The stairs I once took three by three, as a quick warm-up when I was running late for class, I now climbed one by one, grateful that I still could.

As soon as I entered the reception area, I heard the piano. My heart leapt. I pictured Bebe readying herself for class, her hair dyed to a blond frizzle and flowing down over the caftan she always wore. I whipped around the corner and through the door—but instead of Bebe found a young girl tying the pink satin ribbons of her pointe shoes. The music came from a tape deck, not the piano. The girl was as surprised to see me as I was to see her.

"I'm allowed to be here," she said. "I got permission—"

"Relax. I used to do the same thing." Young talent is tender. It can only grow when safe from the icy glares of competitors. "I'm looking for Bebe."

"Oh, Miss Browning isn't back yet."

"When do you expect her?"

"The end of the semester, I think."

I tried to remember when I'd last seen Bebe. Late last fall? Once I moved in with Dmitri, time slipped away. "Is she vacationing?"

"She got a grant to study South American dance…I'm sorry, but I have to get to work."

She was a cute little bunhead. Watching her mark through a sequence brought back memories of simpler times, when trying my best was always rewarded.

On my way out, I saw the nutrition poster Bebe had put up when I was a teen. It was basically the food pyramid—with a few custom modifications. She'd added a new base—*DANCE: It's all you'll ever need*. Above that she'd completely replaced the bread group (which she called "dough") with glasses of skim milk and water. The layer of vegetables and fruits she'd left untouched; above them, she'd flattened the proteins and dairy to half their former height. The triangle typically sitting up top—representing sweets, fats, alcohol, and other "foods used sparingly"—she'd lopped off altogether. We called it the "Food Mesa." She'd had it laminated, and although it had yellowed a bit, its advice had held up well over time. I ran my hand fondly down its surface. Bebe had offered me the discipline and focus I couldn't get at home.

Beyond the food mesa, someone had tacked a snapshot of Bebe to the wall. She stood against a backdrop of mountains, surrounded by a gaggle of sun-bronzed kids, her closed mouth turned up at the corners. Bebe would not let that brown tooth be photographed. Beneath the picture hung a collage of postcards she'd sent from Argentina, Ecuador, Brazil—the dance world was clearly spinning fine without me.

I wondered if Bebe had any sense of the miracle that allowed me to read her words. She had probably contributed to it—if I'd drunk soda instead of the buckets of milk and water, who knew how many of my bones would have succumbed to the stress of my fall?

Ever since I left her apartment for Dmitri's, I'd acted as if he was all I'd ever again need. That was a mistake. Now she was off feeding her own inner artist, as she had every right to do. But there was a time, before she fired me, that I was special to Bebe. Her protégé. Now I was an anonymous recipient of group greetings.

Outside, the early morning rain had tapered to mist. Beads of moisture collected on my clothes as if they'd been sweating. On South Street, I passed my favorite mural, a massive mosaic that had always spoken to me. Pieces of broken mirror highlighted waves of color splashed across the side of a building. A line of tiles spelled out a message that still held hope: "Art Is the Center of the Real World." I ran my hand over the mural's uneven surface. From a reflective shard, one of my own eyes looked back at me.

I rounded the corner onto Broad across from the Arts Bank, where we'd premiered the first pieces Dmitri and I worked on as a team—*Puma*, *Arena*, and *Zephyr*. Margaret MacArthur, in the *Philadelphia Sentinel*, deemed them successes. I had read her review with conflicting emotions. I was flattered she had used such rich detail and imagery—we not only captured her attention, we inspired her writing. Yet she failed to note my contribution.

The omission ate at me for days until I finally asked Lars to see the program he'd printed.

❧

"Why'd you leave me out of this?" I said, after scanning it.

"Your name is there, two times." Lars pointed once to the roster of dancers, and once to my listing as rehearsal assistant.

"But not as assistant choreographer. You know I helped with every piece on this program. Especially *Puma*."

"Take it up with the boss." He stopped short of a smile, but I could tell my distress was of no concern to him. "Dmitri gave me the copy."

"In English?"

He laughed. "I just typed it up."

I didn't want to confront Dmitri in front of the others, so I waited until he was heading home. I grabbed my stuff and caught up with him.

"Were you happy with MacArthur's review?" I asked.

"Yes. Like me, she thinks the company looks strong."

"And you're happy with my contribution?"

"Every day I grow because you are beside me." He put his arm around me and squeezed.

"Why wasn't my name listed as assistant choreographer in the program, then? We worked on those pieces together."

He stopped walking and dropped his arm. The queer smile on his face revealed his uncertainty as to whether we were still having a friendly chat.

"The ideas were mine, Penny. You were helping. If you want to make a name, you can make your own piece." The mist escaping his mouth into the chill of the night underscored the import of his words.

"And Dance DeLaval would perform it?"

"If it fits the program."

I threw my arms around him. He peeled them away.

"Work on your own time. We will see how good it is. Show me what you come to, *oui?*"

Life continued as usual by day, but back at my little room above Bebe's, I couldn't sleep. Couldn't eat. This was a chance beyond anything I'd hoped for. I wouldn't be adding my fingerprints to the surface of one of Dmitri's ideas; I'd have a chance to leave my own footprints in Philadelphia's dance world.

I didn't have the confidence to call a rehearsal without knowing what I'd do—I couldn't, wouldn't waste the dancers' time, and risk their ridicule while choking in front of them. So I sketched their bodies in a primitive fashion on a piece of paper. Four perfect bod-ies—I wasn't so presumptuous as to cast Dmitri in my piece—and my own larger frame. They remained on the page. Stick figures, incapable of expression.

Dimension—that's what I needed. I emptied my change purse onto the table. For hours, I pushed around four thin dimes and one penny. It might have helped to put on some music, but I didn't want my dance to serve the music—I wanted the music to serve the dance. So I sat in silence, scraping coins across the little table in my apartment until I'd the scratched the finish off. I ended up with nothing more than meaningless floor patterns.

As an artist, even I had to admit: that penny didn't fit in. I'd either have to: (1) draw attention to my size difference and make something of it; (2) feature myself as a soloist; or (3) take myself out of the piece. I'd fought too long for equal opportunity to choose option one. And while I considered myself talented enough to compete against any dancer working today for a solo, I didn't have the hubris to bestow one upon myself. Unbelievably, I drew the same conclusion Dmitri had. Option three it was—I was out.

Even with this decision behind me, my anxiety mounted. It wouldn't suit for the piece to be "good." I wanted to blow the company's tights off. If we couldn't be friends, then I wanted at the very least to earn their respect. I wanted to surpass Dmitri's expectations. Win my own self-confidence. I had incredible resources right downstairs—Bebe, her dancers, and her studio— but I couldn't bring myself to ask for them. Besides, I had a grow- ing sense that not all choreography was transferable from dancer to dancer. When coaching Dance DeLaval, I encouraged each dancer to think about the work's larger theme, and infuse each step with his or her own experience of it. For me, it was this prismatic perspective that brought modern dance to life.

To do this my way, I'd have to develop the work the scariest way possible: live, in the studio, with Dmitri's dancers. I called each of them to tell them our weekend rehearsal would start two hours earlier, and trusted that when push came to shove, my inner artist would burst forth within me.

On Saturday, they faced me: Karly. Lars. Tina. Mitch. Four perfect bodies, capable of anything my imagination could cook up. A quartet? Two couples? A trio and a soloist? No matter how I subdivided, the same math failed me. Only now, eight eyes looked on, with only slightly masked annoyance. I dug deep, but inspiration refused to surface. I'd suffered too much criticism for too many years to expose my inner artist in an environment tinged with hostility. The silence pressed. My stomach cramped. I had no moisture in my mouth. The moment stretched, on and on, with the ramping inevitability of Ravel's *Bolero*—but without its climax.

Tina finally broke the silence. "So what's the big secret? Why did we have to come early?"

"I, um, wanted to surprise Dmitri with…" I couldn't complete the sentence.

"You okay, Penny?" Mitch said. "You look a little yellow."

"Sure." I went over to my dance bag and finished the roll of antacids I'd picked up on the way to the studio. I needed to set these dancers in motion, and I had to do it now.

Even though they were clueless about the hell I'd just endured, I couldn't look at the rest of them when I gave up. I spoke only to Mitch. "Can you put on the music for *Arena?* That group movement during Dmitri's solo—I think we can develop it a bit further."

My big chance—I could have given myself a solo!—and that's all I made of it. Without Dmitri to summon it, my inner artist refused to emerge. It remained walled off, like a spore. Dmitri, as it turned out, was *my* muse.

Hundreds of millions of dollars had been spent since 1993 to turn this section of Broad Street into the Avenue of the Arts. Ticket holders coming into town generated $10 million in Pennsylvania state taxes each year. Its venues held more than 14,000 people, who traveled into the city to see performers like me. The "me" I used to be, anyway. That day, I blended in with every other person on the sidewalk. My picture was not on a poster at the Wilma; my visage was not dancing across the big screen outside the Kimmel. Nor was Dmitri's—he'd used the Avenue of the Arts as his launch pad and the work we'd developed together as his fuel, and left me behind to breathe his exhaust. I had to face it: art was no longer the center—or the reality—of my world.

With only that twenty still in my pocket, I had a sudden need for a makeover.

I passed two pricier beauty shops before I found a wizened barber sitting on his Locust Street stoop, smoking a cigarette. I asked him what he charged. "Ten for a cut, five for a buzz."

I looked at his nicotine-stained fingers. "Will you wash your hands?"

He sat me in his chair, made a big show of sanitizing, and caped me. He pulled my hair out of its habitual ponytail. "What do you have in mind?" I had no plan. I simply wanted to see a refreshed image the next time I looked in the mirror. I was so literal in this intent, I asked him to turn me from the mirror while he cut so I couldn't see what he was doing.

"Ay, ay, ay," he said as he spun me round. "Ya better give me something to go on, missy, or you might be sorry. We just talking a trim?"

I perused the photos of local male celebrities on the wall before me and chose an old shot of Jon Bon Jovi. "Can you do something like that?"

Long hanks of hair fell to the floor, each metallic scrape of the scissors cutting my remaining ties to Dmitri. What loss I felt was balanced by my desire to see myself anew. When he finished, he said, "Want to see what I did, or walk outta here not knowing who the hell you are?" He unlocked the chair with his foot and spun me around. "See that, missy? Stick-straight before. Now this hair has movement." He flicked at layered wisps that accented eyes and cheekbones and jawline.

The result was both jarring and fascinating. In a lifetime spent before the mirror, in which I had called every aspect of my body into question, this was the first time my face had been my focal point.

I smiled at myself in greeting.

"Stop in often! New items every day!" promised the sign outside the Bibliophile, but the used bookstore looked stagnant and over-stuffed. I found Angela bent over, taking books from a pile at her feet and packing them into a box.

"Whatcha doing?" I said.

When she turned, the dark mask strapped to her face startled me. A happy face sticker brightened the nose.

"Angela? Is that you in there?"

"Penny? I love your hair!" she said, her voice muffled.

I ran my fingers through a style so new I couldn't quite picture it again. "It should be easier to detangle, anyway."

"Did you stop by and show Marty?"

When I shook my head no, the hair tickled my jaw. "Been on the move all day. What's with the mask?"

"Books are magnets for molds and mildews. This keeps them from irritating my lungs."

"Ah. Well, I'm on the way to physical therapy now. I wanted to thank you again, for having me overnight and taking me to the gym."

One of the books at her feet caught my eye. "If I had any money left, I'd buy you that one as a thank-you gift. It reminds me of you."

"*Living with Chronic Illness*? I've read it. I'm pulling together a box for the CF kids at Children's Hospital." She flipped open the cover. "See, we have a date stamp in each book. If it hasn't moved in a year, my boss donates it."

"I meant this one." I bent down and picked up a book decorated in bright greens, reds, oranges, and yellows. "*Tree Frogs*. A couple of these critters would look cute on your Tree of Life, wouldn't they?"

We laughed. "I've been thinking," she said. "Maybe we could give the roommate thing a shot."

"Really? You didn't seem so into it."

"Forgive me for not rushing right into rooming with someone who so recently flung herself off a building." A man at a nearby bookcase scooted away. She looked after him with wide eyes, looked back at me, and we cracked up again. I smacked her on her good arm. "Anyway, I guess I couldn't imagine why someone like you would want to live with someone like me."

"I like you."

She pulled the mask from her face. It left a triangular impression on her cheeks and chin. "When most people look at me, they see 'someone with CF.' But yesterday, in front of the Independence Suites, you were sharing stuff with me. Like an equal. As if I might have something to offer back, beyond calorie loading or what kind of IV port is easiest to flush."

"But you have other friends outside the hospital. Everyone at the gym knows you."

"They're acquaintances. It makes them feel good to be nice to me, but they're afraid to get close. They look into my eyes and see…I don't know, the reflection of their own mortality or something." Now she looked at me. Her eyes weren't simply brown, as I first thought. They were streaked with slivers of amber. "My own mother treats me as an illness that needs to be healed. Besides my landlady, you and Marty are my first healthy friends."

I burst into laughter. "You're holding me up as a picture of health?"

Angela offered something I'd waited way too long to find: the fertile soil of friendship. Alongside the Avenue of the Arts lay an entirely different world, one I'd never explored. Perhaps here I could sink some roots and let the new Penelope Sparrow grow.

# CHAPTER SIXTEEN

When my trunk was all repacked and I had nothing else to do but wait for Kandelbaum and Angela to pick me up, I realized how much I'd miss hearing my mother play the piano.

"One more 'Moonlight Sonata'? For the road?"

I sat next to her as she played. Listened for the slow, purposeful build. The loss, and its echo. A tinge of fear, a final resignation. When my mother spoke to me through music, our hearts always connected. This time we saw the drama through together, all the way to the end.

I hugged her warmly, then patted the piano. "Daddy must have loved you very much. He gave you a great gift."

She put her hand on my cheek. "I know. He gave me you." Tears glistened in her eyes.

"I'm not abandoning you. But I can't keep circling the living room floor, you know?"

I saw the Independence Sweets van pull in the driveway, heard doors open and shut. I stood and placed my hand over the heart of the piano one last time. "Don't stop playing just because I'm not here, promise?"

She nodded. "Promise."

"When I come back, I'll want to hear some new pieces."

My mother dabbed at her eyes and smiled. "Yes ma'am."

When the doorbell rang, I asked my mother to tell my friends I'd be right out. I had one last thing to take care of. Back in my room, I took from the desk drawer that framed picture of me standing in the wings. I slipped the picture and backing from the frame and looked between them. The rosebud my father had given me before my first recital was still pressed flat, along with the little card explaining that pink roses meant admiration and appreciation. I secreted the items once again and reassembled the frame.

I set the picture back on the desk as a quiet promise to my mother, then walked out of the room. If I was to make anything of this extraordinary second chance at life, it was time to find my own muse.

Living with Angela, the movements in my life gained purpose. Just three months after my fall and with my bruises faded to yellow, I was cleaning and laundering, caring for Angela the same way my mother had cared for me, even shopping for her considerable groceries. One day when she wasn't feeling well, about three weeks after my move, Angela decided she wanted to paint. It was late in the day—I was beat and I knew she didn't have the strength—but I humored her by spreading newspapers on the floor and setting up the stepladder we'd borrowed from Mrs. Pope.

"You're not up to this, Angela."

"That's why I have a ladder."

I climbed up to my bunk, kicked off my shoes, and flopped down. "Why don't you rest?"

"I'll soon have plenty of time for rest. This fatigue is from lack of oxygen, not a need for sleep."

Her breath was a low growl as she climbed up the ladder. The weather had grown warmer and more humid since I'd moved in. She lasted only ten minutes before she asked me to help with her chest therapy. I'd stopped in for a demo at the CF Center, but I'd had difficulty getting the hang of it. I could see faint paisley marks on her back where my cupped hands had bruised her. She didn't complain. I knew now to listen for the right sound, like a drummer: *chawp, chawp, chawp.*

My new and improved efforts were rewarded with a rasping cough, and she removed herself to the bathroom. Then she climbed back up the ladder, dipped her brush into the can of blue paint, and swirled it across the ceiling.

I looked up into her sky. "After my father died, I always pictured him looking down on me from the comfort of a fluffy white cloud."

"My vision of death is a little darker. He's a neighbor—a face I see on this street every day—but I don't know which one he is. And he's plucking friend after friend from my life." She rested her paintbrush on top of the ladder and looked down at me. "The group of CF kids I grew up with at Children's? I'm the last one. There's one lady at Presby in her forties, but I didn't grow up with her. And she's made it without her original parts."

"Meaning?"

"She had a double lung transplant."

"They can transplant lungs? Could you get some?"

"It isn't time yet. And it's risky. Lungs are scarce, and the rejection rate is pretty high. It's considered a last measure." She resumed painting.

"What do you think dying is like?" I could almost hear my mother—*Penny, your manners*. Yet Angela inspired such directness. Like all of us, she was going to die. Since her death was likely to come sooner, I figured she had given it some thought. I wasn't wrong.

"I suppose we die in as many ways as we live. But whether your heart or brain stops first, you ultimately die because oxygen can't reach your cells. Clogged lungs sure don't help."

"Do you think it will hurt?"

Angela looked out over the dunes and lowered her voice, as if death might hear her and rearrange the grains of sand. "Not if I'm in the hospital. They'll have me all doped up." She shifted her focus to me. Her gaze was a test. A challenge. "Most people won't talk about stuff like this."

I forced a smile. I didn't want to ruin her good impression of my fortitude.

"I've heard the doctors say that before clinical death, there's this wrestling match between the soul and body, as if they aren't willing to part."

"I'm not so sure I see body and soul as separate anymore. You saw how far I fell. You'd think my body would have expired, freeing my soul for some sort of cosmic dance. Yet I woke up alive, my soul still attached to this body as firmly as if it were imbedded within my connective tissues. If the soul wrestles to leave the body at death, that must be one hell of a battle."

151

"That part freaks me the most." Angela's voice faltered. "There's no controlling what's going to happen. People even shit their beds. And I know myself—I'm gonna fight like hell not to leave."

She briefly lowered her face to the sleeve of her shirt, then returned to painting her sky blue. I closed my eyes and matched my breath to the whisper of the bristles against the ceiling. I was almost asleep when she spoke again.

"How's the job hunt going?"

"Huh?"

Silence. I opened my eyes. She looked disappointed.

"Penny, maybe this isn't the best arrangement. You need to be pulling your life together, and here I am talking about grinding to a halt."

"I've been trying to pitch in as much as I can—"

"I don't want a wife. I want a roommate. Someone to help with expenses."

"You're right." Angela's fight for life felt so elemental; I wanted to be near the heart of it. Lightening her load or bringing her cheer was like giving myself a life force transfusion. So I'd been stalling, and decided to come clean. "I want to be here with you, you know? In case."

She climbed down the ladder, stretched her neck, and looked me in the eye. "That's not a game worth playing. I've returned from the realm of the near-dead so many times they're propping the pearly gates open these days so the keeper won't get bursitis."

I smiled at the image.

She ripped off a piece of cellophane and wrapped it around the bristles of the paintbrush. "Have you applied anywhere?"

"I have retail experience in a dancewear store, so I did stop in at Baum's, down the street, but they aren't hiring."

"At the risk of sounding obvious, you could teach dance, right?"

"I'd feel like a bit of an impostor at this point."

She cocked her head. "Explain."

Since she seemed truly interested, I sat up and took a moment to put my thoughts together. "It's more than telling someone how to put one foot in front of the other. Dance isn't the steps, it's the motion connecting one step to the next. To suggest meaning, the dancer must create intention by directing energy through a series of linkages and…well, my links are broken. How can I inspire others when I don't know where I'm going?"

"So taking steps isn't the problem, but intention is?"

"Exactly." The fact that Angela could follow my twisted reasoning made me feel more capable already. I slid off the bed, folded the stepladder, and leaned it against the wall behind the door. "Don't worry," I said. "If something doesn't turn up soon, I'll clear out so you can get a better roommate."

"An object in motion tends to stay in motion," she said, suddenly channeling Newton. "Let's head to the gym. I can take you one more time on my pass."

❧

The expanse of exercise equipment before us must have overwhelmed Angela. She said, "Three reps, each piece, three minutes on the bike. No aerobics."

Beneath her eyes were dark pillows, yet I knew not to suggest rest. I no longer assumed she pushed herself to exercise as a way to entertain me. She aimed to clear her lungs. To draw air. To stay alive.

We split up, working machines on the perimeter of the aerobics floor. I was over on bench press when I heard the collective gasp. I turned. The disco beat was still driving, but those taking the class were frozen in a huddle around someone on the floor.

I raced over. I couldn't believe this was happening. *Not now. Not so soon.*

But it wasn't Angela who had collapsed. It was the aerobics instructor, clutching her knee, her lower leg bent at an odd angle.

"What happened?" I said.

"I was turning and then I was on the ground," the instructor said.

"Do you have knee problems?"

She took in a sharp breath and nodded.

I looked up at the gathering crowd. "Is someone getting ice?" They stared at me as though hypnotized by the disco music. "You, go to the front desk, tell them to call 911, and bring back ice. You—run into the locker room and grab a pile of towels."

When the towels arrived, I piled them under her knee to support it so that she could lie down, and held the bag of ice on top. Shortly thereafter, the Adonis from the front desk, Joey, arrived.

"Are you okay, Suze? What happened?"

"My knee again," she said, dissolving into tears now that he'd arrived.

He pointed at the towels and ice I held and said, "Did you do this?"

"It was reflex."

The paramedics arrived, immobilized the knee, and lifted her onto a stretcher.

"You riding along?" an EMT asked Joey.

"I don't have anyone to watch the gym…"

"I could do it," I said. "I'm—I was a dancer for many years."

"I don't suppose you're certified?"

So many of the machines looked familiar. "I was recently in physical therapy, and used a lot of these. Between Angela and me, we can cover you for a couple hours."

"Angela Reed?"

Suzie moaned. "We'd better get going," the EMT said.

"Put Angela at the front desk. She knows the drill," Joey said. "You cover down here. I already have a guy on the men's floor upstairs. I'll call from the hospital once I know how long I'll be."

It was longer than they thought—at least for Suzie, who would be out of the aerobics business for the foreseeable future—and I ended up with a full-time job at the Fitness Evolution, due to qualifications I'd never thought to put on my résumé: rehabilitation after an inexplicable fall from a high-rise, credibility by association with Angela, and someone else's rotten luck.

Yet I thought it might work out. It was a snap for me to keep a group of women moving to a predictable beat for a half hour—kind of like dance, but without creative risk. No intention beyond elevated heart rate. The paycheck would be a godsend. An employee membership would also give me free workout and whirlpool time, not to mention the lap pool, steam room, and a sauna I hadn't yet tried. I could ease my muscles back into the kind of fluid strength dance required. Make a concerted effort to maximize my physical potential and find out, post-fall, what Penelope Sparrow was really made of.

And, I had discovered the secret weapon of the exercise underworld: the measuring tape.

Before things got cranking my first day, I filled out a chart for myself, measuring calf, thigh (ugh), hips (ugh), waist, bust (ha-ha), shoulders, and biceps. That much was pain-free. I'd never measured my body before in my life; I didn't need proof of inadequacies so obvious to the naked eye. Whatever numbers Dance DeLaval's seamstress came up with, she took down covertly.

But then, heaven help me, I had to face the scale. My partner in crime, my lover, and my nemesis. Its base heavy and squat, its back tall and thin. The notched beam, whose numbers I'd once craved daily, now ready to damn me for turning my back.

I stepped on, holding my breath as the beam clunked to the left, then slowly and fastidiously moved the weights. The numbers didn't have the decency to lie. Cold, hard fact: since I stopped dancing, I'd gained four pounds. I jotted down my results and hid the paper away in a bottom desk drawer.

Knowing my numbers were in that desk burdened me as much as the extra pounds. What if someone else found them? They'd know more about me than I'd been willing to tell myself.

The other girls were trying to show me the equipment, give me tips. But I couldn't concentrate. I hovered closer and closer to the desk, protecting its contents. Finally, I couldn't stand it anymore. I retrieved the paper, tore it into tiny pieces, and threw it away.

I didn't need it anyway. The numbers stayed with me, as if tattooed on the tender flesh of my inner thigh.

Angela's health improved, as if our brightening financial picture lifted a burden from her overtaxed chest.

"Joey seems really happy with you," she told me after I'd been working a few weeks. "I heard he wants to move you into sales soon so you can make commissions. Let's call Marty and celebrate."

Angela thought about Kandelbaum every time she wanted to celebrate something—and she'd celebrate anything. My new hair, my new job, the blue ceiling getting finished, the clouds added. I was starting to worry about his intentions; the guy had to have at least twenty years on her. One day, when I knew Angela was tied up taking another load of secondhand books over to the CF kids at Children's, I stopped by the bakery to talk to him about it.

He was behind the back window, making doughnuts, and a couple of small kids stood on the step he'd installed in front of the window for that purpose. They were spellbound as they watched him frost the doughnuts and sprinkle chocolate jimmies on top.

He held up a tray of finished doughnuts for their approval, and they clapped, as did I. He waved, wiped his hands, and came out to the children now gathered at the counter. He carried a misshapen doughnut. "This one doesn't pass my inspection," he said. "I'll cut it up, and you can each have a piece."

The children squealed with delight. The mother thanked him by buying a dozen more, and they left.

"One of my favorite parts of this job," he said. "I'm disappointed not to see Angela with you. Is everything all right?"

# CHAPTER SEVENTEEN

*W*e parked in the Penn's Landing lot and ate on the steps of the Great Plaza. While looking out over the Delaware, Marty ate his cheesesteak and I alternated bites of pear with spoonfuls of nonfat cottage cheese from the container balanced on my knee. "Angela says she comes here every New Year's Eve and Fourth of July for the fireworks," he said.

The poor man was consuming so many calories, what couldn't fit in his mouth oozed out. I held my breath as I wiped some grease from his chin, and he smiled rather sweetly. With food choice alone he was in enough trouble. Did I have any business adding to his problems? If Angela might soon be gone, did it matter if his wife knew about her?

And who was I to get involved? I never meddled in other people's business, let alone love affairs. What did I know of love? How it fails. How it can freeze-dry your heart and scatter your remains. I didn't even remember what love looked like between my parents. Yet Angela made me want to matter—to her. If it took all the fight she had to keep from drowning in harsh medical realities, I'd do what I could to make her air sweeter to breathe.

I stood up. "Could we walk?"

We trashed the containers and headed down the esplanade in the direction of the river's flow.

"Listen," I said. "Angela isn't well. She doesn't need these kinds of complications."

"Is it the cystic fibrosis? From what complications is she suffering? Tell me."

"What are you doing, keeping a diary? Angela is more than her disease. And if you're going to hurt her, you'll have to go through me."

"Why do you raise your voice?" he said. "I am in complete agreement. I'm lucky to have you both in my life."

"And what about your wife?"

He looked baffled. "Of course, I was lucky to have her as well."

"So you've left her?"

"I guess Angela didn't tell you." He stopped, took a deep breath, and let it seep out through pursed lips. "My wife died four years ago. It's still difficult to speak of."

I stopped and turned to him. "Wow. I had no idea."

He nodded with his head bowed, then resumed walking. "I fear I broke down a bit when I shared it with Angela. She has been protective, and very sweet. I can sense the god in her."

"If you'd rather not talk about it—"

"The sun is shining, and the bread rose today—I'm fine. It happened at a friend's house, on a summer day. You know how steamy Philadelphia can get. She asked for a glass of iced tea to cool herself, and drank it right down. One moment she stood next to me, smiling and laughing—I keep seeing her that way—and in the next she blacked out and struck her head on the pavement." He drifted off, watching a tugboat tow a freighter upriver.

"And she died from that?"

"She had an undiagnosed bleeding disorder. She'd been so healthy we never knew. For a week she lingered while blood filled her brain…" His voice grew rough. During a long pause, I sensed some inward struggle. When he spoke again, he said, "It was not meant to be."

"I'm so sorry—"

"Well. A glass of iced tea should have been no match for my wife's will to live."

"There was nothing you could do."

"Oh, but I tried. I knelt by her bed, every day, begging for her eyes to open. For her lungs to gasp for breath of their own accord. For her blood to do what it was supposed to do and keep her with me. But she just kept leaving. And I have been…so…angry."

I touched his arm to stop his shaking. "It wasn't her fault."

"Wasn't it?" If he didn't look just like the gentle soul I'd come to know, I would have feared the blade of his passion. "She was only forty. So vibrant. Look at what you survived, Penny. What Angela rises above, every single day. There is such beauty in the fight to live. We must all find the courage to go on."

I nodded at the truth in his last statement. "Angela has more of that courage than anyone I've ever met."

His whole body seemed to relax at the mention of her name. He smiled. "And I love that about her."

My love life intervention had gone so far astray I now wondered if Kandelbaum and Angela might be well suited for one another.

Maybe I should stick to the world of dance. Here, walking along the river of real life, I was completely out of my element.

Or was I only out of my element when it came to love?

"Contract the abdominals, it will help me, yes." Holding me beneath the arms, Dmitri lifted me out of the split while I wondered if making things easier for him should continue to be my goal. For months I had continued to help him create roles he would ultimately let Karly or Tina perform.

"Dmitri, we need to talk."

"Tsh," he said. He stood behind me and watched himself in the mirror as he reached out to the left, gathered space with his arm, and then returned to hold it over my head. When he lowered his arm, all those bits of air he'd energized rained down over us. He ran his hand along my rib cage and down my thigh before allowing its downward motion to pull him into a dramatic fall to the floor. He popped back up to try it again and said, "I like when you say 'we.'"

"About taking the company to Russia. I need to figure out how I can best support your goals while still performing."

"You are a bewitching dancer, Penny." He never took his eyes off the mirror. He began again, scooping and circling his arm, running his hand down my rib cage and thigh, this time spinning to the floor.

"I like that better," I said.

"What?"

161

"It was different that time."

"How so?"

I posed him in my former position and demonstrated. "The second time you spun down to the floor *sans* drama. It was better, like dissolving into a whirlpool."

"'Whirlpool' means?"

I made a swirling gesture toward the floor with my arm and a swooshing noise.

"Yes, perfect."

"We're a good team." I smiled at him in the mirror.

"Nothing is more true than this." He put his hands on my shoulders to place me before him again and hesitated, smiling at me in the mirror, before repeating the reach, the scoop, the overhead circle. But this time, when his hand reached my rib cage, I felt something different. A sensitivity to his touch, an appreciation in his fingers. As if he were reading me with his hand in order to see me in a new way. His palm slid across the front of my rib cage and came to rest on my abdomen. I verified the sensation in the mirror, then shifted my focus to the reflection of his eyes. His hand reversed direction, as if to check out the goose bumps left in its path, moving slowly enough that its exploration of my breast could not be construed as an accident.

Until then, I thought I'd had an intuitive sense of Dmitri's moves, but I had not anticipated this one. I pulled away and turned to look at him. I could barely breathe enough to say, "What's going on?"

"Penny."

It was like he called to me from the back of his throat. I looked at the way the pink of his lower lip didn't quite extend all the way to the edge of its fleshy ridge and wondered how it was, in all the times we'd worked together, I'd missed this extraordinary detail. I had to divert all resources to the effort to remain standing.

He said, "I want you for myself all the time. You know how I feel about you."

And I was thinking, *I do?* He moved behind me. To start the sequence again, I thought. But he pulled my body back toward his and kissed my neck. He murmured, "Having you near makes me wild." He gently squeezed all my most vulnerable parts—my thigh, my hip, my ass.

"I need you, Penny." He pulled me off-balance and rocked my body against his. He continued the dance then, allowing his left hand to slur down my rib cage and ooze down my thigh before he spun down to the floor. But this time he never let go of my hand, and pulled me down on top of him. He traced my ear, my brow, my nose. Then brushed those imperfectly pink lips against mine, tickling and tasting until I slipped my hand beneath his curls and pulled him to me, almost losing myself in his pliable strength and the feel of that baby-soft neck hair curled against my fingertips.

It was only a small but demanding morsel of pride, way down in my right pinkie toe, that protected me from letting anything else happen in the University of the Arts, where at any moment a college student or professor could walk in on us.

"Not here."

After a walk in the brisk night air, we rode the elevator all the way to the fourteenth floor of the Independence Suites next to a disheveled man who reeked of alcohol and cigarettes. After closing

Dmitri's door, we laughed when we noticed each other take a gulp of fresh air, then laughed again when the heat coming on sounded an awful lot like "Tsk, tsk, tsk." If the spell had dissipated, I needed to find a way to preserve our relationship without any undue awkwardness, but before I could say *you don't owe me an explanation*, he leaned his face so close to mine I could feel the warmth of his breath on my face.

"You understand me, Penny. Sometimes it feels like you are under my skin, inside, where the heart beats and movement begins."

Was it so easy for him to access his heart? What I couldn't protect with calluses was too vulnerable to survive the abuses of my dance life, so I'd splinted and wrapped and plastered what was precious to me until I felt full no matter how little I ate. Dmitri's whispers peeled back that protection like clothing, layer after layer, until nothing remained between us but my heart, frantic and fully exposed. One snide word at that moment and it would have stopped beating. But he spoke no more. He pressed his lips to mine, so gently, as if to taste my wounds. In return, I gave him all of me.

Kandelbaum's voice intruded. "I'd better get you out of this sun. You're flushed."

I was wearing SPF 50. It was Dmitri. The man still had the power to stir such memory that my very blood responded. I wanted to believe that if Dmitri's interest in me had been as obvious as Angela's in Kandelbaum, I would have picked up on it sooner. Why can't we see love when it's staring us in the face?

To turn me back around, Kandelbaum put his arm around my shoulders, and left it. "Our universe holds many mysteries. In one way or another, it seems we move toward them, not away."

"Yeah, well, you know I'm a fan of movement." I looked at him and smiled. "You're pretty philosophical for a baker."

"Baking inspires philosophical thought. You should try it."

Had to laugh at that one.

"Really. Every day, after mixing simple ingredients into a gluey glob, I test dough to the limit by kneading it. Then I leave it alone. All bread wants is time and warmth. When I return, the glob has doubled in size and is covered by a smooth dome. I punch it down until I beat the air right out of it, yet still it rises. It's an act of resiliency, and great hope."

Talking about Angela and the resiliency of dough had restored Kandelbaum's spirit. On this sunny day, with my new friend's arm draped protectively over my shoulder, I felt some good may have come from my own trauma: because of it, Kandelbaum and Angela had met.

When we reached the van, he opened the passenger side door for me. A philosopher and a gentleman—the type of person Angela deserved. I shook my head at my own cluelessness. I'd come here to flag him away from Angela. Now I hoped he'd head straight toward her.

# CONTRACTION

"[Martha Graham's] theory of 'contraction and release' was built on the act of inhaling and exhaling. The dancer, whether sitting, standing, kneeling, or lying down, caves in as if suddenly hit with a blow to the center of her body."
—Deborah Jowitt, dance critic

# CHAPTER EIGHTEEN

*I*'d been working at the Fitness Evolution for a month when my mother waddled into the gym. It was the end of June.

"You still aren't very good about staying in touch," she said.

"How did you know where to find me?"

"This isn't exactly a hideout. Angela told me."

Is it ever possible for a daughter to break free of her mother? "I needed time on my own for a reason."

"Well, excuse me." She reached into her large handbag. "I'm still getting bills from the hospital."

She plopped a rubber-banded bundle on the countertop—right on top of a fitness evaluation sheet. Inspiration hit.

"Come here." I slipped a measuring tape, extra-long, from a hook on the wall. I put it around her waist and marked down the number—55 inches. More than twice my own measurement, and I was a head taller.

She gently elbowed me away. "What are you doing?"

"Selling you a membership."

"Why? I don't exercise."

"Mm-hmm."

Bicep: 16. I had to watch how tightly I cinched the tape. So much of her strength was bluster, so little of it muscle.

"It's too late. I'm fifty-five—it's all downhill from here."

Bust: 49. Hips: a whopping 62.

"I don't think I could fit on some of these machines."

"That'll give you something to look forward to. We have a pool, though. You could start with water exercises." Thigh: 32½. Calf: 17. Tears pushed at the back of my eyes. My mother had been such an overblown, unstoppable force in my life. I would have thought the size of these numbers would prove that. They didn't. Seeing my mother bullied by numbers in the same way I was made her seem smaller. Weaker. More relatable.

I took a deep breath to steady my voice. "Step on the scale."

"Can't I work out first?"

"It doesn't work that fast."

At least she hadn't lost height—she still measured five-foot-five—but she weighed two hundred forty-two pounds.

I showed her the sheet. She gave it a good long look.

"I guess I can try," she said.

"Trying won't be enough. You've got to commit for the long haul." I held out my arms and spun around. "Look at me, Mom. Four months ago I couldn't walk. Now I'm doing aerobics."

She put her hand on my cheek. "It couldn't have been easy."

"It won't be easy for you, either. But now that it looks like I'm going to be staying around…" I lowered my voice. "It would be easier to love you if I knew you cared about being here, too."

My mother glanced nervously at the people around us. "Good mother of god, what's gotten into you?"

"Nothing new, believe me. I'm just finally letting a little something out."

She let out a long sigh. "What would I have to do?"

I took her around the room and led her through a pretty easy program. I didn't want to be the one responsible for her heart attack after berating her for all the damage she'd done to herself. I had her finish on the exercise bike and showed her how to set it at the easiest level. I had to break away to tend to another client, though, and when I returned, sweat was trickling down her face.

"You have to start slowly." I turned the intensity gauge back to where I'd left it.

"It must have slipped."

"Right." I handed her a towel. "That's enough for today. How do you feel?"

"I never thought I'd be in a gym in my life. It feels weird."

"Weird good or weird bad?"

"I don't know. My heart is pounding, my lungs are on fire, and this sweat is coming out everywhere. Even my eyeballs." She dabbed at her eyes with her towel to convince me.

"You described what it feels like to be alive, Mom. *Really* alive. It's about time." Something about our role reversal emboldened me to close the deal. "It's forty-five dollars a month."

She dismounted. "That's a lot of money."

"You used to spend more on my toe shoes."

"But now I have to save for retirement."

"So you can do what, sit around, bored? You need to get in shape so you have a retirement to enjoy." She wanted to sit, but I made her walk around the room with me until she looked less flushed.

"How often would I have to come? With the price of gas and all, this will add up."

"Three times a week. We have a gym west of Allentown, too, but if you buy the membership from me, you'll be my first commission. In a couple of weeks, you can transfer, then just come back every now and again to visit. And to get measured—I'll keep tabs on your stats from this end."

"You've gotten quite bossy." She smiled and snapped at me with the towel.

Another instructor, Haley, called to me from across the room. "Hey, Penny, next aerobics starts in two."

"I have to teach. Make the check out to Fitness Evolution."

For the first few minutes of my class, I caught my mother bopping along to the music out of my peripheral vision. I'd purposely put on Tito Puente. She'd left by the time I returned to the desk after aerobics. I picked up the clipboard with her fitness evaluation sheet, hoping to see a check. Looked under it. Moved things around on the desk. Even looked on the floor around it, once again succumbing to the irrational hope that she might give a crap about herself—and once again coming face to face with my own impotence in our relationship.

Joey greeted me at the front desk the next day. "Congratulations on your first sale. I hear you give a mean pitch."

"I do?" Maybe he was joking. A lot of guests had come in for my aerobics classes lately, and come up to talk afterward. I wondered which of them had decided to join.

"And I haven't even put you on the sales staff yet," he said. "Guess I'd better catch up. But I need to talk to you about something else. Can you come into my office?"

Since Joey had never formally interviewed me for my position, I'd never been in his office. The walls were plastered with training certificates and pictures of him all oiled up and dressed in a teeny blue Speedo. The floor was edged with trophies. "You're a bodybuilder. I don't know how that escaped me, Joey."

"That's Mr. Pennsylvania to you." He shut the door behind us. "But I didn't always look like this. I was overweight as a kid. That's why I think what you're doing for your mother is so awesome."

"My mother?"

"Oh, and her paperwork is all complete. She stopped by the office on the way out yesterday."

He invited me to sit—not in the comfy leather lounger wedged into the room, but on a folding chair from which he cleared a pile of jump ropes as tangled as the skepticism and hope and pride and fear of disappointment his news inspired within me. Was this a commitment on my mother's part, or a token purchase meant to placate a fragile daughter?

Joey perched on the arm of the lounger. "It's about the schedule. Karen and Haley came to me on behalf of the other women's fitness instructors to complain about your aerobics classes being so big."

"This is a problem?"

"Afraid so."

"Increasing participation in a program that promotes health and fitness—in a gym, of all places. Gee, where did I go wrong?"

"They say their prospective clients are distracted during sales tours."

"Because the room gets so crowded?"

"Because your music is weird."

"People like it!"

He crossed to his desk and opened his planner. "I think they're really worried that members are flocking away from their classes."

"With a little effort, they could find interesting music, too."

"They feel threatened by you. They aren't as creative."

"For crying out loud. Did they give Suzie this kind of crap?"

"I'm filling in the blanks on some of this. Their official complaint is that since you took over for Suzie, you're getting all the choice shifts." He consulted the planner, on which he had drawn arrows reordering all the information. "I'd like to start you at five a.m. for a week or two and see if things calm down."

I sighed, stood. "Whatever. Should I stay for my shift today?"

"Yes, but Karen will teach your noon aerobics."

The noon class. A choice time, to be sure, with so many giving up their lunch hour to work out, but I was the one who made that class what it was. It had doubled in size since I started teaching it. I thought about walking out in a huff.

The thing was, I'd started to care about some of the women who came to the gym. I'd heard stories of abuse, broken hearts, surgeries, accidents. Some of them showed a lot of courage in facing the limitations of their bodies. They were starting to feel like family. I wanted to keep my job, and if they wanted to sideline me for my noon aerobics class, so be it.

But I did get a kick out of watching what happened that day.

At five of twelve, the usual suspects gathered in the middle of the aerobics floor. First a few, then seven or eight, then, by noon, a good thirty-five or forty. When a B-52s disco beat started blaring from the speakers, people looked at each other, wondering what was going on. I thought I saw one of them pointing over toward me, but I pretended not to notice and continued filing evaluation forms. In my peripheral vision, I saw Karen strut to the front of the room in her thong leotard.

"Okay, people, get your feet moving. Let's run in place." She lifted her knees and pumped her arms, exaggerating the effort it took to go nowhere. A flurry of false activity ensued and the crowd dissipated. They weren't rude about it; they just acted as if they hadn't really meant to be in the middle of the room at all, and continued on across to a piece of exercise equipment. Only a handful of prancers remained. It was all I could do not to laugh.

# CHAPTER NINETEEN

$\mathcal{B}$y midsummer, my bruising had been replaced by darkened skin, as if I was doomed to wear my own shadow. Dressed in sweats, a tee, and sneakers, though, I passed for any normal aerobics teacher. But July 23 would be no normal day: I had been working at the Fitness Evolution for eight weeks. I arrived early to have the measurement station to myself.

A shiver of excitement ran through me. I'd adhered to a dietary regimen that would have met with Bebe's strict approval, even while stocking Angela's calorie-laden foods. I'd burned calories in dozens upon dozens of aerobics classes. I'd been working out on the machines with low resistance and high reps—the formula, the other instructors told me, for long, lean muscles. Soon, I'd have my numbers. The numbers never lie. All my life the scale had told me what the mirror couldn't: I was staying on track. Sticking to the plan, doing what I could, and doing it well.

But this time I did not seek the simple pat on the back the numbers had delivered before my fall. Now I needed them to predict my future. I knew I had to get my body into peak physical shape, and I'd tried. Problem was, I no longer had any idea what shape that peak might take.

I held the measuring tape…but couldn't unroll it.

The rigorous workout, the spare diet, the injuries, the rejection—before the fall, I'd accepted all that and more for dance. For those moments of communion with a timeless creative force whose flow bestows power and life, whose ebb humbles. But that glory was fading from my muscle memory. Leaving me to deal with the only thing I hadn't been able to accept, the one thing that had undeniably passed directly from my mother to me—my body.

I stood before the mirror and closed my eyes. Ran my hands over my neck and collarbones, felt for the pin in my shoulder. Navigated the swell of my breasts, the flat of my belly, the bulge of my hips, the barrels of my thighs. My nerves—not my mother's—registered the touch. My brain registered the pleasure. I owned these sensations. It wasn't dance, but it was something.

Why let another set of measurements devil me? The two sets I had told me all I needed to know: objectively speaking, my body was nothing like my mother's.

But the scale. My heart rose in my throat; the scale looked back with cool detachment. Truth came easily to this dark guardian.

In the end I don't know if it was bravery, or fear, or some long-lost instinct to protect myself. But I turned my back on both tape and scale, and prepared to teach my first class.

That summer I kept hoping things would heat up between Kandelbaum and Angela, but she was in no shape to romance anyone. She was getting weaker, shortening her work shifts to no more than four hours. The onset of diabetes necessitated self-administered insulin shots, and she had to check into the hospital for more frequent "tune-ups." That's what she called them. With the biological images so scary, I also preferred thinking of her medical needs like car maintenance.

Then in early September I caught a cold. I didn't take it seriously at first. For whatever reason, ill health had never before struck me down. I took over-the-counter meds and tried to keep working. For Angela as much as for me, so she wouldn't worry about our finances.

Kandelbaum and I had made plans to take Angela to the Jersey shore after my morning shift on Labor Day. When I didn't meet his van out in the parking lot as planned, he came into the gym to look—and found me sitting at the front desk, shivering.

He touched the back of his hand to my face. "You're burning up."

"Get Angela." The interior space between my vocal cords and my ears was so stuffed up I didn't recognize my own voice. "You guys go ahead."

"We'll cancel."

Kandelbaum drove me to the ER, and then to the pharmacy to fill my prescriptions. When he got back to the van, I said, "I've got to call my mother. I can't go back to the apartment."

Saying that much brought on a coughing fit. Until then, I had always thought of my lungs as two balloons that expanded and contracted. Their wheezing now inspired a different image:

natural sponges soaked in honey, with only a few recesses empty enough to accept air. I wondered if this was what Angela felt like, every day.

"That's too far in your condition. I'll take you to my apartment."

I woke up when he parked in front of his apartment building, across the river in Pennsauken, New Jersey. Once inside, he steered me past a kitchen area to the right, a living area to the left, toward the bedroom straight ahead.

He fussed about a fresh pillowcase, but all I could think was, no way in hell was I sleeping in this man's bed.

"I'll sleep here," I said, flopping onto the couch.

"Not yet. You need to take these."

I sat at a small round table in front of pills and water while Kandelbaum unfolded the couch and made it into a bed. "I should sleep here, Penny. It's lumpy. You'll be much more comfortable—"

"No, I won't. Really, thanks." I had trampled all sorts of boundaries in my life, but this would not be one of them. Kandelbaum's bed, if she wanted it, was Angela's. Chills rattled my bones, so I slipped off my shoes and climbed beneath the sheets, clothes and all.

Kandelbaum was a good nurse. He wrote my medication schedule on a pad next to the couch and checked off each dose as I took it. He put a bent straw in my water and made me drink it all the way down. While I slept, he slipped out and picked up a bag Angela had packed for me.

The next morning, when Kandelbaum peeked out from his bedroom, he found me sitting up. "Feeling better?"

"My fever broke. I'm afraid the sheets are all wet."

"Are you hungry?"

"Actually, yes."

While I sipped tea and nibbled at one of his maple oatmeal muffins, he said demand for the new products was growing and they were struggling to keep up. "Even the dishwasher boy is baking," he said.

"They need you more than I do. Go."

He wouldn't think of leaving without changing the sheets first. I asked if I could use his phone to call in to work and touch base with my mother.

"Of course, you don't need to ask. But Angela has been in touch with Joey. He's not expecting to hear from you for the rest of the week. She also said to say she and the other ladies have registered a complaint with Joey about the 'renaissance of disco.'"

I laughed. He sat down next to me, on the only other chair at the table.

"Your mother knows you're here and called in for an update. She's at work now but will call again this evening. I disconnected the phone out here so it wouldn't wake you."

"You are a total sweetheart, Marty."

He smiled. "I don't think I've ever heard you say my name before."

"Don't get used to it. In my head I call you Kandelbaum."

He cocked his head to one side. "Why?"

I shrugged. "You were this stranger who showed up in my hospital room at the worst moment of my life, acting like you belonged there. Guess I needed to keep you at arm's length. You deserve better. Hey—maybe when I get back to work I can get you a free workout."

He shook his head and chuckled. "Perhaps this preoccupation with fitness isn't as healthy for you girls as you think."

"What do you mean, 'you girls'? Is Angela okay?"

He hesitated a beat; I was sure of it. "She says it's nothing to worry about."

He had his hand on the door when I said, "One more thing. Do you have any more tissues?"

"I'll run to the store and get some now. It's just a few doors down."

"Thanks. I've been resorting to toilet paper. Which reminds me—"

"I'll get more of that, too."

Angela insisted she could have picked up germs at the gym, same as me. Even over the phone I could hear her wheezing.

"And here I am with Kandelbaum waiting on me hand and foot. We should switch places."

"You stay right where you are and concentrate on getting better. I've got everything I need for the time being. I'm already on antibiotics, and Mrs. Pope checks in on me now and then. Who knows, I may just beat it."

"And if you don't?"

"That's why I keep a stable of handsome young doctors at Presby."

"You *are* sick. I've seen some of them."

She pretend-laughed—"Heh-heh-heh"—to avoid coughing.

"Seriously, Angela. At least stop in for a tune-up."

"I am. Tomorrow. I don't want this thing to get too far out of hand, either."

A sense of impending doom loosened my tongue. "Kandelbaum really is a sweetie, Angela. I can see why you're in love with him."

I heard jagged coughing; the phone collided with the floor. "Angela? Angela—are you okay?" I shouted into the phone. "Can you hear me?"

She got back on the line. "I'm here. Sorry, you got me laughing. You think I'm in love with Marty?"

"You haven't exactly hidden it. And he loves you, too. I can hear it in his voice."

"You are so wrong. I don't have the kind of body men fall in love with. He's just a loving person. You hear loving-kindness in his voice."

"If there's nothing going on, why do you keep orchestrating reasons to have him over?"

"So he can spend more time with you."

"If he wanted to spend more time with me," I said, "he could just ask."

"This is Marty we're talking about. If he wants an apple, he isn't going to go out to the orchard and pick it. He'll stand under the tree and wait for one to fall on his head. Has he told you about his wife yet?"

"That she died? Yes."

"And that he prayed to God to ease his loneliness. Like every day."

"Not in so many words."

"So one night he's driving to work," Angela said. "It's earlier than usual, not long past midnight, and the streets of the city are so deserted he's talking to God while he drives. He asks God for a sign. Will love ever come into his life again? Well, right after he thinks this, he notices that every single

light on his way to work has been green. 'Is this a sign, God?'
he says. Could be, he's thinking, but on the other hand, this
isn't his usual travel time, he can't be sure. Then he gets to
the last light between home and work and hits a yellow. He
slows, but this yellow is longer than usual, a lot longer, and
since no other cars are coming, he decides to pass through. He
says, 'Was that a sign, God? Because if these are signs, I can't
read them. Can you be clearer?' Then he parks the car in the
alley and you enter the picture—by falling from the sky and
landing on his car."

# CHAPTER TWENTY

*A*ngela's story left me reeling. Could I have had this all wrong? If Kandelbaum had ever thought of me as a potential love interest, I'd know by now. And I loved Kandelbaum like an uncle, not a lover. I had to get this sorted out.

But how? I was certainly no expert on dating. Before Dmitri, I'd madly loved only one other dance partner—my clumsy, rhythm-challenged father. But he worked long hours at the store and traveled for business, and as soon as my mother was done at the candy factory, she'd run me to classes and rehearsals. What chemistry may have passed between them I hadn't witnessed. At my performing arts high school, the boys in my dance classes only had eyes for each other. I didn't go to prom; instead, my mother banked the money she would have paid for the ticket and dress toward my participation in the Young Dancers Workshop at the Bates Dance Festival—an arrangement I negotiated. The only heterosexual male flesh I'd pressed belonged to the dads at Bebe's meet-the-teacher events.

So Dmitri—oh Dmitri—he threw me for a loop.

Every time he came near me in the studio, my muscles

contracted with anticipation. At first, accustomed as we all were to touching in front of the others, only a sharp observer would have seen the suggestive glance or lingering touch that made us desperate to get to Dmitri's each night. I ran back and forth to my place to pick up new clothes, exhausted but deliriously happy. After a couple of weeks, we gave up the charade. I left my little room at Bebe's for the last time, and made Dmitri's penthouse our home.

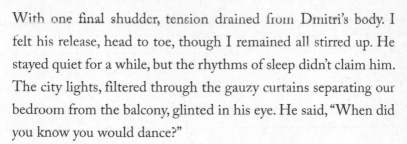

With one final shudder, tension drained from Dmitri's body. I felt his release, head to toe, though I remained all stirred up. He stayed quiet for a while, but the rhythms of sleep didn't claim him. The city lights, filtered through the gauzy curtains separating our bedroom from the balcony, glinted in his eye. He said, "When did you know you would dance?"

It took me a minute to shift into verbal mode. "I just always danced. As far back as I can remember. My mother would play the piano and I'd twirl around the room."

Dmitri kissed the top of my head and brushed his thumb down my nose. "One day I will meet this player of piano to thank her."

I thought it best to change the subject. "How about you?"

"Like you, I did not decide. I always knew I would bring modern dance to Russia."

"That's precocious."

"Child of plumber is plumber, child of soldier is soldier. I am the son of a dancer and an ambassador. I will make a company that travels. My mother trained me for this."

With that line of thinking, I was destined to be either a quality control inspector for chocolate-coated deer jerky or an outdoorsman with a wicked sweet tooth. It seemed prudent to keep the focus on him. "When did she start this training?"

"My mother said she started to stretch my hips when she changed my *couche-culotte*."

"Your what?"

"Baby pants…for sleeping? What is word…"

"Diaper?"

"Yes, diaper. Later I biked up hills near our apartment to develop the leg muscles. Each day she wrote out exercises for me. I learned to read this way."

"Sounds like she was training you for Olympic gymnastics, not dance." He rolled away from me to face the wall. I snuggled up against his back and slipped my arm around his chest. His body felt tense. "What's going on?"

It took him a while to answer. "This body is trained, yes. But is my art prepared? Do I have something to say to the people of Russia?"

"Why are you suddenly uncertain?"

He was silent for some time before saying, in a thin voice, "I have only a few ideas for the new piece."

I smiled. "That's artistic flamboozlement."

"I do not know this word."

"That's what Bebe used to call it. It's that normal, healthy doubt that accompanies the artistic process. While you're working on the new piece, casting about for the right material, it's normal to have doubts. You have to trust the process." A wise little lecture from a

186

dancer who'd been artistically flamboozled ever since Dmitri had offered her the chance to choreograph.

"My mother was beautiful dancer, like jewel in the Communist crown. But Europe wanted to see her also and asked for her by name. Officially, the Soviet government cleared her to tour, but the KGB got another dancer to drive a sharp tack into her toe shoe. Next time she put it on, she tore her foot and needed stitches. It just missed a tendon. Another time they poisoned her food. She understood the message: she would dance for the Soviet Union or dance no more."

"How did she escape?"

"She married my father, a French citizen, and had me. She told them she retired, but when she got to Paris, she still had many years of dance inside her. But she never stopped feeling inside her shoe with her fingers before putting it on."

"That's horrible. But you can't rewrite history."

"But I could play a role in history. Soviets took away expressive freedoms that should be the right of every artist. U.S. gave political asylum to Baryshnikov. Before that, Paris gave asylum to Nureyev, then my mother. All became great artists. You see what it would mean to carry freedom back into the land that hurt my mother? Young dancers could grow up believing in a world where all is possible."

"It's a beautiful vision, and I love you for it." I stroked his back. My hand instinctively found a knot of tension and kneaded it.

"When you take the germ of my ideas and grow them, you make this look easy. What if I don't have enough inside?"

I kissed Dmitri's pale shoulder, tasted its salt. "You have enough inside, Dmitri. Remember the love of movement that inspires you." When he didn't speak, I tried to help him reconnect to his passion. "Tell me. When did you first feel that love?"

Dmitri turned back toward me, kicking the covers aside, and pressed the full length of his naked body to mine. "All my life dance was business for me. Then I saw you."

"Charming as always." I kissed him on the nose. "But when did you fall in love with dance?"

He whispered, "The moment I saw you do my movement."

"So what do you think?" Kandelbaum said after dinner. "Do you want to watch some TV, or go straight to bed?"

I giggled.

"That sounded odd."

His sheepish look was endearing. The couch was folded, but he stood at its edge, as if he'd already made permanent room in his life for me. "You may approach," I said, patting the cushion next to me. His hair smelled of flour and fryer grease. I smiled again at Angela's notion of us as a potential couple. Despite everything I loved about him, I would never date a man with a body as soft as a marshmallow. Yet I leaned against him, arm to arm, burrowing into his warmth the way I would with my mother when I was little.

"When we first met, you said God might have had a reason for providing your car as a landing pad," I said. "Do you…still think about that?"

He nodded. "After my wife died, I would pray every day for a sign that God would relieve my loneliness. One day, as I am doing this, you fall right out of the sky onto my car."

I smiled. So Angela didn't make that up.

"My prayer was answered. I have not been lonely. For that I am very grateful. My path joined yours and Angela's, and I never really knew why. But I have shown up every day to see what God has in mind."

"I think God's telling you. In here." I laid my hand over his heart with a confidence I did not feel. I was not used to such faith-based pronouncements. "It's so you could find love again." His gaze snapped to mine. "With Angela."

He deflated back into the couch and picked up a foot-high object sitting on the end table that looked like a dried gourd. "And what makes you speak with God's authority on this?"

"What I know of love—true, unconditional love—you and Angela have shown me. You do love her, don't you?"

He spun the gourd in his hands, smoothed it with his palms. He gazed through a hole drilled into it as if the gourd were some sort of Magic 8 Ball with answers written inside.

"The situation is complicated. I'm sure you understand better than most that love requires great courage. The god within you loves dance, for example, yet still you don't embrace it."

"Yeah, well. God flubbed my particular project." I moved to the other end of the couch so I could face him and burrow my cold toes beneath his thigh.

"What makes you say that?"

"Why would God make me a dancer and then give me a body like this?"

"Your body is irrepressible. You survived a fourteen-story fall—"

"You don't get it."

"Perhaps you could help me."

"This is how the world defines a female dancer: something like five feet, five inches, ninety-five pounds. Shorter than the male partner and light enough to lift. Lean legs that end just south of the armpits. Hips that are nothing more than the skeletal breaking point between thighbone and spine in a six o'clock arabesque."

That much came easily. But my next words had been buried within me for so long they wouldn't take shape on my tongue without some movement to unearth them. I stood and paced. Sharing such thoughts with any of my dance friends was out of the question—dancers were pack animals constantly vying for the role of alpha; my admission would have exposed my weak underbelly. Bebe seemed blind to my contour; I never wanted to burst the bubble of her inflated expectations for me. And I would never share these feelings with Angela—compared to hers, my body was freakishly reliable. And Dmitri. He may have found the courage to share his fears with me, but I couldn't return that kind of intimacy. Not about this.

It's what I could never tell my mother, because my disappointing flesh had come from hers. I found it so hard to love her unconditionally, though I wanted to believe my father had. In his eyes, would I have found the acceptance I was unwilling to extend toward myself?

I almost choked it down again. Words so long unexpressed take on a horrific power—maybe it was best to leave them festering where they'd found comfort, in the black, bubbling cauldron of my soul.

But then I looked at Kandelbaum; his crooked face a kind

190

question mark, his pillowy body leaning toward me to accept whatever blow I might be ready to hurl. I teetered at the brink of a declaration that would single me out from others of my kind and yet I felt…safe.

"I'm too tall for many partners. My hips are too wide. I've got thighs like Schwarzenegger. I don't fit the mold."

I heard a little puff of air—Kandelbaum was stifling a laugh.

"You are such a jerk." I bopped him with one of the throw pillows.

"I'm sorry. But I was trying to imagine Schwarzenegger's thighs attached to small hips."

"Easy. Picture Schwarzenegger."

"But you are a woman, Penny. You have wider hips for a reason."

I pressed the throw pillow against my unneeded reproductive center and sank back into the couch.

Kandelbaum thought for a moment. "How does the world define the perfect singer?"

"I don't know. Someone like Pavarotti, I guess."

"And yet Rod Stewart did pretty well for himself."

"That's not the same."

"Isn't it? Surely things other than size matter in a dancer. Flexibility, artistry, commitment—"

"I learned the hard way: that is not enough."

Pressing his palms together beneath his chin, Kandelbaum closed his eyes.

"Are you praying, or what?"

"I'm trying to imagine a world in which we all look alike. We'd think alike too, no doubt. Without differing perspectives, the arts wouldn't be necessary. Hitler would have won."

"Yet clothing would be cheaper. One size fits all. We could skip the body politics. And we could all get health insurance."

Kandelbaum ran his hand over the gourd—its narrow top, its wide bottom, the blemishes on its surface. "We don't get to choose our gifts, just as we don't get to choose the shape of the vessel into which they are poured. If you fail to claim the gifts, what will you have? The same vessel—just empty."

My eyes and nose and sinuses started to fill. I fetched a new box of tissues and opened it.

"All I know, Penny, is that Mother Nature shaped you with loving hands. For a specific purpose. She wouldn't shortchange you."

I returned and dabbed at my eyes. "You don't know how badly I want to believe you. But belief is irrelevant. I tried so hard—the jobs aren't out there for me."

"Belief is never irrelevant. If you want to believe me, it's because the god inside you knows it's true. Until you hear what she's saying, I can't see how you'll ever be happy."

I sat down again and let all he said sink in.

"So you think love is a gift," I said.

"The very best gift."

"And you think love isn't complete until you act on it."

"Exactly."

"So we *were* talking about Angela."

Kandelbaum sighed. "Penny." He wrapped his arms around the gourd and pressed it to his heart. His voice was constricted, barely more than a whisper. "I've already lost one great love. How can I bear to lose another?"

"Maybe that's why I'm also in the picture." I nudged him

with my shoulder. "When you lose her, you'll still have me to help you through."

The next day, after Kandelbaum left for work, I sat on the couch and picked up his gourd-oracle. *Will I dance?* I gazed into its depths for an answer. Inside, a nest of small twigs had been hot-glued together. On them sat a small wooden bluebird, its beak lifted in song. I spun the gourd in my hands as Kandelbaum had, as if to read it with my palms. It was then I noticed the black lettering that circled its bottom. Writing I recognized. *Dearest Marty: You are not alone anymore! Love, Angela.*

I called Angela, but got no answer. I called the CF Center at Presbyterian to see if she'd been admitted, but due to new privacy regulations, they wouldn't tell me. So I called back and asked for Angela Reed's room. When the nurse who picked up told me she was in the bathroom, I decided it was safe to move back into the apartment to recover. But when I got home, the door at the top of the stairs was ajar. I peeked in.

Someone was going through our dresser drawers.

# CHAPTER TWENTY-ONE

The woman pawing through our possessions had brown hair flecked with gray. I couldn't tell if she was working alone or not.

I held the key ring in my right fist and let the keys protrude between my knuckles, a trick I'd learned to protect myself at night on city streets. It can deliver a nasty gouge, as Lars learned the hard way when I'd forgotten my dance bag one night and he kindly but unfortunately ran up behind me to return it.

I put my other hand in my pocket and made my move. "Leave now. I'm calling 911."

The woman turned with a start. "May I help you?" she said. She looked more surprised than guilty.

"What are you doing in my apartment?" I kept her in my peripheral vision as I assessed the rest of the room.

"You must be Penelope." She could have learned that from the tag under our buzzer. "I'm Dara Reed. Angela's mother. I'm picking up a few things to take to her."

Once I got a good look at her brown eyes and freckles, I shut the door and relaxed the grip on my key. "I'm sure Angela took what she needed. She has a whole packing system for routine admissions."

"Routine? I can just hear her saying that." She folded a couple of nightgowns into a duffle bag, her spine straight, her movements determined and rhythmic. "To Angela, hospital stays are all routine. This one began with a little more drama, though. She could hardly breathe when she woke up this morning, and had to call an ambulance."

She said this with the same intonation she would have used to say, *Yes, Angela decided to have a pumpernickel bagel this morning instead of her regular blueberry*. I, on the other hand, had trouble staving off panic.

"But she's okay, isn't she? I called the hospital and a nurse said she was in the bathroom."

"She has an infection, which is always critical for someone with CF." She smiled. "But she can still get up to pee."

"She's critical?" I was losing it. I couldn't possibly go see her. Mucus was releasing its squeeze on my head and threatening to avalanche down my face. I rushed to the bathroom for the box of tissues. When I returned, I used an antiseptic wipe on everything I touched. "How can you stay so calm about this? She's been sick for days—why didn't you come sooner?"

"Angela may have CF, but she also has an independent nature. I have to honor both my daughter and her illness. I keep tabs on her. But this is her ninety-third hospitalization, and I have to keep working. As you can imagine, the finances of her situation are challenging. She knows I'll come if she really needs me."

"What if I need to contact you?"

"I live in Bethesda, Maryland." She pointed to a luggage tag on Angela's Tree of Life. "My address and phone number are hanging right there. When I'm not home, I have my calls forwarded."

I took down the tag and considered the distant address. "What do you do that's more important than sharing your daughter's life?"

Angela's mother turned to me, a pair of balled socks in each hand. She looked at them, clueless as to whether her daughter would want the black or the neon green. "I would have thought she'd told you. I was a pediatrician until her sister died. You do know about her sister?"

I touched the baby shoe on the Tree of Life and sent the nearby feathers into gentle motion.

"After we lost Amy, I quit my practice and went into CF research. I'm trying to find a cure."

"Wow." No wonder Angela didn't talk about it—she probably wanted her mother to stay away as much as she wanted her to come. I felt a bit more kindly toward Dara then, but still found her cool delivery unnerving. "Leave the black socks here. Angela calls them her formalwear. In the hospital she only wears the bright colors." Dara put the green socks in the bag and added the orange, aqua, and yellow.

"It must have been difficult for you, raising Angela by yourself."

She disappeared into the bathroom. "Yes, well. My husband was never much use." She stuck her hand back out. "Is this Angela's toothbrush?"

"No, the purple. Angela doesn't talk about her father."

She wrapped the toothbrush in a paper towel and added it to the bag. "Once he took off, life got easier."

"I'd assumed he died."

Dara paused a moment. "No, he's healthy as can be. A mutual friend told me he traded us in for a ready-made family with more perfect children."

Tears sprang to my eyes. I couldn't imagine anyone more perfect than Angela.

"Getting all teary is going to cause a roadblock in that head of yours." She patted a cushy floor pillow. "Sit and rest. I'll get you some water."

"Go see Angela. I'd go myself if I weren't sick." I went into the kitchen to get my own water. "In my world, going to the hospital isn't so casual. It signals an emergency."

"Hospitalization may be routine, but I don't take it lightly. Each time, I know that this might be it, the time she doesn't leave. But I can't always be there to hold her hand."

I studied her face. She was a master at compartmentalizing emotion—if she felt anguish over her daughter's predicament, it was nowhere near the surface. I determined to scratch at this tough shell until I found the woman who could be Angela's mother. "What if you're not here for her at the end?"

"That's a possibility I've had to accept. Unlike you, I cannot allow myself the luxury of emotional outburst. How will it help her if I fall apart? At some point, those of us who love her have to take a step back, as hard as that is, and let her life unfold."

*Unbelievable.* She lifted the sunset quilt from the bottom drawer and stuffed it into the bag.

"Now. Before I go, shall I heat you up some chicken soup?"

I shook my head no. I already felt bad enough that while

Kandelbaum served me a buckwheat pancake with fresh strawberries, poor Angela was dialing 911 to croak for help.

Right then, I made a silent promise to Angela that when the end came, she would not be alone.

A few weeks later, Joey waved me into his office. "How's Angela?"

"Much better. She's coming home tomorrow."

He handed me a folder. "I was going through her chart. I'm sure you understand that this is confidential, but look at the top here and see if you notice anything interesting."

Angela Reed, our address and phone, her height—"Oh my god. She only weighs ninety-two pounds?"

"Not that. Look here." He pointed to her birth date—September 30.

"This Saturday."

"She'll be twenty-nine. Thought you might want to know."

Once I'd arranged a few details, the Fitness Evolution caught fire with the topic of Angela's surprise party. Joey and I made calls all day, to Mrs. Pope, Angela's mother, the staff at the Bibliophile and the CF Center. Those who couldn't come promised to send cards. My call to Kandelbaum elicited so much enthusiasm that I finally begged him to spill.

"Spill what?"

"You know. You've spent a lot of time at the hospital with Angela…have you told her you love her yet?"

Silence. A sigh. Then at last, a small no.

"What are you waiting for? Love shouldn't sound so pained. It's supposed to make you jump up and down. Act irrationally."

"I appreciate your concern, but—"

"Come on. She'll soon be out of the hospital and could damn well use some cheering up. Celebrate your love while you have the chance."

"I appreciate your concern. But I'm not the kind of man to act irrationally. For this to be meaningful, I have to stay true to who I am."

"You're right, of course." She deserved no less. But with Angela turning twenty-nine and him pushing fifty, the luxury of time was not on their side. "So let's plan a party."

Kandelbaum offered to cater with soup, cold cuts, and his healthy breads. He asked a bartender friend to whip up several gallons of fruit smoothies. I asked one of the members with a balloon business to decorate the aerobics room. The very next day cards started arriving, and by Wednesday, I had to ask the bartender for a liquor box to hold them all.

My job: to get her to the gym at noon Saturday.

The Monday prior, when she was due to arrive home, I went out to Walnut to meet the cab. It turned out her bag wasn't the only thing I'd be helping with. Tubing in her nose connected her to an oxygen tank on wheels, which I helped her lift from the car.

"Ick. How long will you have to use this?"

"I'm not thrilled to be hooked to this thing either, but it sure helps me sleep better at night."

"But I thought we could—"

"Sorry, no mountain climbing this week."

"I was hoping to talk you into a pampering. You know, a mani-cure, maybe a nice relaxing whirlpool at the gym…"

She gave me a weak smile. "Maybe next week."

Next week, of course, wouldn't do at all. "Let's see how it goes. You may be ready sooner than you think."

"By the time I make it to the top of our stairs, I'll be ready for a nap," she said, bumping her oxygen cart along the cobble-stone path.

Instead of a nap, though, Angela sat at the desk under my bunk and sketched some camels. She decided to add them to one of the distant dunes, but could only handle painting one before needing a break.

Our track lighting "sun" had not yet risen when I woke up on Saturday. It was still dark out, yet light emanated from somewhere beneath me. I peered over the edge of my bed. Angela sat on a pillow before the floating votives, oxygen off, staring into their flames.

"Hey, no oxygen. Are you feeling better?"

"I wanted to light the candles. I didn't want to blow up." Her voice sounded flat, lifeless.

"Are you okay?"

I crawled down from my bed, pulled up a pillow, and sat beside her. Melted wax spread from a pool at the center of one of the votives and reinforced the candle's edge when it hit the cooler water. I patted her leg and had to fight the urge to recoil. So little meat padded her bones. She held a pencil, and on the table before her lay a sketch of a figure. Its lips were parted, brows lifted, hands bent at odd angles, feet turned inward. A tragic doll whose soul struggled to emerge. *Petrushka*.

"I'm shutting down, Penny."

"You just got out of bed on the wrong side this morning." I knew what she'd say as soon as the words left my mouth.

"Our beds only have one side."

It was no fun playing straight man to a straight man. "Hey. What's going on?"

"All week I've been too tired to do much during the day, but I can't sleep at night because I still have so much to do. I can't work, can't play. Then I get this."

She pushed a bill toward me—it was for uncovered medical services totaling more than thirteen thousand dollars. If I'd had that kind of money sitting around, I'd have given it to her in a heartbeat, but my budget was already strained. What could I do to relieve her burden? I pulled the edge of the bill through the flame and it caught.

"What the hell?" Angela grabbed her drawing and scooted away as I dropped the flaming bill to the glass surface.

"They'll send you another one. For now—no bill. You've got to put it out of your mind. Depression isn't going to help."

"And this from someone who allows herself a steady diet of depression just because it's calorie-free."

The silence between us swelled. I finally said, softly, "Maybe you need to take it easy. Rest a while."

"I've been fighting for twenty-nine years. Do you have any idea how hard it's been to make it this far?"

I understood more than she realized. But if Angela's cheer couldn't be restored, I saw little hope for any of us. "Where's the Angela who would say that was an accomplishment? 'Let's celebrate'? 'Call Marty'?"

She didn't crack a smile. "I'm sorry—anything beyond whining takes so much effort."

I held her while she sobbed and coughed, but she didn't have the stamina to sustain tears for long. When she had calmed, I said, "Hey, a perfect body isn't everything, right?"

This time, she smiled. "Who's this talking?"

I laughed, and dabbed at her eyes with the sleeve of my nightgown.

"It's my birthday and my friends—I mean my CF friends, the ones who would really understand—are all gone."

I slipped my arm around her. "It hurts to lose a life you've loved. It amazes me the way you square off against your loss, both eyes open. No one will blame you if you blink every now and again." I kissed her temple.

"You've changed, you know. The Penelope Sparrow I met at University Hospital wouldn't have said that." When she turned to me, I saw some peace had returned to her smile. I gave her one last squeeze.

"I believe Kandelbaum would say love does that to a person. Or the god within. Or maybe it's the same thing. I don't know, he's still tutoring me. But you, young lady, are going to get that pampering I promised." I had to get her to the gym. With any luck, Kandelbaum would have the courage to say the words that could fully rekindle her spirit. "I have to get to work now, but I'm going to have a cab waiting for you at noon."

"A cab? The gym is one and a half blocks away. Anyway, I can't afford a cab." She pointed to the ash. "Remember?"

"I'll pay for the cab. You'll have a nice long soak in the whirlpool, then lunch, then—"

"You're sweet to offer. But I don't know if I can muster the energy. The most well-rounded meal I've had in the past week is a can of Ensure."

"Maybe just the whirlpool? How much energy does that take?"

I gave her a hug. She felt delicate, as if her bones had hollowed out like the shafts of the feathers she collected. If I could light the fire of Kandelbaum and Angela's love so she could experience the pop and snap of pure joy in her life, I could believe God really did have a hand in setting me on Kandelbaum's car.

❧

A quarter to noon. Joey and Suzie set up tables for food and drink. Karen and Haley helped the balloon lady tie a floating rainbow of orbs onto the exercise equipment, which I thought was pretty big of them considering they were angry with me for creating an unprecedented following for the dawn class, now some sixty strong. Kandelbaum was such a mass of nervous energy he finished setting up well ahead of the bartender and followed me around. He bumped into me twice before I posted him at the front door as a lookout.

The preparations were complete. The only way it could have been more perfect would have been if Angela's mother had come, but it was no big surprise when she'd told me she couldn't leave work.

"Excuse me, coming through." The crowd parted, and Joey backed into the room. He and one of the male instructors, biceps bulging, were carrying Joey's leather lounger into the room. Angela's box of cards rode along on the seat. Taped to the back of the chair was a handmade sign: "Angela Reed: Queen for the Day."

"I never thought I'd see the day when that chair left Joey's office," said Suzie. "He's never even let *me* sit in it."

An hour later, though, that was exactly where Joey's wife was sitting. People checked their watches and said they'd have to get back to work. I'd called Angela fifteen minutes earlier, and when no one was home, I assumed she was on her way. Before everyone left, I ran up to the front desk to get the report from Kandelbaum. He had no report. The phone rang. In the absence of other staff, I answered.

"Fitness Evolution, may I help you?"

"Woohoo, first try. That is you, Penny, right?"

"Angela?" She sounded—well, drunk. I waved Kandelbaum to my side and held the receiver so we both could hear. "I was getting worried. Where are you?"

"Presby. I doubled over with pain on the way to the cab you sent and had to hijack it. It could be another abdominal blockage. They need to run some tests." In the background, I heard horns and laughter and someone calling out Angela's name.

"It sounds like a bar."

"They're giving me a party! They must have scrambled around like crazy because they have balloons tied to the beds, and cup-cakes, soda…"

I wanted to tell her about our balloons and our food and all of the people waiting down in the gym, and about the tightly wound man sharing the receiver with me who had taken the day off work to set up a small feast for her, but I couldn't bring myself to burden her with it. "You sound happy."

"Pain meds! I'm higher than a kite. And my mom said she'd drive up to see me tonight. Listen. I owe you an apology."

"Why?"

"I was foolish to let myself get so down this morning. I'd forgotten all the sordid biological details of my life are constantly on view here. Someone remembered my birthday after all!"

"Sure did." She'd know soon enough how very many people had remembered, when I dropped off the box with all of our cards. I pushed the receiver toward Kandelbaum, but he pulled back and waved me off. I elbowed him in the ribs and got back on. "Okay, I'll see you later. Have a good time."

Partygoers drifted away. Kandelbaum left to get the uneaten food back under refrigeration. I was glad. I could no longer put up with his hopeless lovesickness.

"Why don't you go over to Presby and tell her how you feel?" I said.

"I can't."

"It would cheer her up."

"She'd think I said it out of pity. I have to tell her when she feels strong enough to believe me."

I wanted to argue, but he had a point. His declaration of love would have to wait.

# CHAPTER TWENTY-TWO

*P*enelope Sparrow!" On Monday morning, a new dawn aerobics participant took a half step back and looked me up and down. "It never occurred to me—in a gym!—but then of course I thought you were still in Allentown. How are you? You look well." Margaret MacArthur pumped my hand. "Oh dear, that wasn't your broken arm, was it?"

I almost didn't recognize her in a tracksuit and sneakers. For fun, I pictured her wearing the little pillbox hat as well.

"How did you track me down?" I asked.

"You give me too much credit. One of your gym members works at the *Sentinel* and mentioned she'd discovered a love for movement through this class. I thought it would make a good story—and here you are at the center of it." A photographer joined her and she directed him to set up in the corner of the room.

"I can't let you photograph—"

"I have approval from the owner," she said. She started taking down names of the ladies coming into the gym.

Joey might be on board, but I wasn't. Things were finally going well with Karen and Haley, and the last thing I needed was to draw more attention to myself. Anyway, I thought I'd put an end to the notion of a MacArthur interview months ago.

MacArthur circumnavigated the room and made her way back to me, notebook in hand. "You're a little overqualified for this sort of thing, aren't you?"

"I could say the same of you."

A voice sang out through the doorway. "Penny, hold up, I'll only be a second."

Good god. I'd asked her to check in now and then, but what the hell was my mother doing here at five-thirty in the morning? She would have had to leave home by four. She bypassed the locker room convention and dropped her handbag and coat at the edge of the room before giving me a hug. She looked drawn. I hoped she wasn't ill. MacArthur joined us after stripping down to a tight tee shirt and stretchy black pants that revealed a boyish figure. She had no intention of watching the class—she was taking it. My mother stood right next to her. The professional and personal lives I'd carefully compartmentalized were about to collide. And if my mother should trip on those triple-X workout pants she was wearing, she would squish MacArthur like a bug.

My mother made the first move. "Hello, I'm Evelyn Sparrow."

"Sparrow? So you would be—"

I cranked up the stereo with a Trans-Siberian Orchestra version of Beethoven's Fifth.

After class, MacArthur asked if we could talk. I said I had another appointment. I pulled my mother over to an office area separated from the rest of the room by a half wall and a sheet of glass. I handed her a towel and a water bottle from my private stash. "Are you all right?"

"Of course I'm all right. Didn't you see me dancing?"

I put my hand to her cheek. Her skin was moist, flushed but not flaming, and she was able to speak without panting. I asked, "What are you doing here?"

"I'm here to treat myself to that warm, fuzzy feeling you get when you surprise someone."

"Sorry, I'm on edge. Angela is having surgery today."

"I'm sorry, honey."

"You look different."

"It's been so long since you've seen me, your eyes probably changed."

"You're not sick, are you?"

"Oh stop." She wiped a towel across her face. "Hey, did you see that movement I added with my arms?" She showed me again, holding her arms above her head and letting each inscribe its own conical shape. "Like you did in *Puma*."

I looked around to make sure MacArthur was nowhere in sight. "How do you know what I did in *Puma*?"

My mother couldn't possibly know that choreography. I hadn't spoken with her about that performance since we premiered the piece. And I'd only performed *Puma* once—in Washington.

"You didn't think I'd miss your Kennedy Center premiere, did you?"

"How did you know about it?"

"*Dance Magazine*. I followed Dance DeLaval in the listings."

"You went down to Washington to see me?"

208

"Twelfth row. You were a lot better than Tina in that role."

But Karly had finished out the Washington run. Tina had only performed it—"You saw it in Philadelphia, too?"

"It was a public event."

"Of course."

"Sweetheart. I went to all your Philadelphia performances. Anyway, your movement didn't look right on Tina's little body. Your long limbs slice through the space. She just pokes at it."

My mind swirled. She'd called it *my* movement. Dmitri had never credited me, and I was sure the fact I'd been feeding him ideas hadn't been in *Dance Magazine*. "How did you know it was my movement?"

"I've been watching you dance since you were old enough to walk. I know how your body moves. That dance had your thumbprint all over it."

I struggled to take in what she was telling me. My mother had been with me, performance after performance, step after step? "You never came backstage."

"I did, once. I got close enough to see you through the stage door. You and the other dancers were hugging. When I saw how happy you were, I knew that's all I ever wanted."

For a long, confusing moment I tried to find the hidden subtext. The implied comparison to some famous dancer who'd given up at the height of her career. But I sensed no snap to her tone, no rush to judgment. She didn't meet my eyes, but looked down and away. Sad. Wounded, like a mother whose unconditional love for her child went unrequited. I didn't know this woman, or how to relate to her, and I sure as hell hadn't meant to create her. We stood for a moment in awkward silence, my guilt thickening the air.

"But now that we're talking about it, I've been dying to ask about the Kennedy Center. You shined in the first half, but toward the end you looked a little off."

"I broke my toe."

"Oh."

We started to laugh. I threw my arms around her, turning my head to hide my tears from the ladies on the other side of the window who had stopped midexercise to gawk. With her shoulder a soft pillow against my cheek, I remembered a source of comfort I had denied myself during the darkest moments of my life. "I am so sorry, Mom."

"That's okay, baby," she whispered in my ear. "You'll tell me all about it when you're ready."

But I had already said more than I ever intended to on the subject—that day in her kitchen, when I called her fat.

She pulled away and offered the box of tissues from the counter. She acknowledged the onlookers with a nod of her head. "You've always done your best work on a stage, you know."

I turned away to dab at my tears and heard my mother say, "You're listening anyway, Ms. MacArthur, so you might as well hear this clearly."

I whipped around to see MacArthur slip into the room, notebook and pen already in hand. "I actually owe some of the weight loss I've achieved to you," my mother continued. "Every time I want a doughnut, I think of this article I once read: 'Fall of a Sparrow.' I picture my daughter's broken body on the dented roof of a car, with flattened fastnachts all around her. Then I think of how brave she was to put her life back together, even while you waged a continual assault on her privacy." She reached for my hand and gave it a squeeze. "Somehow, after that, doughnuts lost their appeal." My mother turned to me. "I'll see you later, Penny. And Ms. MacArthur? I have a witness—that comment was off the record."

My mother left the office and MacArthur brazenly flipped open her notebook.

"She said it was off the record."

"So she did. How is it that you came to work here?"

"You can just switch gears after what my mother said? Are you made of flesh and blood?"

She lowered her notepad. "Of course I am. But she wasn't attacking my flesh and blood. She didn't care for my work, which is understandable in this case. I'm a critic, Penelope. People don't always see things as I do. That doesn't change my beliefs or my interest in carrying on." She raised the notepad again. "Now—about how you got this job?"

"It was an accident." I excused myself—a woman on the other side of the room was doing squats with form so poor it made my own knees hurt. I went to help her.

MacArthur followed along. "I've never seen floor pattern work in an aerobics class before."

"It decreases boredom."

"Theirs, or yours?"

I had to think. "Both."

"Hmm. You have the soul of a choreographer, you know. Like Dmitri."

I turned on her—like *Dmitri*? She was so small I could blow on her and knock her down, but her bullying hit its mark. I inhaled, raised, flared.

"You think you know what was going on inside Dance DeLaval, but you don't. Dmitri is not the cute little baby in a *couche-culotte* you may remember—"

"I've heard you suffer from an eating disorder. Is this true?"

I froze. Thoughts scrambled, sought new order. What did she know? What had she seen? My private struggle, so carelessly exposed, burrowed deeper within me. Filled my stomach until it ached. I had to wait before forming words; even my soul stuttered.

When I recovered enough to move, I grabbed her arm and pulled her deeper into the room. "Where would you hear something like that?"

"So you're not denying it."

"Who's gossiping about me?"

"I don't reveal my sources. Is it anorexia?"

Had she trumpeted that final word? I looked around, but no one seemed to be staring at us. Did she not know how important public perception was in the life of a performer? Between health and danger lay a tightrope I'd been walking my entire adult life. I'd perfected my skills. If I'd left that line behind, everyone would know it—there was no safety net. I lowered my voice. "I will not honor that with a response."

"Then tell me why Dmitri left for Europe without you."

"Why should I?"

"Because I need your input for my article. It's important that women with unconventional bodies—"

"Enough with that. Can't you allow me the smallest bit of happiness?"

"Don't tell me you're happy here. Doing"—she waved her hand around—"this."

"This is all the dance I can handle right now."

She actually had the gall to laugh. "This is hardly dance."

"I was injured, you know." I pictured myself the way my mother had: lying on a dented car roof. Falling so far…with no safety net.

Had I finally screwed up? Pushed the line too far? MacArthur babbled on but the cold, dark balcony of the Independence Suites once again claimed me. What if I had fainted that night? Loss of consciousness would explain my memory loss. I couldn't believe it—refused to believe it, I'd always been so careful—but my own dark potential rattled me so badly I had to sit.

MacArthur stepped closer and looked expectantly into my face, as if she'd asked a question.

"What?"

"I said your shoulder has mended, yet still you don't dance." She closed her notebook and slipped it into her back pocket. "Perhaps it's your spirit that's still broken."

Perhaps so, but an interview with MacArthur was not going to heal it. And I couldn't unburden myself to my mother. How could I tell the woman whose arteries gave me life about the black vein of self-hate that had damned thighs sturdy enough to survive a fourteen-story fall, and stilled the joyous sway of hips made to mambo?

This was the sort of thing I could only share with a best friend. Now that I had one, I hoped it wasn't too late.

# CHAPTER TWENTY-THREE

*M*y soles squeaked against the hospital floor as I walked down the hall to Angela's room. I didn't realize I had been holding my breath until I saw her name still written on the placard outside the door, albeit in dry-erase marker that could be removed with nothing more than a tissue.

I found her with her eyes closed, breath raspy, Kandelbaum holding her hand to his lips. Her mouth and nose were covered by a new kind of oxygen mask.

"Has she woken up yet?"

Kandelbaum shook his head. "They told me she would come around any time now, but that was five hours ago."

Feeling helpless, I set down the box of belated birthday cards and started taping them to the wall.

A nurse sorted out Angela's tangle of tubes. "I'm adding morphine to her drip," she said. "Her breathing should quiet down in a bit."

"So soon?" I said. "I mean, isn't morphine a one-way trip?"

The nurse raised the bed rail and clicked it into place. "All of life is a one-way trip. Can't go back, no matter how hard you try. This makes the final ride a little easier."

How long did she have? Days? Hours? Minutes? Would her mother have time to get here? I stood behind Kandelbaum and slipped my arms around his shoulders.

"Her doctor put her on the transplant list," he said. I pressed my cheek to his. "I'm about to read to her." He produced a folded copy of the *Philadelphia Sentinel's* entertainment section and read aloud, "'Dance Aerobics Dawns at the Fitness Evolution.'"

"Don't read that drivel here." I tried to grab the paper, but he yanked it away.

"Miss MacArthur quotes Angela. Joey told her how long Angela had been a member, and she called Angela for an interview before…well. She had a bit more pep then. Right, Angela?"

Breath in, breath out.

Kandelbaum turned to me and whispered. "I want her to know she was in the paper." His lip quivered.

I rubbed his shoulder. "It's okay. Sorry. She didn't tell me she'd been interviewed."

Kandelbaum took a steadying breath and began, while I read over his shoulder.

"'The sun hasn't yet risen over the streets of Philadelphia. Indeed, many are still curled in their sheets, sound asleep. But a burgeoning group of fitness buffs is already gathering downstairs at the Fitness Evolution on Twelfth Street, awaiting the start of what used to be one of the town's best kept secrets—a dance aerobics class taught by professional dancer Penelope Sparrow, formerly rehearsal mistress of Dance DeLaval.'"

"Best kept secret," I said. "That's a good one."

"'Most members see the class as an alternative way to get the heart pumping and the metabolism cranked up. But what they are really getting is an introduction to choreography and its building blocks—rhythm, effort, motion, and floor patterns."

"I can just hear Mrs. Weinstein at her next bridge tournament," I said. "'Ladies, if you sense a change in me today, it's because I have recently experienced the most fabulous rhythm…'"

He collapsed the paper so I could no longer see. "Are you going to let me read this, or not?"

"Sorry." I circled the bed to sit across from him.

"I'll skip to the part where Angela is quoted, since you aren't appreciative." He ran his finger down the page. "Here is a quote: 'With Penny's class to wake you up, your day starts singing,' said member Angela Reed in a telephone interview from Presbyterian Hospital, where she is currently hospitalized with complications from cystic fibrosis. Because of her fragile health, working out is vital for this ten-year Fitness Evolution veteran. 'To stick with a fitness program,' she says, 'you have to understand the link between the energy you expend now and the energy you'll gain later.'"

He looked up at Angela, lying so still. His eyes sought comfort from mine, for a moment, before returning to the article.

"'Penny's passion for movement creates that link. A lot of people have joined the gym just to take her class.'"

I took Angela's hand, pressing her lifeline to mine. When I'd had no clue how to rebuild some semblance of life, she was the one who gave me a home. Inspired me to help others. She put my muscles back to work, one foot following the other. Slowly, at first. Now I was doing so at tempo, to a variety of rhythms, and in floor patterns, no less—while she was lying here, drained of that precious energy she'd been hoping to bank. It wasn't fair. I never would have crossed the threshold of that gym if it weren't for her.

I squeezed her hand. Though she had to reach across the border of consciousness and through a morphine cloud to do so, I felt certain she squeezed back.

"It was a lovely article." Kandelbaum stood. "But now I have to get back to the bakery." After I assured him I planned to stay for a while, he leaned over, combed his fingers through the kinks in Angela's hair, and pressed his lips to her forehead. I remembered when Angela called that kind of attention "loving-kindness." But this time, when he left the room, I believe he left half of himself behind.

If I thought about it too long, I would chicken out. I shut the door behind Kandelbaum and returned to the chair beside Angela's bed. As the October sun sought its tired zenith over my shoulder, I dove into the story about the night that ended my delusions about my role in Dance DeLaval.

Dmitri and I had been working for twelve weeks on a new work for the company, I told Angela, a multimedia extravaganza titled *No Brainer*. We planned to juxtapose live dancing with videotaped segments projected onto screens of various shapes, positioned either upon or suspended above the stage. The live dance would evolve; the taped dance would loop over and over. We wanted to make you wonder which was more real: what was unfolding, or what was captured? Events, or your perceptions of them?

While working on the piece, our days fell into a pattern: Dmitri and I would get up for company classes at the college in the morning, teach the new material to the others in afternoon rehearsal, work late into the night at the studio, then crash when we got home. He was going through some artistic flamboozlement, but once the concept solidified, ideas flew out of me, and as he watched the piece take shape, Dmitri got more and more excited. His happiness was my happiness. I felt like part of the company again, because my role in the dance was as large as anyone else's. I was in a good place.

One day after rehearsal, he asked me to speak with him in the office off the dance studio. Dmitri sat in the desk chair and dropped his head onto his hands.

"Penny. You are driving me mad."

"What's the matter?"

"You keep stepping out of the dance while we rehearse the movement!"

"I have to, to see the big picture."

"We must learn the steps."

"I know the steps. I made them up."

"Others do not know the steps. They do not know where you stand, what your body is doing, how much space you take up."

"Unless I step back, we can't figure it out, either." I pulled an extra chair in front of him and stroked his arm. It was tense. "It's going to be fine—"

He shrugged my hand away. "You disrespect me in front of others."

I put my hands on his chest and shoved him so hard his chair rolled back a few inches. "Maybe it just feels that way because you don't bother thinking things through. How do you plan to pack the tour bus?"

"What do you mean?"

"Someone needs to think about it, you know. Touring this piece will be a logistical nightmare. Each theater has different lighting and sound capabilities, not to mention different stage sizes and proscenium openings. We may not be able to use all the set pieces at each location—have you thought about that? Our spacing will have to remain fluid, so we might as well get used to it now."

The silence in the room underscored the volume and edge my words had taken on.

"I'm trying to support you every way I can," I said. "If you loved me, maybe you'd see that."

In sharing this memory with Angela, I noticed it didn't spring from my muscles. I could no longer feel the anger rising through my gut or taste it on my tongue. It was just something that happened last year that I wanted to tell my friend about.

I looked up at Angela. She lay still, her beautiful face sucking for air. Here I was, again, seeking connection with someone incapable of responding. But she did seem to be comforting me, in a way, through the hiss of oxygen and the rhythm of her breathing: *Shh…shh…everything is fine.* I pressed each of the fingernails on her cool hand, taking heart that after each nail turned white, it flooded pink again. *Where there is life there is hope*, Kandelbaum once said. *L'chaim.*

"I do love you, Penny," Dmitri had said. "You do much for me, I see this. I show you too many of my nerves. This is not good." He took my hand. "This will be a big piece for me."

"And me," I said, allowing him to pull me onto his lap. I felt the heat transfer from his hand to the small of my back. I'd been on my feet all day, sewing stretchy fabric over metal frames to make the projection screens for the set. We had liked the effect, and had ordered enough material to complete the project. We were waiting now for the store to deliver it.

"Exhausted?" Dmitri said.

"I can handle anything when you let me dance." I rubbed my nose lightly against his. It took me a moment to realize he was shaking his head no.

"You aren't just another body. You are smarter. Many can dance. Who else can do what you do?"

I put my arms around his neck and gave his ponytail a tug. "There are many roles in your life I wouldn't want to lose." I kissed him, and within moments exhaustion was the furthest thing from my mind. My passion for dance and my passion for Dmitri could no longer be separated; I didn't know where one ended and the other began.

A knock on the door—Mitch. "Delivery truck arrived. With the bolts of fabric? Penny wanted me to let her know."

"Ignore it," Dmitri whispered. He slipped his hand beneath the stretchy tee shirt I was wearing and brushed my nipple; it had been too long since we'd been intimate. Since he'd told me, body to body, that I was a perfect fit. He playfully bit the inside of my arm. "Come home with me."

It took all I had to pull away. "You know as well as I do we need to get the material cut tonight. The New York premiere is Friday—as in this coming Friday? Six days from now."

"I need lover, not mother."

"What's that supposed to mean?"

"You don't need to worry so much. Already some things are coming together—"

"We need to simulate a full tech here in the studio before we leave. With this many variables, we can't rely on good luck. You won't return to Russia the homeland hero with quotes like, 'Although the movement was scintillating, the sparks weren't enough to illuminate the work after the lights went out.'"

"Sin-lating?" he said.

"Scin-til-lating. Lively, sparkly," I said, miming small fireworks by flicking my fingers in the air.

"Ah, like you."

He reached for my breast again, but I grabbed his hand and tugged it. "We'll have time for this soon enough, Romeo. Say, Friday night? At the hotel? I'll share a room with you if you ask nicely. Now let's get to work."

He sank back into the chair. "I have no more work in me tonight," he said. What energy the promise of sex had temporarily revived in him now receded beyond my reach. "Too tired. I will not watch even Letterman."

"If I have to do this alone, I'll be here for hours." Yet when I saw how exhaustion weighed on his features, I felt bad for whining. "Never mind. Go on home. Maybe I can get one of the others to stay."

He stood and gave me one last hug. "What would I do without you?"

We went out into the studio, but I had no heart to ask for volunteers. Lars had already left. Karly shouldered her dance bag and shuffled her feet to the end of the studio. She'd thought she had her shin splints licked, but they flared up again with the running involved in this piece. After fetching the bolts of fabric from the truck and depositing them in the studio, Dmitri, Tina, and Mitch left together, talking and laughing as they headed down the stairs.

Their receding footsteps left behind a hollow silence. I put the music for the new piece on the stereo, a quirky mix of classical strings and incidental noise, and got to work.

I had one frame traced and cut when Mitch returned. I smiled up at him, glad for the momentary company. "Forget something?"

"I felt too guilty leaving you here alone. I'm here to help. And this is from Evan."

"That's so sweet." He handed me a wrapped tuna fish sandwich. "No mayo, I hope?"

"Just pickle relish," he answered. I tossed the top of the sandwich and ate the salad off the bread.

"He's a good husband. And thanks so much for coming back. This'll go a lot faster with two of us working."

"About twice as fast, I'd say."

We laughed at the math. Inside of two hours, we'd completed the task.

On the way home, my muscles ached with every step. I couldn't wait to get home and slip into a bath.

"You get to know someone's habits when you live together," I told Angela. Now that the story was flowing, I'd quit poking at her nails, but I appealed to her consciousness by squeezing her hand every now and again. "I know you like a morning shower, because it loosens up your lungs and refreshes the wave in your hair. Shower gel with juniper scent instead of soap. But Dmitri, after a day at the studio, loved to soak in a bath. He was like a kid that way—he even loved the bubbles—and he wouldn't come out until his hands and feet were all puckered."

By the time I got home, my dance bag felt so heavy I suspected a stowaway, but the contents I emptied were only rumpled, smelly dance clothes. I dumped them on top of Dmitri's in the corner and headed for the bedroom.

I heard the television—at least I thought I did, but the way sounds bounced around in that building, you could never be sure—and was greeted by its bluish glow when I opened the bedroom door. I slipped out of my shoes and cushioned each step in case Dmitri was already asleep. The people at the party below us weren't as considerate—occasional bursts of laughter rose up through the floor. The bed was still made, making the strip of light from beneath the bathroom door a welcoming beacon. I quickly slipped out of my clothes to join him in the tub. I could already feel his lathered hands slipping over my body. I remember thinking that sometimes the diligent *are* rewarded.

I opened the door to find Tina Franke astride Dmitri in the tub.

Stark naked, dumb-ass smile and all, I tried to make sense of the scene in front of me: my lover fucking a thinner, smaller, younger version of me.

All of us gawked for a moment. I took a few steps farther into the room, unable to detach my gaze from Tina's body. She looked so youthful, her pink nipples like rosebuds about to bloom. And below her spine, against the dark hair of Dmitri's thighs, her ass nestled like two pale orbs, one in each of Dmitri's hands.

"Penny—" Dmitri started.

Hearing his voice connected me to mine, but still I did not take my eyes from Tina. "Get out."

"This is awkward," she said. "Could you give us a little privacy?"

"You forget, Tina. I live here."

"I marched right past them, closed the toilet, and sat down on the lid," I told Angela. Nothing amused me about it at the time, but in the telling of it, I started to laugh. "I sat and watched while Tina climbed out of the tub and wrapped herself in my towel." When I looked up at Angela, she just lay there, breathing. Listening.

I waited for Dmitri to say something, anything. Maybe Russians let the womenfolk duke these things out. I stood. "Get out, Tina." I thought I was on firm ground. What had he said, just hours ago? *You aren't just another body. You are smarter. Many can dance.*

Tina's eyes darted to Dmitri for affirmation of their—whatever. Dmitri closed his eyes and shook his head as if to tell her "not now."

Tina got dressed and left. Left the bathroom, left the apartment, left the planet for all I cared. Dmitri lay in the tub, offering nothing.

I suddenly felt way too exposed. I wrapped myself in Dmitri's towel and left him in the bathroom with nothing to dry off with but the nonslip rug. I was so angry I would have walked right out of his life except for one thing: Dmitri was the center of my world. I needed him. So although he never asked me to, I stayed.

For the next few days, Dmitri swung wide of me at the studio. I didn't see him much. At night, my muscles stood guard so I wouldn't accidentally roll toward him in bed. I wanted him to be the one to slip his arm around me, pull me back from the edge, beg forgiveness. But the magic we had conjured was an illusion that had vanished. I felt diminished. Empty, even of tears.

I told myself we'd be okay. We had the big premiere coming up. He needed me. But my quiet certainty soon devolved into a hysterical grasping at straws, as lack of productive sleep gave way to exhaustion. Dmitri ordered me about on errands; I tried to please him.

Perhaps a nice hot soak would have relaxed my muscles enough to bring on the rest I needed so badly. But the night I found him with Tina, I scoured that tub with Comet until its finish was gone and it was a lighter shade of beige. I would never again surrender to its warmth.

Angela's hand stirred in mine. She never opened her eyes, but she used her other hand to pull the oxygen mask from her mouth. In a breathy voice she said, "You got a story with a happy ending?"

# CHAPTER TWENTY-FOUR

*W*hat do any of us know about the schedule of our own demise? Angela may have known how she was going to go, but not when. I wasn't any better at guessing than she was—it shocked and thrilled me when she stabilized. By all accounts, my own time on earth should have already expired. And who knew how long my mother might have? Now that I'd shared with Angela some of the clutter in my own emotional closet, it was time to clear a few mothballs back home. Once it seemed safe, I left Angela in Kandelbaum's capable care and went to spend the weekend with my mother.

"So what's this all about?"

I led my mother to the door of the garage and opened it.

"Whatever you want, Penny, get it and come back. With all that junk, there isn't enough room for both of us."

Regardless, I pulled her over the threshold and onto the landing at the top of the wooden steps. After he'd died, my father's belongings had only gotten as far as this garage. Spread before us were clothes still on hangers, rusting tools, piles of magazines, and a few things she couldn't part with when she sold his sporting goods store. The room was so full and musty it was hard to breathe.

I hit the automatic door opener. After a clunk that seemed to signal indecision, the door rose, allowing a wave of spicy air and sunlight into the garage.

My mother looked a little shell-shocked. When she found her voice, she said, "Close that, Penny. The neighbors will see."

"Or we could move this stuff out into the driveway in case they want any of it. We'll need the extra space to get it all organized. What to toss, what to sell, what to give away."

I feared she might turn and run, but she surprised me by descending the steps, picking up a few fishing poles, and moving a step deeper into the garage to look around. She lifted a box lid, peeked at its contents, and took something out.

"Do you remember this, Penny? We were having such a good time at that circus. You could barely read, but you were fascinated with this program your father bought. Then something in it scared you, and he had to take it away."

I couldn't believe this program still existed, or that she remembered anything about it. I avoided my mother's eyes but couldn't help myself: I took it from her, still as drawn to its contents as I was embarrassed to have her watch me open it.

The full-color pages had seemed larger in my five-year-old hands. I had been tucked between my mother and father on the top row of bleachers, turning pages with fingers sticky from cotton candy. I found again the part that had so intrigued me: the gallery of characters in the "Sideshows of Yesteryear." All these years later, the ways in which human bodies could be so different still fascinated me. The Siamese twins, the human rubber band, the married midgets. The handsome strongman.

I had tugged on my father's sleeve. "Look, Daddy, it's you." He smiled and ran his hand down my hair. Nothing made me happier than earning that smile. A few pages later I found the fat lady, who had my mother's curly hair and kind eyes. I tugged his sleeve again. "And look, here's Mommy."

He ripped the book from my hands so fast I started to cry.

"What is it, honey?" my mother had said.

"She's thirsty," my father said, picking me up. "We'll be right back."

I would mull over my father's lie and our swift escape for years, finally realizing its significance: it was the first of many times I would associate body shape—my mother's, and by extension mine—with shame.

These days, my mother no longer resembled the fat lady. Rather than soft and weak, she looked sturdy and strong.

I moved to the far end of a canoe resting upside down on sawhorses, pushing stacks of boxes to the side to make a path as I went. "Let's set this out in the yard for now. Can you grab the other end?"

Moving the canoe revealed our recreational roots: stored beneath were croquet, badminton, volleyball. I pictured my dad, jumping up over the net to spike, Uncle Pete diving low for the save. My mother on the side, cheering.

I laid all the sports equipment on the slope beside the driveway.

"Would you look at this." She brought a box out into the light and set up a camping chair beside it. "These are programs of performances I took you to. Must be two dozen 'Nutcrackers' alone. And look—this was from that talk Edward Villella gave at Lafayette College. Remember?"

I grabbed a handful and leafed through them. "I can't believe you kept all these."

"Guess I couldn't face the end of it all."

"The end of what?" I looked up at my mother.

"Our partnership, I guess. You were growing up."

"It was a special time in our lives." I hugged her shoulders. "I know it's hard. Let me." I took the programs from her hand.

"Wait! Give me back Villella."

"Mo-om—"

She plucked the Playbill from my hand. "He signed it."

For some reason, only the circus program seemed worth saving. I tossed the rest back into the box and carried it to the curb.

My mother fiddled with the latch on a trunk and opened it. "I can't believe I still have this."

"What is it?"

She went over to sit on the steps. Due to her weight loss, there was enough room for me to sit beside her. She held a framed photo. My mother smiled at the camera, her cheeks chubby and radiant. My father supported her elbow with one hand and enveloped her shoulders with the other, looking into her eyes with a magnetism that seemed to have defied the photographer's attempts to get him to look forward.

"Of course you kept it. This must have been your wedding day."

"Notice anything?"

They wore suits. His was navy pinstripe, hers ivory with a jacket and pleated skirt.

230

"I guess I'm surprised you weighed so much here," I said. She looked at me askance, but didn't jump down my throat. "Daddy used to say your weight was baby fat, so I always assumed you gained weight when you were pregnant with me."

A moment of awkward silence stretched long between us. "I was pregnant," my mother said, slowly.

"Wow." I didn't know how to react to this. "You'd think I would have done the math."

"Why would you? You were still pretty young when your dad and I stopped having anniversaries."

"But you were in love, right? I mean, you can see it."

"He adored you from the first." She traced her finger over her contours in the picture. "It's no wonder I put this picture away. Even if I was pregnant, I can't believe I really looked like that." Her cheeks flushed as if she were embarrassed for herself.

"I don't really like to look at pictures of myself, either." I peeked in another box, hoping not to find too many more surprises. "Had you always been big, Mom? I mean, if you don't mind talking about it."

"I guess I can, now. I've lost so much weight it feels like I'm talking about another person, anyway." She sighed, and looked again at the picture. "I couldn't play softball and dodgeball and all the games your dad loved. While other girls played jump rope and roller-skated, I stayed in to practice the piano. But I became a decent pianist." She looked over at me and forced a chuckle. "Your father never let me despair over it. If I felt low, your dad would pinch my cheek"—here, her voice wavered—"and tell me not to worry, that it was baby fat, and if I was meant to grow out of it, I would."

I slipped my arm around her shoulders and gave her a squeeze. "Dad would be proud of you, you know. For finally losing the weight."

"You think so."

"He might even call it heroic."

She rolled her eyes.

"I often think about how Dad died. All alone, away from home on that business trip. You haven't mentioned it in so many years—do you still think about it?"

My mother slumped forward, elbows on knees. "I didn't think you remembered."

"How could I forget? It was a Sunday. I was watching cartoons and eating Cocoa Puffs."

"You know what you were eating?"

"Even you had food standards back then. You wouldn't let me have chocolate cereal on a school day."

She cracked a smile, barely. "What else do you remember? About that day."

"I ran up the stairs to wake you and tell you Uncle Pete was at the door in his fire chief uniform. You were inconsolable, carrying on about the hotel fire in Allentown, how bad it was, how Uncle Pete had found him burning in the flames of hell."

My mother started crying. I went inside to get her a tissue, fearing the rest of our project would dissolve into more wallowing. I'd always suspected the grief she'd packed away was part of her weight problem. Part of our problem. But it was time to move on. "That was fifteen years ago. Come on, let's get to work."

I scrapped the idea of a yard sale, though—my mother would never hold up—and decided instead to donate the sports equipment to the township for their summer rec program, and call Purple Heart to pick up the rest.

"Let's grab a bite, Penny."

I whisked balsamic vinaigrette at the kitchen counter while my mother assembled ingredients for a salad.

"It's time I told you the rest of what I know about your father's death," she said, washing greens in the salad spinner.

"Like what?"

"For one thing, he wasn't on a business trip."

"But he was in a hotel."

"In Allentown."

"Oh."

"When your father didn't come home that night, even I didn't know where he was until Uncle Pete came the next morning to tell me."

"You'd had a fight?"

"Your father and the woman he was with had been drinking—"

My life suddenly seemed to depend on the thorough emulsification of oil and vinegar. I could not look at her.

"She was smoking, they fell asleep… They both died."

My arm ached. Pressure built in my gut.

"God, Mom. All these years—" I slapped the whisk into the bowl too hard. Brown drops spattered the wall and counter. "Why didn't you tell me?"

"When, exactly? You still needed to believe in your father. You needed to believe in me, too. I'm afraid there's no good time to say your father found your mother lacking."

She lifted the knife and slammed it through the cucumber so hard it made me jump.

I still wanted to believe in my father. Still needed to. His genes, I'd always felt, would be my salvation. And Dmitri's betrayal had cut me to the bone; for so many reasons, I had to know my father was the better man.

"But most of the time, when he was away at night, he was on purchasing trips. Right?"

Each chop of her blade scored my heart as I awaited the result of my genetic testing. She chopped faster; I bled. She said, "His partner did the purchasing."

I could think of only one just reason for the subterfuge. I said softly, "He must have been in love."

"Yeah, well, there was plenty of that going around."

I felt like she'd struck me with her own wedding picture. "You don't have to be crass."

She turned to me, the cucumber now a weepy mush. "Why are you defending him?"

"Could you give me a few minutes to catch up here? All this time I idolized him." As I'd idolized Dmitri. I felt his betrayal again, doubly deep, and threw the whisk into the sink. "I can't believe he'd hurt you like that. Hurt us. Choose to leave us!"

"How did you think I'd feel when I heard you'd jumped off a building?"

"We do *not* know that's what happened—"

"Don't give me that crap, Penny! How else could you have parted from that balcony?"

Her words summoned the darkness once again. I saw the void, felt the wind, dizziness struck—I had to grab hold of the sink.

She sprinkled the dressing on the salad and gave it a few angry tosses. "Well?"

"I can't tell you what happened!" Tears had their way with me. "I run over and over the facts, but I can't remember anything, or make sense of what happened. I just feel the dark and the cold of it. And I'm scared because once I do know, the memory will be stuck inside me forever, and I won't know what to do with it!"

Now that I'd named it, my fear decompressed and all that was hidden rushed up my throat. I leaned over the sink and retched, over and over, putrefied emotions spilling out like an imagined waterfall even though only a thin line of drool hung from my lip. The sweetness I'd tried to preserve—my adoration of my father, of Dmitri, of the career I'd longed for—now tasted like bile on my tongue. I fought to swallow them back down. What would I be without my most precious dreams, especially once Angela was gone? Alone. I retched again.

Sobs wracked my belly. My mother did not rush forward to take me into her arms, nor did she speak. But she didn't turn away, either. She stood her ground, witnessing my pain.

Once my sobs died down, I splashed cold water on my face, rinsed the sink, and made my way to the table. I felt hollow. My mother got out forks and plates. Dropped a napkin in my lap. A moment ago the entire foundation of my world had cracked, and now it all felt so normal. I was not alone—my mother sat beside me, at the head of the table. Had anything changed, really? Dmitri had still left me. And my father hadn't been around much when he was alive—this new knowledge didn't change that. With no startling revelation about my fall, I'd have to continue piecing together what life I could. Still, I struggled for orientation.

My voice was hoarse when I finally spoke. "So you weren't consumed with grief all these years?"

"I grieved plenty, for a while, for all the ways he had left me," she said.

"He left *us*, Mom."

She nodded and put her hand over mine. "More than anything I didn't want you to suffer. I worked hard to give you what I could of a stable home life, however flawed that was."

Something had changed after all. Sitting here with my mother, with her talking to me this way, felt an awful lot like love.

I looked at her and smiled. "You did good."

My mother used the tongs to transfer modest portions of salad onto our plates. "And it's a good thing you're still here, because God knows without you in my life I wouldn't be eating a lunch like this."

Out of habit, I teased out the fatty olives with my fork and pushed them to the side. "So if it wasn't grief, why is it you never cleaned out the garage?"

"That was his crap. I was too damned pissed at him to do the work."

This made me laugh. My mother joined in. When she looked up at me again it was as if she was seeing me anew. With her salad only half eaten, she set down her fork.

"I underestimated you, Penny. You didn't need a fantasy about your parents to pull you through." Her bottom lip quivered. "Look inside. You are…exquisite."

My mother's edges softened as once again tears collected in my eyes. I wanted to believe what she said. But until I knew what happened out on that ledge, I didn't know what demons I had yet to face.

Later, while setting the final box of sports magazines at the curb, my mother tossed the wedding picture into one of the boxes. The speed with which I snatched it up surprised me.

"Why, Penny?"

"He looks so happy here. And it's a kind of proof. At least we were two of the women he loved." I pressed the photo to my belly. "I need that."

As the sun set, my flesh and blood mother and the image of my father returned to the garage with me to take one last look around.

"What to do with all this space?" I said, my voice reverberating against bare concrete walls.

She slipped her arm around me. "We could dance."

# CHAPTER TWENTY-FIVE

*L*ife kept punching her down, and Angela kept rising back up. Two weeks later, Angela had begged enough doctors to autograph her medical chart to earn her discharge from the hospital. When I protested her move back to the apartment, she said, "I don't want to die in the hospital." How could I argue?

If she wanted to be home, then I'd make sure it was a homecoming to remember. And for that I only needed one thing: Kandelbaum.

I'd asked him to come along with me to help get her home, but he said no, he needed for her to perceive a clean break between his hospital visits and this homecoming. So I'd given him my key. Knowing what lay ahead made keeping up idle chitchat in the taxi with Angela difficult.

When we pulled up in front of the row house, I let Angela get out first. Kandelbaum was so eager to greet her, he pulled the front door open before she reached for the handle. For a moment they each took in the surprise of their new positions on opposite sides of the door—even this first embrace, Kandelbaum would not rush—then he slipped his arms around her tiny body in the gentlest possible way. The moment seemed suspended: him loving her, her allowing love, my heart swelling with the joy of behold-ing it. He murmured to her and kissed her cheek and smoothed her hair and kissed the top of her head, and I couldn't pull my eyes away.

I took on the rent. Stretched myself thinner to take care of Angela's daily needs. Ignored my exercise regimen so I could leave work early enough to fetch prescriptions, wash clothes, borrow library books, and shop for foods she hoped to eat. Waxed bags accumulated in the kitchen as each day Kandelbaum brought her a treat from the bakery. Our laughter ebbed as the coughing grew more painful—no one wanted to bring it on—but as long as Kandelbaum was sitting beside her, telling stories about everyday life at Independence Sweets or reading her a short story from one of the library books, those bright eyes radiated contentment.

I struggled with her decline. I showed up to work at the gym one day with an Adidas shoe on my left foot and a Saucony on my right.

One day in early November, Angela and I were watching one of the soaps on her little television when she started a coughing fit. I held a paper cup to her lips, but she couldn't seem to gather up the strength to expel any mucus. Yet she hacked and hacked, as if her lungs were filling up and closing off and there was no longer much she could do about it. Finally, she spit into the cup—and when I pulled it back, the mucus was streaked with blood. She fell back against her pillow, panting. Her physical presence a mirage fading into the wall of desert behind her. I tried not to hold my breath as I waited for the reassuring hiss from the oxygen tank. An IV pole, now a fixture at the corner of her bed, fed her antibiotics through a port in her chest. Her body seemed smaller in relationship to a face now swollen with steroids.

Her struggle was getting harder to watch. I averted my focus; it fell upon the growing stack of newspapers by her bed. She had not let me recycle them or suspend the subscription while she was in the hospital. She wanted every day accounted for. *Life goes on whether I'm in the hospital or not*, she'd say. *I'll catch up, you'll see.* But to me the growing pile was a bar chart of her waning engagement with life.

I said, "Hopefully a new set of lungs is on the way."

Her head jerked up.

"I know you're on the list."

"It's not a cure. I'd still have CF."

"But you could breathe again. It would buy you time."

"I can't risk handing myself over. It could drain my willpower." Her gravelly voice defined the jagged pockets of air that her lungs strained to billow forth. "Most days, willpower is the only thing I can count on."

"What do you mean, hand yourself over?"

"To the transplant team. To another person's lungs. To the possibility of rejection and infection and even depression if lungs aren't available—"

"But maybe you'd be handing yourself over to the possibility of life."

"I am *not* an experiment," she snapped.

I sat down beside her and waited until her features settled. "Is this about your mom?"

She took her time before speaking again. "I took myself off the list."

"What?"

"I've seen what my friends went through. I do not believe God ever intended to torture me. He gave me this mind and these lungs to shape me."

"But maybe God could shape you through the doctors. They've dedicated their lives to finding treatment—"

"Let me finish. I must believe I've had a purpose, Penny. If this body is on its way out, then so am I. Maybe God's telling me we're packing it in."

I lost it. Were we to sit here and watch while she drowned in her own fluids? I had to do something. I pulled out her suitcase and started packing her stuff.

She said, "I'm not going back to the hospital."

"I'm not taking you to the hospital. We're going to Oregon. I am going to call the airport and get—us—tickets," I said, accenting the words by throwing in one toiletry item per word. I couldn't hide my anger anymore. I was angry at her for fighting so damn hard to live and angry with her for giving up and angry at her mother for not being angry and angry at myself for being so helpless, and I was ready to explode from acting like none of it was bothering me.

"Why Oregon?"

"Did you think I'd only been holding your hand these last few weeks? I've learned things. I know about Oregon's Death with

Dignity Act. Doctors will prescribe pills so when you can't take it anymore, you can put an end to all this."

"Penny." Her wheezy whisper commanded my full attention. "That's not how I want to go."

I stood up and squared off. "Well, look at me, sister, because I am living proof you can't control how you go." The words flew from my mouth. Added up. Resonated within me. I started to shake.

"Exactly." She drew several breaths, waiting until I had calmed enough to catch up with her reasoning. "I understand the desire to escape from pain. But I can't turn back. This is my life. I've got to fight."

"Then fight better. With new lungs."

She shook her head, gently waggling her nose tubing.

"This is such a big decision. Are you sure?"

She rested, a chorus of crackling noises accompanying each breath. "I'm sure of this body. Trying to trade up feels like Russian roulette to me."

I wanted to run, to scream, to do physical battle on her behalf. "I want to make your suffering go away."

She smiled and closed her eyes. "You help"—breath—"by being here."

I took her hand in mine, slipping my fingers up high enough to feel her pulse. Her fingers were delicate, more sparrow's foot than human hand. I remembered my silent promise, to stay by her side. I hadn't done this enough. I pressed my palm to hers, hoping to infuse her with my energy.

She looked into my eyes as if searching for something. "I'm worried about you, Penny. You need a way to manage your stress."

"Unbelievable." How could she worry about me?

"When I'm agitated, I paint."

"Fine. Where's a brush?"

"Seriously?"

I nodded.

"This should be good." She settled back onto her pillows and told me where to find her supplies. To protect the floor, I grabbed a newspaper from her pile. "Not that one, I haven't read it yet." I took one from the recycling pile instead and tried to act confident as I dabbed a slim paintbrush in burnt sienna.

I stared at the wall but didn't know where to start. Angela suggested adding another camel to the rolling sand dunes, but after a half hour my dromedary still looked like a humpbacked sawhorse. I added a smile to its face, in blue. Angela was kind enough not to break into painful spasms of laughter when I tossed the brush into the bathroom sink.

"Oh what the hell," I said. "I'm not a painter."

"No, you're not. *I'm* a painter."

When I went to pick up the newspapers, she grabbed my hand. The ferocity in her grip stunned me.

"What is it?"

Tears formed in her eyes, and her breathing grew shallow. "It also hurts me, you know. To watch you suffer. Penn—" My name choked off. "You're starving."

She let the gentle hiss of oxygen and the rhythm of deeper breaths steady her voice, then said, "You've got to find a way to feed yourself."

# RELEASE

"What I long for is the eagerness to meet life, the curiosity, the wonder that you feel when you can really move..."

—Martha Graham

# CHAPTER TWENTY-SIX

*M*y body knew what it was doing before my mind caught up. Still a bit winded from my run up the stairs, I strode to the desk where Bebe was shuffling papers and plunked down my fifteen dollars.

"I have to dance."

She took a moment to study the face and haircut.

"Darling, it is so good to see you! And in one piece." She reached for my hand and squeezed it, then motioned to a chair. "Sit, sit. I heard about the…well, your…and then DeLaval left…"

I winced.

"I'm so sorry, dearest, I was out of the country."

Something seemed off about her. "You got your tooth fixed."

"You cut your hair." She shrugged. "We do what we can. So tell me what you've been up to."

I had just suggested that my best friend consider suicide, that's what. As good as it was to see my mentor again, holding still—holding a conversation—holding anything was torture. I needed to spill, not hold. To thrash, leap, bounce, and swing until anxiety loosened its grip on my body.

A tide of twittering adolescents washed into the reception area through the door of the back studio.

"Can we talk later?" I said. "It's going to take me a while to get ready for class."

"Adult intermediate? Penny, you started teaching that class when you were nineteen years old. Come back in the morning for the professional class."

"Give me a break, Bebe. I haven't danced in eight months." My tone was sharper than intended and sliced through the buzz of conversation around us.

Bebe raised her meticulously drawn eyebrows. "Go on in."

Stripped down to my leotard and sweats, I walked around Bebe's front studio. Without their calluses, my soles felt as soft and sticky as a newborn's.

I rested my hand on the barre in the back of the room. My body knew what to do: shoulder blades slid down the back, navel pressed upward and inward, hips squared off. This preparation, repeated mindlessly countless times in my life, rendered my body taut yet resilient. Fully engaged. Ready. I marveled at this. I massaged each sole against the floor, over and over, allowing the wood to suck away moisture and toughen the skin for the fight ahead.

Bebe clapped her hands and we arranged ourselves center floor. She began: *plié, relevé, bend again, and straighten.* Bebe never demonstrated; she spoke in shorthand augmented with small hand movements. But her voice and hands clicked my body back into a long dormant groove: I was a student of the dance. *Tendu, roll down through the foot, push away, and close.* I hadn't been using my feet enough. All of those little muscles, tendons, and ligaments had gone stiff. *Flat-back, release, roll up, arch, hold, hold, return, swing down, swing up, plié, repeat.* Oh my god, Bebe, that felt great. Repeat, repeat—do it twenty more times. Nothing about everyday life offers the spine such sweet release.

When she moved us across the floor, I almost wept with the joy of it. Mauricio was wrong—I could dance! The galloping and skipping of acrobics had never satisfied; it left me feeling flat as an animated cartoon character with a thumping chest. Dance added shading, perspective, texture. I was at once tortoise and hare, antelope and inchworm, coyote and sailfish.

For ninety blessed minutes, I left my stress outside the door, and when class ended, I was in no rush to greet it. As the number of dancers in the studio thinned, I caught a glimpse of my body in the mirror. I saw those same intractable hips, yes, but my face glistened with the sweat of hard work and the joy of movement.

"Miss Penny, is that you?"

Behind me stood a petite black woman, no more than four foot ten, with dreadlocks in her hair and a diamond stud in her nose.

"I'm Jeannie Richards. I used to take your beginner class. Of course I was fifteen then."

When I mentally subtracted six years, cropped her hair, and removed the stud, I found a face I recognized.

"Goodness, Jeannie, you've changed."

"You haven't. I mean, your hair is different, but I wouldn't forget that body."

I smiled and excused myself to cover that unforgettable yet quickly chilling body with a sweatshirt. Jeannie followed.

"I wanted to grow up to be just like you, but I stopped about a foot short," Jeannie said. "So where've you been?"

Heat rose to my face. Desperation had precipitated my rush back to class. I wasn't prepared for bumping into people I knew, hadn't rehearsed a quick answer. "I took a break."

"I heard about that night, you know, last winter. How awful."

"I guess I'm trying to work my way back."

She told me about a class she liked in Manayunk. André's. "It's a great workout. Thursdays at six. Maybe I'll see you?"

"I thought I'd take Bebe's improv tomorrow night."

"Bebe hasn't had that class for a while now."

"But it was so popular."

Jeannie shrugged. "I gotta run, but it was so good to see you again, Miss Penny."

When I emerged from the studio, I found Bebe at her desk, catching up on paperwork. I flopped into the chair across the desk from hers.

"I thought you'd retired," she said. "Or given up."

"It was more like Dmitri hijacked my career."

"So life's a bitch and he's a bastard. That's no reason to turn your back on everything you are."

"You don't even know what happened."

She shrugged. "This theme doesn't have many variations. You fell in love with him and found out he was gay."

I stood and gathered my things. Tears threatened. "If you think it was easy for me to come here tonight, you're wrong. I am not in the mood for this, Bebe."

"I apologize, darling. Sit." She tipped her head toward the chair. "Enlighten me."

I hesitated for a moment, but the release the dance class offered left me eager to rid myself of everything I'd dammed inside of me. I took the seat. "You know what it meant to me to get that job with Dance DeLaval. Dmitri saw me the way you did—the way others never could. The dancer I was on the inside. He gave me a chance, and when he saw what I could do, he promoted me to rehearsal assistant."

"So he wasn't completely without faculties." Bebe punched numbers into a calculator while she spoke. I wasn't going to go through the anguish of relating this story if she only planned to lend half an ear. I waited until she closed her attendance roster and checkbook and turned to me. "I'm sorry, darling. The back studio has a leaky pipe, and I've had to shuffle the schedule."

"Can't you get a plumber?"

"Sounds deceptively easy, but with plumbing this old you never know what it's going to cost once they start fiddling with things. They remove one joint and break the next—but go ahead, I'm listening."

"We had a huge piece due to premiere later that week, and since I was buried in final production details, Dmitri pulled me aside to say he worried about all the pressure on me. I figured he was being extra sweet because the night before I'd walked in on him having sex with—"

Bebe nodded as if she knew this part of the story. "A hidden boyfriend."

"He is *not* gay, Bebe. Sometimes I think that would've been easier. She was in the company."

"Ooh, that is extra sweet."

"This was his bright idea: take on a new dancer. I said no way in hell. He said he'd already hired her. I said he couldn't possibly have hooked up with a new dancer already, and he said Margaret MacArthur had recommended her. He said the new girl would take my role in *No Brainer* for the premiere. I told him that was bullshit. He said it was his company. I said pull her. He said she'd already learned the steps. I said that after all I'd done for him he owed me my job. He wouldn't meet my eyes. I stood, shaking—he'd taken everything. I begged him: Please, Dmitri, I need to dance."

Bebe shook her head.

"My anger wasn't fazing him, it was only hurting me. I knew the only way to get my life back was to forgive him. I was heading down the hallway toward the studio for that very reason when I overheard Dmitri's voice. Turns out, I had happened upon a company meeting—one which I'd known nothing about."

I moved to the window but couldn't take the smell of dust on the blinds any more than the glare of the late-day sun reflecting from the windows across the street. I turned to look at the woman who had nurtured my love of modern dance. She stood with her arms crossed, caftan wrapped around her like a chrysalis. She gave nothing away in her face, but her voice was soft when she said, "Go on."

It was the night before the New York premiere. I walked through the studio door, and they all looked up at me—Lars, Mitch, Tina, Karly, Dmitri, and the new girl—then, as if they'd choreographed it, they all looked back down to the floor.

Dmitri said, "Penny, we are in a meeting. Could you wait at home?"

I demanded to know what he was talking to them about. The air in the studio thickened until I could hardly breathe before Mitch said, "They're heading toward Russia early. Next week."

"That makes no sense," I said. "You have a year left in your residency "

"What do you mean, *they?*" Dmitri said, looking at Mitch.

"I can't go," Mitch said. "My marriage is on shaky ground as it is. Evan doesn't want to raise our daughter in Russia. I can do the premiere tomorrow and that's it." I hated to see Mitch go. Of all the dancers, he'd been the kindest to me. So before he left the room, I gave him a hug—but he responded with only one arm and a weak pat on the back. As if he'd had a stroke.

Silence once again swelled within the room. I broke it.

"It's a good thing I'm here, then. You'll need me." I read the confusion on Dmitri's face as a translation problem. "Because I know all the roles."

But he said, "Please Penny, I will talk to you at home."

"You have it wrong, Dmitri. What's between the company members should happen at the studio, and what's between *us* should happen at home." I glared at Tina as I said this, sure that by now all of them must know Dmitri had slept with her.

I waited for Dmitri to speak. He worked his mouth as if

chewing words whose taste troubled him. "The company asked for this meeting without you. Lately, it is too intense in the air. They think it better if…if you do not come for the tour."

"Then we're lucky they're not in charge, aren't we?"

He paused. Too long.

"Dmitri?"

He took the time to commit fully to his next words, then finally sputtered: "I am not taking you, Penny."

I grabbed him by the arm and pulled him into the office. I wanted to slam the door, to scream, to knee him in the groin, but I held it in. Someone had to take the lead and restore order. And I would not allow him to see my anguish. I searched his eyes for the man who called me his muse, who said he had fallen in love with dance when he saw me perform his movement.

With a level voice, I said, "Was this Tina's idea?"

Dmitri shook his head as if he pitied me and with his next words imploded whatever slapdash foundation had been propping up my self-respect. "It is unanimous."

I was already falling, but made one last attempt to reach back for him. "And this is what you want too, Dmitri? You would choose them over me?"

"I need the company. Offers to perform in Europe are coming. If I could see earlier what problems our relationship would cause, I never would have—"

"Don't. Don't finish that sentence." I would not listen to him reduce what we'd had together to lack of foresight. I let myself crumble, then, and landed in the office chair.

"You can stay in the penthouse until you find a new place. I will pay you for two months."

⚬

Bebe guffawed. "Guilt money."

"I know. He always liked to think of the company as some big American corporation, but I had wanted it to be more like a family where everyone is loved for the part they bring to the whole. *No Brainer* was like our baby, but I would never see its birth."

"And that was it?" Bebe said.

"He said good-bye to me that night, and I sat motionless in his office chair until the studio lights went out and every faint sound of the retreating dancers had faded to silence. I left alone, feeling my way through the dark. When I got home, his stuff was gone." I paused to honor my emptiness. "I never saw him again."

I wanted Bebe to wrap me in the wings of her caftan, but comforting had never been her strong suit. She had sharper edges, and used them well to poke and prod and keep her dancers moving. She stood beside me at the window.

"He yanked out my heart and held it up so everyone could watch it wriggle. I lost everything."

"No. It was Dmitri who lost everything. A parasite disengaged from its host has to move on, darling, in search of fresh blood. Have you been reading about the progress of his European tour?"

"Jeez, Bebe, I'm not that hard on myself."

"Margaret MacArthur wrote a small update in the *Sentinel* last week. Seems that starting new relationships isn't the only thing

DeLaval does too quickly. The critics haven't been kind. They say he's lost focus. He wasn't ready for that tour."

I was surprised MacArthur would speak ill of her pet choreographer. Maybe she was more discerning than I'd given her credit for. Yet Dmitri's failure didn't make me feel any better. "Dmitri was the best thing that ever happened to me. I wanted so desperately to make him proud. His goals were big. Important."

"Goodness, darling—if I felt my work had to be big to be important, I would have stopped teaching long ago." Bebe turned to me and, to my surprise, took my face in her hands. "Listen to me. People do stupid things for love. But you don't need to host a heartworm to know your creative blood has value. And there could be no stupider move in a life full of promise than jumping off a building."

Shame dark as night swept through me. Angela fought so hard, every day, for her life. I tried to turn away, but Bebe held tight to my jaw, forcing me to look at her, until at last a tear slid from my eye to her hand.

"It hurt, Bebe. To lose Dmitri. And now I'm about to lose someone else I love."

"Of course it hurts, darling. Use it! It's what artists do. Life has wisdom of its own. It dumps shit on you and stirs you up until your soil is fertile. Accept the challenge and plant some seeds. This is how artists grow."

I knocked softly on Mrs. Pope's door. From the other side, I heard Shakespeare squawk, "Spread 'em, baby," before his owner answered.

"How'd it go?" I said. If I was going to take time for myself to dance, someone needed to know where to find me. I chose to confide in Mrs. Pope. I figured her expectations about my dancing would weigh less than anyone else's.

"You're back," Mrs. Pope said. "Did you enjoy your class?"

"Shh." I pushed my way into her living room and closed the door behind me. I didn't want Angela to overhear that I was dancing again. I still needed to sort out my motives and goals in my own mind. "I'm not limping. Yet. How'd things go here?"

"The world didn't stop spinning because you took some time to yourself. Marty came to pick her up about an hour ago."

"Oh no. Did she need to go back to the hospital?"

"She told me earlier she was feeling much better this evening."

That was Angela-speak for "don't you dare pity me." The knot in my gut would not release. "I don't know…"

"I do believe she wore a spot of makeup. Honest, Penny, they looked so nice I snapped a picture. Marty wore a suit! I'll make a print for you."

When I got home, I gave waiting up for them my best shot, but my body wouldn't hold out. I sank into a heavy, dreamless sleep.

Early the next morning, before moving from my bed, I tested my range of motion in the dark. From my huge quads to the threads articulating my hands, my muscles had organized a revolt. I made my way to the bathroom in herky-jerky fashion.

I either had to dance regularly or never, ever do it again.

I left the bathroom light on and cracked the door so I could get ready for work without waking Angela—allowing enough light into the room to see that her bed was empty. I lurched to the phone to call Presbyterian. As I was dialing, I thought I heard footsteps on the stairs, then giggling and coughing. By the time I reached the door, Angela was opening it from the other side. I felt a blast of cool air from the outside door down below.

"You scared me half to death."

Angela crossed over to her bed, sat down, and reattached her oxygen. When I flipped on the track lights, she was holding up her finger, signaling for me to wait until she got some air into her lungs. She sat with her legs folded beneath her—when her slacks rode up I could see her best black socks. I sat down beside her. One thing I could intuit: she was not in dire straits. She had a big smile on her face.

"Is that a new bracelet?"

She waved her wrist, now wrapped by interwoven strands of pearls held together with a heart-shaped clasp.

"Marty gave it to me. Isn't it wonderful? But that's not all. I am bursting and I've gotta tell someone and you're the someone I want to tell…"

No wonder she needed oxygen. That was the biggest bundle of words I'd heard from her in one breath in a long time.

"Go ahead."

"I feel kind of bad, because Marty and I were out having fun and here you were home by yourself—"

"You're straining your lungs. Spill."

She took a few more breaths. "Last night this used-up body of mine was the source of mind-blowing pleasure—"

"How much morphine did you take?"

She laughed, coughed. "Come on, Penny, I was with Marty."

"Right, he wouldn't do drugs—"

"I mean, I was *with* Marty."

"I know, I was just teasing." I grabbed her hands. The brightness in her eyes blew a hole in my heart. "Did you go to his place? I've slept on his couch too, you know."

She pushed at me weakly. "He took me to this beautiful bed and breakfast up in New Hope. The whole night was so…magical. I never would have met him if it weren't for you."

Her breathing turned rapid and shallow.

"Angela? Are you okay?" I started thumping on her back, just in case, until I realized she was crying. I put my arm around her. "What's going on? Tell me."

"I feel…insane. Cracked open. Like air is reaching new surfaces deep inside me that I'd walled off. It hurts and it tickles and I'm scared and it's wonderful all at the same time. Look at me." She held up a shaking hand. "I am completely out of control." She sobbed and coughed until she brought up some phlegm. I handed her a paper cup so she could spit. "I'm sorry, I'm going on and on, but this is the best thing that's ever happened to me. And it happened in *this* body."

I knew exactly what she was talking about. I'd felt that same frightening euphoria myself.

In this body.

Last night—when I danced.

After my shift, I returned home to find Kandelbaum pounding on Angela's back.

"Call 911, she can't breathe."

He said the words calmly, but the frantic beating of his cupped hands revealed his heart. I pounded the numbers into the keypad, Angela's eyes bulging, her skin a scary purple. A paramedic intubated her right in front of us. It looked like a collapsed lung and another trip to the hospital. As they wheeled her out the door, I told Kandelbaum I'd take over if he needed to get back to work.

"I need to be with her," he said. I gave him a hug. "And you look exhausted, Penny. A little unsteady on your feet. Why don't you lie down and take a nap. I'll follow the ambulance and make sure she gets settled in okay."

"Give me fifteen minutes and I'll be right behind you."

When I next opened my eyes, it was after four-thirty in the afternoon and the sun was starting to set. I jerked up, swung my legs off the bed, and slid to the floor—but my legs gave way and I landed in a clump. I rolled onto my back and tested my joints. Everything functional. I grabbed my cell phone and called Presby as I stretched. When they connected me to Angela's room, Kandelbaum answered the phone.

"How's she doing?"

"It was pretty frightening for a while. She's quiet now."

"I'm so sorry. I overslept." I could take the fire in the hamstring I was stretching; it was letting Angela down that had me struggling to push back tears. "I should have been with her."

"She hardly knew I was there. Quite a team surrounded her, and then whisked her into surgery. She has a chest tube that will have to stay in a couple of days."

"Oh my god." I rolled over and reached for my shoes. "I'm on my way."

"There's not much point in coming tonight. They suspect she'll sleep through till tomorrow."

I felt like such a loser.

"And Penny? She knows you love her."

I checked the time, put on my shoes, and then did my best impression of someone capable of jogging to the Market East station to catch the train to Manayunk.

# CHAPTER TWENTY-SEVEN

ndré's Manayunk class was athletic and taxing. While walking to work Friday morning, my muscles complained so loudly I was surprised others on the street couldn't hear them. Joey noticed the hitch in my step. "You look like Frankenstein in leg braces," he said. "What's with you?"

"I think that's obvious." Muscle soreness was always worse on the second day. If I could get through my shift at the gym and keep getting to dance class, I should feel a little better each day.

"You working with a trainer someplace else? Because if you want to compete, I'm your man."

"Compete?"

"Weightlifting. I know you're doing it, the squats always give you away. That's how I bulk up my thighs, too. But they hurt something wicked until the muscle tears heal."

I didn't know whether to laugh or cry. "Why the hell would anyone want to bulk up her thighs?" I made a grab for my paycheck, but Joey pulled it out of reach.

"I said, I want to know what you've been up to."

I looked around me. People were filtering in for early morning workouts, but I didn't see MacArthur.

"Are you checking for spies? What kind of secret is this?"

"Have a heart, Joey." Saying this was big for me, and felt as intimate as sharing my sex life with him. I braced myself against the front desk. "I've started dancing again."

"Oh, is that all." He tossed me the paycheck. "I guess that's good timing."

"How so?"

"Suzie's ready to come back to work. I can only afford to keep you on for the early morning class, so I'm glad you're—" He looked both ways and whispered. "*Dancing again.*"

I was too embarrassed to tell him that my dancing was no longer an income stream, but an added expense. With Angela so sick, though, she needed my support now more than ever. "Could you keep me on another month? Until I find something else? Please. I need the money."

He shook his head. "I appreciate all the new clients you've attracted, but I can only stretch the payroll so far. You can finish out the month. If short words will do, I'll be glad to write you a recommendation. Oh, and wait." From beneath the front counter he retrieved an ivory envelope, hand addressed. "You have mail."

I decided to skip the stairs. Once alone in the elevator, I opened the envelope. It was lined in gold, and an inner envelope was addressed to "Miss Penelope Sparrow and Guest." I pulled out a card from beneath tissue paper protecting its embossed lettering. An R.S.V.P. card and envelope were enclosed.

KATHRYN CRAFT

As an esteemed member of the Philadelphia Arts Community
The Philadelphia Dance Alliance
cordially invites you to attend a luncheon
at one in the afternoon on December twelfth
Rose Garden, Park Hyatt Philadelphia at the Bellevue
honoring
Margaret MacArthur
Critic for The Philadelphia Sentinel
In celebration of her thirty years of service to the dance
community
R.S.V.P. by December 1

Was this a joke? I wondered how many other aerobics instructors would be breaking tofu with the Philadelphia dance professionals. When the elevator doors opened, I stuffed the invitation deep into my bag.

After my shift, I went to Presby to see Angela. I packed her favorite things into her wheeled suitcase to make her feel more at home, and in deference to my sore muscles, treated myself to a taxi.

I sensed that talking was painful for her, so I kept up the chatter while I redecorated her room. Soon she was covered with her own quilt and illuminated by her own reading lamp. I'd also brought a new item—the photo of Angela and Kandelbaum that Mrs. Pope had taken, now framed. I held it out to her. "Look."

Their arms were around one another, their cheeks pressed

264

together in a pose so full of life and hope that anyone coming across such a picture in the engagements section of the newspaper would predict a long and happy life.

She smiled.

I gestured toward the bedside table. "Shall I put it over here, where you can look at it?"

She shook her head no and pressed the picture to her body. Not to her heart, which was way too close to her chest tube placement, but low on her belly, right above her center of gravity.

"Thank you," she said. Her face twisted into a grimace.

"Shh," I said. "Don't cry, sweetie. It wasn't any trouble."

She shook her head. "Mrs. Pope hasn't asked for the rent in two months. I'll pay you back."

My chest seized. I kissed her forehead. "Of course you will."

"This is—it's a tough stretch."

"I know."

From its emaciated tube, I squeezed what remained of her moisturizer. Rubbed it on her arms. Sought, with long strokes, what remained of the meat beneath her skin.

"I can apply my own lotion, for god's sake."

I smiled. "I know."

Bebe stood by the door of her studio, shopping bags balanced in both arms while fiddling with the lock. I heard her curse as I approached.

"You tell it, Bebe. Need help locking that?"

Bebe looked at me, let her load slip to the ground, and tried the lock again. "Oh, Penny. I'm going in, not leaving."

"Did you forget something?"

"I live here. I moved back into the little apartment."

"But you loved your brownstone."

"Well. I never needed that much space."

A VACANCY sign hung in the window where the Chen laundry used to be. My hopes for a job took a nosedive. Bebe was their landlord. "Is it money problems?"

"I'm simplifying my life. And you can't argue with the commute." She took a deep breath and picked up her packages.

"Let me get those." I was surprised she had struggled with them—the packages held nothing heavier than cotton balls and light bulbs.

"Thanks, darling." I pretended my thighs didn't find the steps a challenge. "A few health issues have crimped my cash flow, and I haven't been able to swing some needed repairs—"

"Are you all right?" I turned on the stairs to look down at her.

"It's nothing fatal. What did you stop in for? I've never had a Friday class."

Bebe's face looked puffy. A two-inch spot of silver on her crown gave away an uncharacteristic lack of hair color maintenance. Her movements were more cautious. It occurred to me she could use my help at the studio, maybe on a per-student commission, but it would take time to rebuild her class schedule to its former glory. I needed something full-time, and now. I set that goal aside. "I need a class tonight. Something not too expensive."

She stopped at the second floor landing. "How does free sound?

Go in and use the studio. You still have a key—come whenever you want."

"Just me, and all that space?"

I waited for Bebe at the top. She continued to speak as she climbed the stairs.

"You don't need a teacher to tell you what to do. Your body knows. I could sense your vision maturing within you as a teen. For the life of me I can't figure out why you don't have the courage to use it."

She squeezed past. Cramped as we were in the narrow hallway with the added bulk of winter clothing, I grew painfully aware of my size.

"That's because your body is perfectly acceptable to the dance world. Mine isn't, and there isn't a damn thing I can do about it."

"My talent isn't as great as yours and there isn't a damn thing I can do about that, either."

I leaned against the wall behind me. "You taught me almost everything I know."

"Because I am a teacher. That is my gift. But you are an artist, Penny. Are you so blind to your own talent you never noticed when I stopped teaching, and started nurturing, instead? Didn't you sense the shift from listening to me to listening to your own inner voice?"

"Whatever voice that was went silent. At Dance DeLaval, I had these perfect dancers at my disposal and Dmitri's permission to choreograph my own work on them, and I couldn't think of a damned thing."

"Perfect, you say? That was your problem. It is our imperfections that make us endlessly fascinating."

I loved what she said and recognized the truth in it. Privately. But I was shocked as hell to hear Bebe utter the words aloud. Wasn't striving for perfection the very basis of our efforts, in all my years of training?

She unlocked the door to my first apartment, the place she now called home. I handed Bebe her groceries.

"You're stronger than you think, Penny. Look how many times you've been tested, and yet here you are. Go downstairs and dance."

I tried not to let her see the way my sore muscles' spastic contractions jarred me as I descended the steps.

I chose the back studio for its relative intimacy. Since the night of my fall, space and I had had an uneasy relationship. Too much of it and I feared I might disappear.

# CHAPTER TWENTY-EIGHT

*T*he princess-seamed camisole in aquamarine, or my black cap sleeve leotard with the low-cut back? I glanced at the clock—I had hoped to arrive early, but it was only fifteen minutes until Bebe's Saturday morning class. I laughed at my reflection in the mirror. It had been a while since I cared what the hell I wore. When I stripped down at the studio, it was to a raspberry tank and my gray knit warm-up pants.

Center floor, stretching and chatting, were Jeannie and some of the other dancers I recognized from André's. They'd invited me out for coffee after the Thursday class, and I was struck that most of them knew of me, whether from rumor or reputation. I had enjoyed their easy camaraderie, but I'd lived in a world where dancers climbed on the injured and aging bodies of their friends to get noticed. Instead of joining them, I gave a noncommittal wave and took a place at the barre to warm up.

During the class, I had trouble concentrating. It wasn't fear for Angela—according to her doctors she was "as stable as could be expected," which was code for "unstable," but I also knew I couldn't do a blessed thing about it.

The problem was my overactive mind. My love for Angela and the push-and-pull of her duet with Kandelbaum had awoken within me a new sensibility; I now saw relationships everywhere. Jeannie was the embodiment of Bebe's earthy fluidity, while the short jock from André's—was his name Luke?—translated the same into a language with harsher edges. Made it look male and athletic. They'd make interesting partners.

A woman named Rhonda had on enough makeup to perform at the Met: pancake, fashion model eyes, rouged cheeks, painted lips. It seemed to conceal massive reconstruction on the left side of her face. But she also put extra detail into every movement—a flexed foot here, a cocked head there—as if carefully embroidering her name onto every square of a patchwork quilt. The approach was quiet and patient. Her soft middle made me think of inner conflict—what was going on inside of her?

The guy next to me, Vincent. He wore a sleeveless Villanova sweatshirt, but the black footless tights beneath had me checking out his legs. After we'd cycled into the front row, our bodies displayed their similarity, side by side, in the mirror. We were the same height, had the same sturdy thighs, and he matched me "powerful glute" to "mambo hip" in the butt department. Why had I never seen my hips as the product of powerful glutes?

Each dancer offered something different. Our class became a skyline of heads, lowering and raising with each plié. One of those heads stood out as if lit by a spotlight: her hair was pure white. Bebe called her Stella.

Stella was narrow-shouldered, with a pouchy abdomen. Sagging breasts cushioned her rib cage. Despite her age, she could really dance, with movements as delicate and classy as fine bone china. She used everything her body was still capable of doing to draw attention to the way she moved through space.

Bebe taught a pretty intricate sequence. Stella kept her eyes on Bebe, yet didn't mark along with her the way some others did. Instead she internalized the movement through small nods and wiggles of her head. The rest of the class was still struggling to nail it when Bebe said, "Now reverse to the left. Penny, demonstrate."

The request was at once commonplace and shocking. How could she single me out this way, when she knew I only had a few classes under my belt? "I'm sorry, my head was somewhere else…"

When she looked at me and cocked her head, I started to laugh. Bebe smiled. I got it—I didn't need my mind. My body knew what to do. It always had. I tapped into the beat of my heart and the flow of my blood and listened for the movement. I performed Bebe's sequence to the right in my head, and then trusted my muscles to reverse it to the left. I thought I heard Vincent say, "Wow."

"Did I get it?" I asked Bebe.

"As if it were yours," she answered.

She broke us into small groups to perform. My group included diminutive Jeannie and a buxom redhead named Gayle whose height was a step between ours. We performed the movement almost identically at our different levels of atmosphere. *Triplets*—a title?

Outside, after class, I thought I'd lost Stella until I caught a tuft of white escaping from beneath a black knit hat up ahead. She stood at the corner of Tenth and Lombard with a small group waiting for traffic.

"Excuse me." I touched her sleeve.

"Yes?"

Out here she looked like any aging woman. Only the erectness of the spine housed within her camel coat suggested her dance habit. "I couldn't take my eyes off you in class today."

I felt powerful and alive and in the moment, for once trusting my instincts to lead me exactly where I needed to go. She smiled as if strangers came up to her blathering such drivel all the time. "Will you walk along with me then? Penelope, isn't it?"

"Penelope Sparrow," I said, offering her my hand. "I'm a friend of Bebe's. And you're Stella…?"

"Just Stella. At this point I've had too many last names to believe they illuminate my identity in any way."

I laughed and fell in beside her. "You've been dancing for a long time."

She nodded. "I once danced with Twyla."

"*Tharp?*"

She smiled at the reverence in my response. "Back in the late sixties. I was only with her a few months, but it's still fun to say."

"Why on earth did you stop?"

"I got pregnant. Then married…Each day I drifted further from the life of a dancer. After a point, I forgot to tend to my own needs altogether." She turned left onto Spruce; I followed. In a voice I could hardly hear above the rumble of a bus accelerating beside us, she said, "Time slips away."

"You're still a pleasure to watch."

The corners of her mouth turned up. "The dancers in this city would love a critic like you."

"Do you take class anywhere else?"

"Just at Bebe's, every morning. I take the yoga first, and then Bebe's class after. At my age it takes longer to warm up."

"So when did you get back to dancing?"

"Not until my late forties. It was like my body reawakened after a long hibernation. Now I'm sixty-six," she said, with the frank enthusiasm of a child claiming she is six-and-a-half. "Who knows how much longer I'll have to dance?"

The notion of still dancing in my sixties had never occurred to me. Not so long ago, I feared I might grind to a halt this side of thirty. "Who knows anything? Maybe you'll perform again."

She laughed. "The odds are against it."

"I fell fourteen stories and lived. The odds were against that, too."

She stopped walking and looked at me with an expression so queer it could only have matched my own. The moment passed, and when she resumed walking, she said, "I wouldn't count on that again."

Stella stopped outside the Independence Suites. "This is it for me."

"You're kidding. I used to live here, too."

"Oh no, I have a studio over at the Versailles. But this is the best bakery in town. I always stop in for a little something on my way home. Would you like to join me? His new health breads aren't too much of an indulgence."

Kandelbaum looked up from behind the counter when the bell dangling from the door announced our entrance. "Hello, Penny. Look at your bright eyes and pink cheeks—the picture of health. And Stella, sit anywhere you please. I'll be with you in a moment."

Stella and I looked at each other. She said, "You know the baker?" I burst out laughing.

"And how do you two know each other?" Kandelbaum said.

"We met today," said Stella. "In dance class."

"Dance class." Kandelbaum's unspoken questions pushed his eyebrows higher on his forehead. I removed my coat and hung it over the back of a chair.

"That's why I couldn't get to Presby this morning. How was Angela?"

"Resting comfortably, they say. Although I heard her tell an intern that if he pressed his stethoscope to her chest one more time she'd wring his neck with it." His smile was skewed with the uncertainty of whether she just might do it.

"That's our Angie." I squeezed his hand. "I'll be spending the afternoon with her. Can we get coffees?"

When Kandelbaum brought the coffee, Stella ordered us each an applesauce pumpkin muffin, then captivated me with stories of dancing with Twyla Tharp, her retirement to raise children, her string of husbands, and the teachers that influenced her path back to dance. Each story pulled me further from my money worries and whetted my parched creative mind. When I asked if she had missed dance horribly when she left, she nodded. "But when I missed it enough, I went back. And found Bebe."

I laughed. She made life sound so easy. And perhaps it was:

I, too, had gone back. I felt giddy with inspiration. If I needed money badly enough, I'd get a better job! If I wanted to create, I'd give birth to the ideas starting to kick within me! And I had an advantage over Stella: I'd had Bebe all along. I should never have left her all those years ago. At this instant, through a mist of joy, I could even allow that my return to dance was sweeter for the career hardships I'd faced. To dance, to feel the power of muscular contraction as it propelled me through space —it was all so elemental. Everything that had happened since I'd auditioned for Bebe at Muhlenberg College had led me toward this amazing day, and I couldn't wait to share my appreciation with her. Bebe had always been the one sane voice in my world.

"You mentioned you were taking yoga at Bebe's? I'm surprised to hear she's offering it."

"We need it."

"We?"

Stella nodded while swallowing a bite of muffin. "Bebe takes the class with me."

I thought of the food poster, where Bebe wrote that dance was all we'd ever need. "Back when I first started class, Bebe ran a modern dance studio. Period."

"Hard to argue with her success, though, with the way she's been able to put off surgery. Of course I'd just as soon take a rod down my throat as one up my spine."

I nodded somewhat blankly, unwilling to acknowledge the fact I had no idea what she was talking about. Was this why Bebe was moving awkwardly? Losing spinal strength and mobility would be devastating for a dancer. I'd faced the possibility myself, not too long ago. And here I was chatting over coffee while the woman who shaped me—mostly by telling me not to eat the kind of crap sitting before me—was in crisis.

"I've got to run, Stella. This has been fun."

"But you haven't touched your muffin," she said as I pushed back my chair.

"I'm not hungry. You want it?"

Stella sucked in a breath and put her hand to her mouth. "How thoughtless of me. I forgot about your problem."

"What problem?"

"You don't need to be defensive. An eating disorder is a disease."

How did these words spring from this delightful conversation, with a woman I'd just met? "Where would you pick up such a notion?"

"Well, let's see. We were talking. During intermission, I believe. At the Pennsylvania Ballet, last month. And—I'm sorry, I can't remember how we got on the topic. But I thought it was bulimia."

"Who was there?"

"Bebe. And me, of course. And Margaret MacArthur."

I stood and put on my jacket.

"I didn't mean to make you angry. Eating disorders are more common than you might imagine. A dancer's need to limit calories can become a dangerous obsession. Any dancer could relate."

I wrapped my long scarf several times around my neck, then said, "I am not just any dancer."

# CHAPTER TWENTY-NINE

*T*he wind hit my face full on as I rounded the corner. I leaned into it. My calf muscles burned from that morning's workout. I thought of Bebe's blond frizzle, that brown tooth of honest imperfection I almost missed in her smile. That spine I could always count on for its sturdiness, now breaking down.

Was her mind going as well? Why would Bebe tell anyone I had bulimia? I tried to think if we'd ever shared a meal. And why would she want to hurt me? This was Bebe. My dance teacher. The woman who'd taught me about balance on the dance floor and balance on the plate and the balance between the two—and I'd adhered to her teachings with religious fervor. Why would she spread rumors about me? MacArthur was probably behind this, trying to stir things up so I'd get angry enough to blurt something she could print.

Classes were over for the day, so I used my key to let myself in. Mounting the worn treads, I chastised myself for thinking ill of my mentor. If I was willing to believe Bebe would betray me—someone who'd always had my best interests at heart—what dark intentions might I have had toward myself while up on that balcony? I felt a blackness rise like bile in my throat and swallowed hard against it.

Bebe met me at the top of the stairs. "Oh, it's you, darling." She put her hand to her heart. "Did you forget something?"

Everything in that moment—the sound of Bebe's voice calling me "darling," the sight of her caftan and bare feet, the air still thick with sweat—grounded me. "Yes. I didn't realize it, though, until I sat down for a cup of coffee with Stella."

"Oh?" Bebe smiled, but the effervescence I'd always admired was missing. Her pale blue eyes looked distant and sad.

"I fear I haven't been the best friend after all you've done for me. Stella told me about your back problems. I'm so sorry."

Despite her odd deer-in-the-headlights look, I reached for her. I needed to pull her to me, and show her how much she'd meant to me.

Bebe flinched as my arms encircled her. "I'll be gentle," I whispered.

I felt what I hadn't been able to see: beneath her thin caftan a hard exoskeleton offered the support once provided by a healthy spine. The buckles on the front of the brace pressed against my own ridiculously resilient rib cage. I couldn't help myself—I wondered what other secrets she was keeping. She patted me stiffly on the back and pulled away.

I walked over to the rack and filed copies of *Dance Spirit* and *Dance Magazine* strewn on the coffee table. Tidying the waiting area and cleaning the mirrors were the first responsibilities she'd given me as a teen. "So what put you and Stella and MacArthur together at the Pennsylvania Ballet last month?"

"Balanchine's *Slaughter on Tenth Avenue*. Can't get enough of it. Maggie was reviewing, of course."

"Maggie? You mean Margaret MacArthur?"

"Sorry. I'm too tired to keep her names straight—my back's been deviling me today. I had to take a pill."

"You two are friends?" The floor beneath me seemed to thin, as if I should tread lightly. "Professionally, you mean. Like colleagues."

"I used to take the same ballet class as Maggie and her sister Laura."

It shocked me, the number of people who actually found MacArthur likable. If Bebe's relationship with MacArthur predated her relationship with me, where did her allegiance lie?

I worked to maintain a conversational tone. "Forgive me if this sounds absurd, but you didn't tell MacArthur I had an eating disorder, did you?"

During a noticeable pause, I tried to fit the last three magazines onto a rack already full.

"I may have posed the possibility."

I slapped the magazines back onto the table. "Why?"

"I was trying to figure out why you'd jumped from a building, and why you didn't call once you felt well enough to dance again. It seemed a logical conclusion."

"I meant why the hell would you pose the possibility to the *dance critic*?"

"It was the first time I'd seen her since I returned from South America, and she had more information about you than anyone else did. You may not know, but she's close to someone with an eating disorder. But that's not my story to tell."

"And mine is?"

"Your jump was hardly a quiet statement. It was news, darling. And anything I added was off the record. Maggie knew that."

Maggie, Maggie—the name ate at me. "How could you think so little of me, Bebe? The only thing I've binged on in my life is your advice. You taught me the food mesa. At its base was dance, the only thing I'd ever need. I gave up a job I loved and moved to New York because you pushed me to. And now you make up stories?"

"Your defensiveness speaks for itself, darling. Denial is part of the disease. I've seen it too—"

"You know why I kept trying all those years in New York, when I was so poor I could barely eat? Because you told me I would make it one day. And I didn't want to let you down." I wound the studio key from the ring that had been its home for thirteen years and broke a nail doing so. When I'd first crossed Bebe's threshold, I thought I'd found my place in the world. Among people who recognized my talents and sensibilities. But the dance world was an exclusive club, and it was clear I would never be thin enough, double-jointed enough, or thick-skinned enough to squeeze back in through its gates without also being labeled as mentally ill.

I slapped the key into her palm. "You and Dmitri are quite a pair. I hope you had fun, trying to shape me. I'm done."

Bebe's rattled voice trailed me: "If you walk away, Penny, you'll regret it."

I paused at the top of the stairs. My entire body was steeped in regret. Couldn't she see that? I had just reconnected with movement; the blush of love was still fresh on my skin. But I knew I wasn't strong enough to take on the entire dance world—I hadn't even managed proper relationships with the icons on my mother's wall, let alone my faulty memory of my father and Dmitri's over-inflated ego.

I turned my back on that harsh world and walked back out into the real one.

For a few minutes, back at our apartment, I suffered a horrible sense of déjà vu: that same paralysis I'd experienced when Dance DeLaval left for Europe without me. But this time no stripped-down penthouse imprisoned me. Dry desert might stretch around me on every side, but I stood in an oasis filled with spirit. Beneath that desert, only thinly disguised, still stood a rich jungle. I could almost hear its birds still calling.

No one had stolen my dance life from under me—this time I'd surrendered it. I'd never felt more present in the world than when expressing myself through movement. Yet somehow, in trying to live up to everyone else's expectations, I'd lost myself.

I couldn't let that happen again. For this second chance at life to be worth anything at all, it had to be more meaningful.

To celebrate the fact that movement itself had not betrayed me, I wound my arm over my head, then pushed it through space like the paddle of a windmill, sending the trinkets on Angela's Tree of Life into a satisfying swirl.

I needed a new plan. I sat at the glass table on one of the floor pillows and lit the votives to help me think. As the scent of euca-lyptus hit the air, I remembered Angela's defeat when she pushed that hospital bill toward me on her birthday. It was the lowest I'd ever seen her. I had to keep paying her rent—but how? If only my decision-making was as simple as Stella made hers seem. Or if my destiny had been woven into my genes, like Dmitri's.

Then again, maybe it was. If I needed money, I'd get another job. That's it—I blew out the candles.

I stuffed a few outfits into my dance bag; I'd come back for the rest. While I was happy enough to put some distance between Bebe and me, I hated to abandon Angela while she was so sick. I'd have to leave the bedside attentions to Kandelbaum for now, and figure out later how I could get back to visit. I'd call the Fitness Evolution and leave a message for Joey. They'd be fine. As MacArthur had so kindly pointed out, I'd never fit in there, either.

I rushed over to Suburban Station, my long strides energized by a purpose that made what I was about to do more palatable. I could do this, for love.

I bought a one-way SEPTA ticket, boarded at Suburban Station, and took the train to the end of the line.

# CHAPTER THIRTY

y mother and I sat in Aunt Mary's office for ten minutes. It was fundraising season, and her secretary said they were "crazed." Good. The longer we waited, the better the chances they needed to hire, I figured.

"I don't know why you're doing this," my mother whispered.

"The same reason you have been all these years."

"But I could contact Randall at the Arts Council and see if—"

"I can't waste any more time and energy squeezing the square peg into the round hole. I need a paycheck." I picked up a magazine from Aunt Mary's desk—*The Manufacturing Confectioner*. New trade, new journal. I flipped through it back to front, trying to look studious, not really focusing.

"There's nothing here for you."

Nothing for a dancer, she meant. "You once told me the candy factory was your inheritance."

"It's been in my family since 1892."

"Well, I'm your daughter. Just getting in line." I grabbed a title from one of the articles. "Cocoa sustainability—I guess that's a pretty hot issue, isn't it?"

Uncharacteristically, my mother got up from her chair and paced. "I never thought this day would come," she said. "This feels all wrong."

Well, join the club. I swore I'd never give up the dream, never cop out. But things change. Since I'd met Angela, I'd experienced a kind of love I'd never known before. It was complete and unconditional, and compelled me to help her any way I could. And for this my mother had been an admirable role model: she had earned money reliably, and used plenty of it to support someone who was struggling to make ends meet. It was time I paid that forward. To do so, I was willing to cross the final line between dancer and candy maker—probably the only boundary neither of us had ever challenged.

We heard the door handle and Aunt Mary bolted into the room as if shot from a crossbow. I hadn't seen her in a decade or so, but my first impression was the same: she was a tad more man than woman. She had none of my mother's softness. Broad shoulders strained against her suit.

"Evelyn, Penny. To what do I owe the pleasure?"

"I need a job," I blurted. "I'd like to learn the family business."

"Aren't you a musician or something?"

I felt my mother tense beside me; I spoke quickly before she unloaded. "Not anymore."

She reached into her drawer and took out a job application. "What did you have in mind?"

It hit me that I had no idea what the various jobs in a candy factory actually were. I looked at my mother.

"I thought she might start in Quality Assurance."

Aunt Mary snorted. "You don't bring on someone new and put them at the top, Ev. She knows nothing about the business."

"Aunt Mary's right, Mom." I scanned the pictures on the wall for a job whose nomenclature I might not botch. "I'd be happy with a job on the line. In packing."

"Our packers are highly skilled. We'll see if you can cut it— next week. I'll start you in our mould washing operation. Plan to work fourteen days straight to get the lay of the land."

"That's an insult," my mother said. "You weren't treated like that. Daddy must be turning in his grave."

"If that music degree qualified you to take over HR, then I guess you didn't need me all these years."

"I'm sorry, how many credits shy of that business degree were you? Daddy made me COO for a reason—"

"Don't worry about it, Mom." I looked at Aunt Mary. "Thank you. I'll take it."

Before she hurried from the room, she pushed the application across her desk and told me to bring it along when I showed up for my first shift tomorrow. I stifled a laugh, as I'm sure Aunt Mary would when she read my qualifications for this work.

"Congratulations, Penny," my mother said. "You're now a dishwasher."

I was used to generating heat from inside my body. Now steam from the mould washer applied sweat from the outside in, through white smock, tee shirt, and jeans, until it invaded my lungs. My hair was plastered to my head beneath my net, and despite the gloves and the rubber drain mat upon which I stood, my hands and feet were pickled by day's end. Used mould trays came at me in a steady stream, and I had to spray them with scalding water, load them into the washing machine, take them out, and before putting them in a box, wipe away the water that always collected in the bottom of the cups. The same minimalist movement, over and over.

The humid air made me sleepy. At one point I leaned against the side of the machine to close my eyes for a moment—and awoke to a man slapping my arm. I pulled the muff from my ear to find him yelling at me in Spanish. I slapped the earmuff back into place, nodded, and tried to take deeper breaths for the rest of the shift.

At day's end, my shoes squished as I walked out front to wait for my mother to give me a ride home. The fresh air that hit my lungs tasted both sweet and tart. When my mother came out, she looked at me as if I'd been sprayed with vomit. She didn't ask about my day.

Aunt Mary sequestered me in mould washing the next day as well. Guess I hadn't quite gotten it down yet. My mother's inheritance might have been hers for the taking, but I'd have to earn mine.

When I got home from work, I peeled off my clothes, took a hot shower, and flopped onto my bed. Where previously my muscles hurt from the added demands of dance, my joints now ached from sheer lack of movement. I turned on my phone and found a text message from Kandelbaum. He'd written: "We miss you." I couldn't help but smile.

Starting the third day, Aunt Mary rewarded my fortitude by rotating me through a series of line operations. I was grateful, since my shoulder had begun to complain in the mould washing room. A day of scoring toffee did nothing to silence it, however. The next day, a dull ache migrated down my spine as I bent over a conveyor, distributing potato chips on their way toward a coating of chocolate. No doubt my pain was exacerbated by disgust. I tried not to knead my muscles or otherwise manifest my discomfort. I caught Aunt Mary staring down at me from behind the huge glass windows of the observation deck often enough to know she was watching me. Even in this performance I did not want to disappoint.

I came home to a message from Kandelbaum: "Listen to the god within you, Penny." If only he could see how the god within me was blossoming from hard, unselfish work—at least in the area of my bad knee, which was now the size of a small cantaloupe. The next day, I had to wear a compression stocking on the factory floor while shoveling nonpareils into little bags. I then weighed them on a scale—better them than me, with the extra water weight. It wasn't long before needlelike pain began pricking my feet and legs. Why couldn't my body ever behave? This was my chance to stop courting heartbreak and despair and fulfill a secure, societally acceptable role. My desire was great—I wanted to do this, for my friend. But physically, socially, and intellectually, this job was killing me.

I had to find a way to keep the blood moving before I lost all feeling in my feet. I began a simple step-touch to the rhythm of the moulds being flipped by the machine behind me—shovel, step, pour-touch-bang; weigh, step, adjust-touch-bang. To keep the noise of the pallet loader from driving me mad, I framed its *beep-beep-beep* as a supporting instrument, like a piccolo. I found when I swung my hips side to side, in a gentle mambo, the ache in my lower back eased.

In my peripheral vision, unusual movement up on the observation deck. I hoped it wasn't Aunt Mary throwing a fit. But no, it was a group of schoolchildren on a field trip, pointing at me through the observation deck windows. When I waved to them, they applauded. That had to have been my oddest performance to date. It made me think of Kandelbaum and the pint-sized fan club of his jimmy-covered doughnuts. Who would have thought Kandelbaum and I would end up having this much in common?

On the drive home, my mother said, "You should start an aerobics class at the factory."

"Sure," I lied. With the fierce beauty of dance so newly reawakened in my soul, I couldn't settle for being an exercise instructor any longer.

In the hope of making it through my Saturday shift in the retail store, Friday evening I kept my leg raised and knee iced. I wanted to visit Angela, but couldn't bear to limp into her hospital room with my knee all blown up, looking like more of a patient than she did. And I would not chance her drawing the conclusion that it was my concern for her that had wounded me. I'd have to wait and see her when I got the swelling under control. I called her instead, although with both of us pirating what energy we could to sound happy, our conversation was strained.

The next morning my knee was a little better. I found two new voice mails from Kandelbaum—they must have been delayed coming through. "Angela found this on the Internet, and it's too long for a text message," Kandelbaum said. In the background Angela countered that it wasn't too long, but Kandelbaum said it was if you were all thumbs. Angela said, "It's from Martha Graham." I delighted at the enthusiasm in her that only Kandelbaum could still inspire. Kandelbaum popped back on. "She was a dancer, you know." I shook my head as Angela read a quote I knew so well I finished it along with her: "…and because there is only one of you in all of time, this expression is unique. And if you block it, it will never exist through any other medium and it will be lost."

I cued up the next voice message and was startled when my phone rang right next to my cheek.

At five a.m.

As soon as I connected—before I even spoke—Kandelbaum said, "Thank goodness you're there. It's Angela."

# CHAPTER THIRTY-ONE

*L*ove and panic amplified the pounding of my heart. "I need you to come, Penny," Kandelbaum said. "Now."

"Just a sec." I met my mother at her bedroom door. She'd heard the phone.

"It's Angela. Can you—"

"Of course."

"I hate to ask." My head kicked into overdrive. I re-sorted my day. "I'll be blowing off work, you'll be late, we'll piss off Aunt Mary…"

"On a scale of my worries, pissing off Mary ranks somewhere after the tuning of my piano and the future of the arts in America. Let's go."

I asked Kandelbaum, "Shall I go straight to the hospital?"

"Don't bother," he said. "I'm at the hospital—but Angela isn't. And no one knows where she went."

Instinct told me Kandelbaum was overreacting. There were only a few places Angela would go. The apartment. Mrs. Pope's. The gym. I called each on the drive down, to no avail.

Sitting in the car not knowing about Angela was as painful as standing still in the factory when my body wanted to move. I needed to take action. If someone required me to be still for one more day, I might explode. I pictured myself on the ledge of the high-rise, leaping far into space for the sheer joy of the movement.

"Where could she have gone?" I said. "Any ideas?"

"I don't want to," my mother said, "but I keep thinking of Merce."

"Cunningham?"

"No, Mercy—our cat. Remember when he ran away, and it was a week before our neighbor found him under the—"

"Angela has not crawled off to die." At least that's what I said. But knowing Angela's stubborn thoughtfulness, I wasn't so sure.

My mother dropped me off in front of Independence Sweets so I could see if Kandelbaum had any news. She promised to smooth things over with Aunt Mary, but I wasn't so sure she had control over that.

The place was swamped. A line snaked out the front door and onto the sidewalk, and the people waiting gave me evil looks as I pushed past. When he saw me through the kitchen window, Kandelbaum came out into the bakery to meet me. "Have you found her?"

I shook my head. "Just got here," I said. Despite the uncertain circumstances, a sense of well-being washed through me. I was home. The bakery, with its close walls and enforced intimacy, seemed to smile in welcome. I wouldn't have to stand around and make candy today. I was needed; movement was called for. I'd walk the city if I had to, but I'd find Angela and everything would be fine. Kandelbaum, on the other hand, shook like an alcoholic with the DTs. I sought to reassure him. "One night—not too long ago, as I recall—I came home to an empty apartment because she was missing—"

"Yes, when she was with me. This time she's missing from the hospital. I waited there for a half hour thinking she was off getting some sort of test before a nurse came in to say she wasn't there. She'd signed herself out, AMA."

Against medical advice. Kandelbaum and I had learned all the lingo. "What's the doctor's main concern?"

"Another collapsed lung. She's at high risk." He waved his hands to indicate the crowd. "I can't leave."

"I'll go now."

"I've been at the hospital so much, I gave Pete the day off. My dishwasher hasn't shown up yet. I'm afraid if I close the bakery I'll lose it." Kandelbaum's heavy brows weighed on eyes already worried.

I gave him a quick hug, then brushed the flour off the front of my clothes. "I'll call as soon as I know anything."

I found her on Market Street, some eight blocks from Presby. Curled up on top of her suitcase, out front of Thirtieth Street Station, she could have been taken for a homeless person.

I hugged her and kissed her. "What the hell are you doing here?"

"I missed you." Angela always knew how to take the bluster out of my sails.

"You scared Marty half to death, you know." I hailed a cab and punched in the bakery number. "He went over to see you this morning."

I told Kandelbaum she was okay and that we'd call him back once she got hooked up to some air. But he would not be appeased without hearing from Angela herself. I handed her the phone. "You're going to get chewed out," I said.

But she just listened for a moment, then said, "Let me rest up for today. I'm not going anywhere, I promise. I love you, too."

⤸⤹

"Now. What am I going to do with you?" I asked Angela once I got her attached to her oxygen and home IV back at the apartment.

"Why don't you show me what's in your hand?"

I'd grabbed the circus program and my parents' wedding picture from my bedroom desk on the way out of the house and had been carrying them ever since my mother dropped me off. I sat down next to Angela on her bed and showed her the photo first. "This is—"

"Your father," Angela said. "You look so much like him. Except one thing." She reached over and touched my belly. "He knew how to smile from here."

"Yeah, well." I handed her the circus program. "Look at this."

She set aside the picture while I struggled with the torrent of emotion any mention of my shortcomings always produced. But as she flipped through the circus program, one by one the pages again drew me in.

"Each body has its own beauty," Angela said, affirming my five-year-old sensibility. "As if it had its own purpose." We flipped through the book one more time, this time musing about ways each of the sideshow characters could be the hero of his or her own tale. Even as my best friend's health waned beside me, I was reconnecting to an excitement and hope that felt an awful lot like life.

This time I would not let my father derail me. I rejected his message of shame. And when I did—for the first time—I could finally let myself feel his smile. It took seed within me, and I let its beauty spread through me until its warmth reached my face. Angela looked up suddenly and smiled back. For a long moment, we sat in happy comfort.

But the moment withered and passed. Angela shut the program and said, "I need a favor."

Immediately I was aware of its importance. Angela didn't ask, she gave. "Anything. You know that."

"Take me home."

"For Thanksgiving?"

Angela lay back onto her pile of pillows. "My mother's team is on the verge of a breakthrough…gene transfer therapy…a cure is close…a breath away…if I can just hang on…"

Angela was quiet for a few moments—as quiet as she could be while breathing. She was sucking in and stowing away enough air to power her vocal cords. I recalled an earlier conversation: *When those final hours come, people want to go home.*

"I need to get to her," Angela said.

"Is that why you left the hospital?"

She nodded. "And once Marty catches on to why I'm asking, he's not going to be able to do it."

"I don't have a driver's license." I hated to let her down at this stage of the game, but our options were limited. "We need Marty."

She thought about this. "He'll be able to do it if you're there. You'll keep his hands on the wheel."

⸺

Later, after extracting a promise from Mrs. Pope that she would stay close, I walked to the bakery. The door was locked; it was after closing. I knocked. Kandelbaum's teenage helper, Pete, looked up from his sweeping and let me in.

"He's in the back, counting the drawer."

I went into the kitchen. Kandelbaum had coins and paper money in tidy piles on the counter.

"Isn't this the same counter you roll dough on? Money isn't sanitary, you know."

He finished counting a pile of quarters. "How is she?"

"Stubborn as all get out." I pulled up a stool and tried to sound conversational. "She wants us to take her home. To Maryland, to be with her mother."

He froze, a stack of dimes in one hand, a small sleeve of paper in the other. "Then the end is near. Angela and her mother must both suspect it. Dara told me she rarely leaves the lab these days."

"You talk to Dara?"

"Of course," he said, returning to his task of rolling coins. "She's had me phoning her with reports on Angela's condition."

Apparently, Dara hadn't trusted me enough to ask.

"So," he continued. "Have you discovered an affinity for candy making?"

I laughed. The question was so ludicrous I couldn't answer.

Kandelbaum walked to the back of the kitchen and into the walk-in. On the way back, he picked up a bagged loaf from a rack. "Have you eaten today?"

"Only a peach I nabbed from my mother's kitchen counter. But no thanks, I don't eat white bread."

He took a serrated knife from a rack on the wall and sliced the loaf. His face grew peaceful. "Today you will."

He opened the wine he'd pulled from the walk-in and poured a small amount into two coffee cups. My heart began to flutter. "You're not going to make me pray, are you?"

He held up two slices of the bread. "Angela was dealt such meager physical resources in this life, not much more than flour and sugar and yeast. Yet she has created more of her life than anyone expected. In her honor, Penny. Please. Eat."

He placed the bread in my hand. It still held some warmth at its center. I hadn't noticed my hunger until I caught its scent, and once I had some in my mouth, I had trouble eating at a polite pace. When we finished our slices, Kandelbaum picked up the cups.

"Even as Angela grows weaker, her spirit gets stronger. She gives me hope. Please, Penny, let her give you hope as well. In gratitude that we were all brought together to know such love and friendship, drink."

I took a mouthful and tried to believe something significant had happened. I tried to sense the bread nurturing my body, the wine infusing my soul. But it was all so invisible. It took such faith.

"I don't get it," I said. "This morning, when Angela was missing, you were shaking like a leaf. Now she gives you hope? What changed?"

"Now, we know where she is." He stared for a moment into the bottom of his empty cup. "And hope feels better than despair."

# CHAPTER THIRTY-TWO

Kandelbaum had our dishes washed by the time Pete entered the kitchen to say good night. His presence reminded me of the point of my visit. I asked if he could cover the shop one day that week so Kandelbaum could drive Angela and me down to Bethesda. Pete said he could do it the next afternoon.

"Tomorrow?" In one moment it seemed her illness had worn on so long I couldn't endure, yet in the next, when relief was offered, it came too soon. "Let me check with Angela."

We moved to the front of the shop so I could use the phone. No one answered. I was sure Angela was too shaky to go out, and the phone was right by her bed, and I'd left Mrs. Pope with her.

"That woman is going to be the death of me. I'll find out what's up."

Kandelbaum reached for his jacket. "Maybe she's back at the hospital."

"Or in the shower." I laid a calming hand on his shoulder. "Don't worry, she said she was staying put. Go home and rest. You've got a bit of a drive ahead of you tomorrow."

Back at the apartment, things weren't right. No one was home. I smelled paint. The glass table was askew, votives had tumbled onto the floor, and water had splashed across the rug. An electronic beeping—the phone was off the hook. A tangle of oxygen and IV tubing lay on Angela's bed.

A sound on the stairs startled me. Steps approached. I looked into the hallway and saw Mrs. Pope carrying a bag up the stairs.

"It's you." I steadied myself on the railing.

"What's the matter?"

"Angela isn't here," I said. "The place is a wreck."

Mrs. Pope shuffled past to take a look. "I couldn't have been gone twenty minutes."

"Maybe her mom came for her?" It made no sense the moment I said it. Angela's suitcase, the one she wheeled back and forth to the hospital, lay open on the floor. Inside it, the feathers, baby shoe, and other trinkets from her Tree of Life lay nestled, motion-less, on top of her clothes.

Mrs. Pope leaned over to pick up a spilled jar of paint. "It looks like some sort of struggle—"

"I'll get a sponge."

I opened the bathroom door. Flipped on the light.

Angela was on the floor, propped against the wall, her snow-white blanket clutched in her hand. Her ashen face looked now, in death, the way it must have looked in the last few moments of life—mouth open, eyes wide, fighting for air.

"Oh dear god, not now. Not like this."

Mrs. Pope was at my shoulder, but only for a moment. She called an ambulance, told me not to touch anything. But nothing could keep me from Angela. Even in death she inspired in me a strength I never knew I had. I knelt, cradled her head in my lap, and pressed her eyelids closed.

*Oh Angela, if only you hadn't been alone. If only you hadn't been so frightened.*

I leaned in close and told her a story. That she was home, safe in the bed she slept in as a girl. That her mother understood that the race was over, and had come to her side. That her father was here, too, begging forgiveness. That Marty had brought bread and wine, and we'd joined him in a ritual celebrating her release from pain. That friends from the gym, and all of the patients she'd ever collected at all of the hospitals, and a whole chorus of CF kids that she'd inspired had come to send her off, their breath energizing the air like noisemakers on New Year's Eve. That we'd all wanted a turn holding her hand before she dozed off.

That she did not slip beneath a thick blanket of morphine. She fought well, even at death's doorstep. We'd all been with her as the snow fell, blanketing her body, and she had heard our lullaby.

I stroked her cheeks as their warmth waned. And all the while, my tears fell on her unmoving chest.

Commotion. Sirens, their sudden cessation. A policeman telling me to step away, tossing her blanket to the side. Pulling Angela into the center of the room. Laying her on the blue-green carpet that created our sense of oasis.

Yes, she should rest there. I reached for her blanket. A pillow.

The heels of the officer's hands thrusting into Angela's chest. *What?* Another siren. Banging in the hallway. Paramedics rushing in—"Are either of you family?" The woman shoving gloved fingers into Angela's mouth, the man cutting open her shirt. Mrs. Pope crying, still clutching the bag she'd held when she first came home from the store, the paramedics attaching electrodes to Angela's chest. A scream ripped from mine: "Don't touch her!"

"Does she have a DNR?"

"Yes. Yes." Crawled to her box of medical papers, heart thumping as I reached in, eyes struggling to focus. I had to stop this; it was wrong; she was finally at peace. By the time I produced the paper, they had turned on the EKG.

The room fell silent. The lifeless desert stretched around us in every direction, offering no breeze to stir its sands or resurrect the fallen feathers. We watched with ridiculous hope as the machine whispered its long, flat line.

The rip when the man took the readout for the policeman. The final click as the woman shut off the machine.

"I understand she suffered a long illness. Had you made arrangements?"

Had she suffered a long illness? All I could remember just then was the way she fought for a long life, and how long she'd waited for love.

Kandelbaum. The thought of him broke my heart. I couldn't tell him any of this by phone. And he didn't need to witness the evidence of her final, frantic struggle. Better he saw her once she was all put together, at the funeral. I opened a drawer and pulled out her black socks.

Eventually, they all packed up. Emergency over. In the absence of known arrangements, they told us to await the coroner. After they left, I pulled the sheet back from Angela's face—after watching her struggle for air for so long, I couldn't take the look of it.

So quiet without the rattle of her lungs, the hiss of her oxygen. Mrs. Pope and I sat beside her.

One last time, I squeezed her cool hand, its inability to respond frightening and absolute. She wore the bracelet Kandelbaum had placed on her wrist. She'd never taken it off. She'd been so excited to show it to me, flipping her wrist this way and that, I hadn't noticed: there weren't two strands of entwined pearls, as I'd first thought. There were three. Like three lives that had come together to make something bigger, more complex, and more beautiful than any one of them could have created alone.

Mrs. Pope pulled a bottle of lotion from the bag she'd been holding. "Her skin was dry," she said. I nodded. She squirted the lotion onto her hands, pulled back the sheet, and rubbed it into Angela's arms. I recognized the familiar juniper scent. "There you go, dear," she muttered. "There, there."

Soon men arrived to lift Angela onto a stretcher and wheel her to the door. Her final exit.

For a moment, I thought of slipping the bracelet off her wrist. But I didn't need to keep it any more than I needed to cling to Angela's body. Both were mere symbols of something more vital anyway. The coroner wheeled her out with the bracelet right where Kandelbaum had wanted it.

When I shut the door, I looked to her Tree of Life. Habit, I guessed. I wanted the toss of its feathers to register the tornado wringing out my heart—already forgetting that Angela herself had stripped the tree.

Mrs. Pope left. I had work to do. Work I couldn't bear to do, but work I would do, for Angela. Before I left the apartment, I took one last look around. So much of her still here. Her tiny camels caught my eye—one an awkward, humpbacked sawhorse with a blue smile—and above, a sky whose clouds even looked sunny. The empty branches of her Tree of Life reached toward me, yearning to be filled. I hit the dimmer, setting the sun on the place where we'd rested. One of us waiting for death, the other, for life.

# CHAPTER THIRTY-THREE

He answered my knock from the other side of the door. It could have been quite late. I'd lost track.

"Who is it?"

"It's me."

When he opened the door, I knew I'd never hold him at arm's length again. I choked out the name I'd rarely used. "Marty."

"She's gone," he said.

I nodded. I'd gotten sleepy in the taxi and walked the final blocks to his apartment so the air could slap me awake. Now the coldness and rigidity of the pavements had seeped up my legs. Only an empty doorframe stood between us, but he seemed so far away.

In one step, he was out in the hallway, and we collapsed against one another.

We sat on the couch while I told him what little I knew about Angela's last moments on earth.

"She was beautiful in every way," he said. "You shouldn't be alone. And I...I...Stay here tonight," he said. "Would you?"

I reached into my coat pocket for a tissue and felt the luggage tag I'd picked up from the floor. "I need to call Angela's mother."

"I could do it if you want."

"I need to do it," I told him.

I dialed Angela's mother from the bedroom. For longer than I thought possible, she spoke in her typical measured manner, gathering facts and repeating them, perhaps attempting to convince herself through even tones that nothing all that earth-shattering had happened.

"So it's over," she said, at last. "Our work."

"But I understand you may be close to a cure."

A brief silence. "It could be years yet. My daughter was my reason for working."

"Angela would want you to help those you can."

"Penny, I know what you've been doing for her, and how taxing it's been. In my absence, you have been a mother to her—"

I heard a sound, something guttural. From her, from me, both. We'd been skating on thin emotional ice and we fell through, flailing for a firm surface. I let the sobs wash over me.

Dara was wrong. It was Angela, with her stubborn, unconditional love for life, who had mothered me.

"Thank you, Penny, for being there. And taking care of…of her tonight."

"What else can I do for you, Dr. Reed? Help you contact friends?"

"I can't think. I'm very tired."

"I'm at Marty's." My voice faltered, recovered. "Do you want to speak to him? Would it help?" I broke then. "He loved her so much—"

"I can't. Not yet. Save the things on her Tree of Life, would you?"

"They're already packed. She was going to bring them. She tried, you know. She wanted to get to you."

Marty's rumpled sheets chilled me through my clothes; I shivered while sleep refused me. I went to the bedroom door and peeked out. He was asleep, a tissue clutched in his hand. I crept into the living room and lay next to him on the sofa bed. His warmth broke down the adrenaline that had propelled me through the evening hours, and I slept.

When the phone woke us in the morning, I was spooning his back, my arm curled around his waist. He looked around the room as if he didn't know where he was, or where to find the phone.

"You going to get that?" The flannel shirt covering his back muffled my words.

He answered in the bedroom but soon poked his head back through the door.

"It's Dara Reed. She hasn't slept. She says she's been waiting till a decent hour to call back and talk to you."

When I got off the phone, I followed the smell of brewing coffee and toasted bread into the kitchen.

"What did Dara say?"

I sat down at his little table. "She's been making arrangements all night."

"This is good," he said. "So many will want to know about the service."

I picked up my toast and set it back down. "It's not what you think. She took her."

"Dr. Reed took Angela?"

I nodded, still unable to believe what she'd told me. "Her voice was so…animated. She said that after we spoke last night, she realized I was right—her work with Angela didn't need to end. Angela could still help with the research. Her daughter may have left clues that could still be a gift. She started listing things: her lungs, her pancreas, her intestines, her DNA."

"An autopsy."

"Her body is already in Maryland. Dara isn't planning a funeral." Sorrow seized my chest. "I didn't call you to come see her and now there won't be a service. Gone so fast…it's like she left a vacuum… no air." I held on to him, gasping. "I'm so sorry, Marty. So, so sorry."

When I had calmed, he whispered, "The god in Angela was fierce. Her spirit had become so large her little body couldn't hold it any longer. I had no need to see it."

I couldn't eat much. Instead, I played with the grapes in the amber glass compote in the center of the table. My mother had one like it when I was growing up. I used to pinch the plastic grapes and watch them spring back to their former shape, until their resilience failed. They eventually looked more like raisins, and she threw them away. When I pinched one of Marty's grapes, the skin split and light green flesh burst from it. I shouldn't have been as startled as I was; Marty wouldn't have anything fake in his house. I let the juice run down my wrist. "Angela wouldn't want a funeral. She would have wanted a…" I couldn't say the word, at first. I felt entitled to my grief. But I forced it, for Angela, from a mouth twisted with pain. "A celebration."

"Maybe when we are feeling better."

"Yes."

We moved to the couch. Since Pete was already set to cover the bakery for the day, we shared stories about Angela until our words slowed and our eyelids closed and we slept, propped against one another, until late afternoon.

We stopped by a liquor store for some empty boxes and took them to the apartment. I expected a more dramatic scene upon my return—yellow police tape over the door, or perhaps the door once again standing mysteriously open, as if God were coming for Marty and me, too—but everything was locked up tight. Then again, sometimes drama takes a more subtle form: Mrs. Pope had brought up Angela's newspaper. It waited for her by our door.

I pulled out clean clothes and went into the kitchen to change. I could bet Mrs. Pope had scrubbed the bathroom, but I couldn't go in. Not yet. Marty packed away Angela's personal effects, which he would ship down to Dara's. She owned so little. Angela was used to living from a suitcase, and her dearest mementos were either small enough to hang from twisted wire or incorporated into the very walls of the room. I tried to lift a file box from the bottom shelf of the bookcase and couldn't. Inside I found years and years of neatly filed medical bills. A three-box chronicle of a life with cystic fibrosis, told in payments. We lugged everything down to his van. The sun was already starting to set.

"Do you want me to hang around?" he said. "It's getting late and UPS won't be open until tomorrow anyway, so if you need me to stay—"

"I'm fine," I said, giving him a hug, although I wasn't sure of it. Something inside me created an uncomfortable pressure. I couldn't stay still any longer.

Did I know what I was looking for? My feet thought so. They took me to Bebe's. On a Sunday evening, the studio could be all mine. It wasn't until my hand searched my jacket that I remembered—I'd surrendered the key to this life. I patted my pocket as if I'd meant to do that and walked on.

Blocks later, I found what I needed at the city's very heart, tucked beneath the historic curves of the City Hall complex. A ball of spotlights dangling from its arch lent the space below a theatrical flair. A lone sax keened from somewhere deeper within the complex; I was where I needed to be.

Would my body hold up? I articulated my feet while prancing in place. Took a few lunging strides. Circled my arms. I had aches and limitations, to be sure, but could no longer allow them to define me. I had to trust this body now. Tonight.

Because I needed, more than any other time in my life, to dance.

I wanted Angela close to my heart, but I already carried so

much inside I couldn't accommodate this new grief. The angry serpent in my belly coiled to strike. I wrenched my shoulders left and whipped my arm to the right.

My own deprivation contracted my abdomen. I fought back with a mighty arch, flinging unwanted memory out through my fingertips: that false food, filling me up without feeding me. Hurt, angst, guilt, shame—their explosive energy rose again within me. Not up my throat, but out through limbs whose choppy movements tugged me this way and that. Misguided love became a spiraling floor pattern that wound inward until I had to reverse just to keep moving. Mistreatment and betrayal shot from me in a dart of long leaps. Holding on to them was no longer an option; I couldn't fight them in that tight, dark space. I needed them out where I could work with them.

The golden light from above glanced off an elbow, a foot, a curve. The globe of spotlights cast multiple versions of me onto the sidewalk. I did not dance alone. My partners were night spirits, a confluence of shadow and light.

Blood surged through me, rejuvenating my muscles and releasing the fluids trapped in my legs. Life itself rushed in and out of my lungs. I was changing the space in this city. With each steamy exhalation, I extended my influence into it; with every breath I took, it became more a part of me.

I stripped down to a camisole and flung my sweater to the side. I swung my upper body down and up for the joy of it, to feel the icy air caress my neck and the crook in my elbow and the underside of my wrist.

Space, the beloved partner I turned my back on when I'd

forsaken my career in dance. It had been with me all along, waiting for me to awake to its presence.

I lifted my fingers to stroke the air. To thank it for this dance. To give myself to it, as to a long-lost lover. Beyond the arch, the Avenue of the Arts stretched before me. Colored lights flashed up its facades, joining my dance: Purple. Blue. Green. Car headlights swept over me like follow spots. Small crowds had gathered on the corners across the circle, pointing and staring in my direction.

High above me, a bell tolled the hour. I stood still, panting, allowing air to reach the newly exposed surfaces within me. Nine times it rang, one for each of the months I'd known and loved Angela. Its vibrations pierced me through, and my grief for Angela rushed in.

Perhaps sensing the show was over, a smattering of applause drifted from across the street.

I pulled back into the shadows and wept.

# CHAPTER THIRTY-FOUR

*I* slept at the apartment that night, alone.

The next day, seeing Marty was the only thing I could think of that might make me feel better, so I stopped by the bakery. Customers milled around on the sidewalk. The lights were out and a sign hung on the door: CLOSED.

❧

I stopped in to see Mrs. Pope. When I joined her at her kitchen table, Shakespeare said, "Spread 'em, baby." I winced at the awkward intrusion; Mrs. Pope cried. I reached for her hand.

"Angela taught him that," she said. "She'd say, 'Spread 'em, baby,' and when he opened his beak, she'd give him one of his papaya treats."

We drifted, each to our own thoughts. The smell of something cooking made my mouth water—I craned to see a pot of soup on the stove.

It was only nine in the morning, but my stomach growled audibly. "It's split pea, Angela's favorite." She got up and ladled some into a bowl. "It was on my mind when I woke up. She always put a heaping tablespoon of sour cream in the middle." She offered me the soup bowl; out of habitual adherence to the food mesa, I shook my head and stood to leave.

So weak my hand jittered on the doorknob. "Squawk—spread 'em, baby!" Heard Angela's voice: *You've got to find a way to feed yourself.* I felt so empty without her. I returned to the table and pulled the bowl toward me. Added a small dollop of sour cream. In honor of Angela, and in gratitude for my own life, I spread my lips and, spoon shaking, started to feed myself.

I curled up on Angela's bed and looked up at the blue sky she'd painted, willing one of the puffs to move, to carry me away. I was not myself. All day I'd nursed a wicked craving by nibbling nuts and raisins. Or was it thirst? The arid wasteland depicted on these walls left me parched. Everything felt wrong—the empty shelves, the votives that once again floated in their pool above the evergreen rug yet no longer created a sense of oasis. The Tree of Life, whose lively branches were now empty, broken hangers.

My eye caught something white still hanging on her Tree of Life. I climbed down to get it, eager to run my fingertips over anything she had once loved enough to live for.

It was the cardboard from the fastnacht box I'd signed. I lifted the yarn from the branch and read the words I'd written when we first met.

*For Angela—*
*Thanks for making me feel like a rock star.*
*Yours, Penelope Sparrow*

I sat in the chair at her desk, the one built in below my bed. Why was this greasy box top the one thing she hadn't wanted to take with her? Tears blurred my vision as I ripped away the stained pieces.

The phone rang, but I let the machine screen the call.

"Angela Reed, who's Angela Reed?" I recognized the serrated edge of Aunt Mary's voice. "Evelyn told me this was the number for Penelope Sparrow. Well, Angela Reed, you can tell Penny that if she'd had her cell on, she could have thanked me yesterday for allowing her a personal day after missing her Saturday shift. But two days is something else. A career is a commitment. For better or for worse, sickness and health, let's get richer not poorer, all that. Her mother will have the pay we owe her. And to formalize things? She's fired."

By the time I finished ripping away the grease spots, I had centered the autograph within a jagged star.

I smiled. Not a smile born of bemusement, but a smile that grew from deep within me, from that place where the heart beats and movement begins.

❧

I mounted the stairs to Bebe's as quietly as I could. Passing the front studio, I caught a few familiar faces, but that class was not my destination. I strode into the empty back studio as if I owned it. I opened my arms and walked around the room, asking Angela—or the space—or the god of the space, as Marty would say—what to do with love that won't quit, hope that won't die, a deep hunger that cannot be sated.

I turned from the mirror so I could listen for my inner voice—*please, let me hear something*—but the voices were everywhere, not just within me but also around me. Feeding me a constant stream of images. I calmed myself by closing my eyes and concentrating on the air entering and exiting my own lungs, accenting its rhythm by hissing slightly on the exhale. In, out. In, out. As I began to dance, the breath magnified. In, out, louder.

Then much louder—I was not breathing alone. I turned to find Stella, Luke, Vincent, Jeannie, Gayle, and Rhonda behind me. They had slipped into the studio and were following my every move, every breath. The last rays of the setting sun angled through the door from the window in the reception area and bounced off their bodies. My peripheral vision caught disembodied curves and angles skidding through the space. Beautiful, gold-tinged night spirits.

I tried to funnel all I was feeling into the thin confines of words. "I lost my best friend…"

"Shh. Turn around." Vincent whispered.

"Don't lose it," added Stella.

Bebe appeared in the doorway. I was struck with shame for the way I'd treated her. So much remained unspoken between us. I turned to her. She was my mentor and this was her space; I would not continue without her blessing. Behind me, the others waited.

She left. Was abandonment to be my sentence? If so, I deserved it. The music ended in the front studio. Bebe returned, and the rest of the students from the front studio filled in behind her. When their footfalls ceased, I watched as her silhouetted head nodded.

My mother said I'd always done my best work in front of an audience, and I only hoped she was right. No longer alone, I reversed the molting process to step into my own long-discarded skin: Penelope Sparrow, choreographer.

It felt fragile at first. But opening myself to the images and letting them rush through me felt so much better than fighting them off. If I allowed Angela to continue growing inside me, and let her spirit effervesce through my movement, she would live on in the form of love.

I took a few steps back, stretched my arm as if gathering the strength of the group, and carried it forward into the night.

# CHAPTER THIRTY-FIVE

*W*e worked three evenings straight on what would become my uncertain tribute to Angela's life: a dance, to be performed for a select audience on Saturday in Bebe's studio. Bebe had sanctioned my rehearsal schedule, then stayed out of my way. Friday night around ten-thirty p.m., after my dancers had left, she entered the back studio with black material draped over her forearm. "You could wear this," she said.

I held up the material so it took shape. "Isn't this your recital dress?"

"I finally stepped on the hem and ripped it," she said. "If you sew it up, no one would notice."

"But I'm so much bigger than you are." The self-deprecation was so habitual the words flew out before I realized how Bebe might take them.

She arched an eyebrow in a way that seemed to say she knew everything, from my first abuses of her food mesa all the way through that shameful retching into my mother's sink. "So it will be ankle length instead of floor length."

"Bebe," I said. "I shouldn't have gotten so angry with you. That day I gave the key back. I know you care."

She flicked some dust from the shoulders of the dress and studied it. "We may be more alike than you think. Try on the dress, you'll see."

"I just wished you could have talked to me about it instead of MacArthur. She watches me so closely. Like...like..."

"Both judge and jury? Why do you think I wear caftans, darling?" A small, crooked smile twisted her lips. "Draping is everything."

I slipped into the dressing room. The material still had a stretch to it that accommodated and supported. I went into the studio to check it out in the full-length mirror. The extra material sewn into the skirt disguised my hips, and its weight invited me to twirl. I lifted my leg and watched the cloth spread like the wings of a great falcon.

Bebe came through the doorway, the hesitation in her step more obvious at the end of the day. "Do you like it?"

"It makes me feel..." I choked on the next word. It was one I'd never before spoken in reference to myself.

I started the piece from the beginning, watching my reflection in the mirror. By adding its own heft and flow to movements I held dear, the dress enhanced the dance. The feeling once again welled inside me, strong and true. I tried again: "It makes me feel...beautiful."

I looked at Bebe in the mirror. She was standing behind me, watching.

"I don't care for the all-black, though. I want this to be a celebration. Do you mind if I—?

"Do whatever you want with it."

Bebe's voice suddenly sounded coarse. I took it for indecision and looked over at her. "I could just do something temporary if you want."

"It's yours. Damn, Penny." She shook her head. "It's good to see you dancing again."

It was after eleven when we heard my mother's footsteps climbing the stairs to the studio. Bebe and I went out into the reception area to meet her. The long flight of stairs no longer winded her, I realized, when she immediately started talking. "Okay, explain the big mystery."

"I'm sorry, Mom, I should have told you. By the time I knew I wanted to quit the factory, Aunt Mary was already firing me."

She laughed. "Well, that was no mystery. I mean, why all the specific instructions? And why did you want me to come all the way down here at this time of night?" She looked me over, head to toe. "The dress looks great, though."

"I'll head upstairs," Bebe said. "You two stay as long as you need to."

"It's good to see you, Bebe," my mother said. "No need to run off." Then my mother turned to me with concern on her face. "Is there, Penny?"

Bebe touched my mother's arm and headed up the stairs to her little apartment. I took my mother's hand, led her into the front studio, and sat her at the piano. She looked at me with a dozen questions in her eyes.

"It's Angela," I said. I hadn't been able to leave the news on her answering machine.

She whispered my name in a way that threatened to crack me open. I took a deep breath.

"I'm barely holding it together, Mom. I want your help, and I'm sorry, but I'll have to call the shots."

"You want my help." My mother looked wary. "Whatever you need."

"I need you not to react when I tell you I've been taking class again." She took in a short, sharp breath, then pressed her lips together. "And I've choreographed a tribute to Angela that some new dance friends will perform—"

At this my mother's eyes widened.

"With me."

"Sweet Mary…"

"And I wondered if we could work up an accompaniment you could play on the piano. Nothing fancy, most of the piece is designed to be performed in silence."

My mother sat for a moment, seemingly consumed with not reacting, practicing the silence. "Is that all?"

"And I'd like you to perform it with us. Here, tomorrow afternoon."

She considered this for a moment. "You must know other musicians. Why me?"

"No one is more sensitive to my movement style. Word has it you've been studying it for years."

She nodded, ran her fingers silently across the keys, and looked up at me. "Is it okay if I smile?"

My mother and I worked late, and then she slept over. After I returned from an early morning errand, we visited the fabric stores on South Fourth to get some supplies. I dawdled, feasting on colors and textures I'd denied myself too long. I hadn't been to Fabric Row since shopping for the set materials for *No Brainer* some ten months earlier. But that was as an emissary for Dmitri. This was for Angela—and me.

When we got back to the apartment, my mother started in on one project while I covered the floor with newspapers and laid the dress out flat. Its full skirt fanned up past the bottom of its arms. I mended the hem and lined up the fabric paints I had purchased, in six shades of blue and green. I sat down at the desk and sketched first, as Angela would have, then applied a river of color to the dress that began beneath my heart and poured down the front of the dress in swirls.

Later that day, eager to see what it looked like, I tried on the still-damp dress and studied it in the studio mirror. The imagery in the swirl of color spoke to me: I had created an oasis in the middle of my pain.

"Guests," Bebe announced. I checked the clock on the wall—our performance would soon begin. Bebe led the contingent from the Fitness Evolution—Joey, Suzie, Haley, and Karen—to their seats. Mrs. Pope scuttled in next. To each of them Bebe gave one of the blue and green scarves my mother had made. Waiting became more awkward with the audience half-assembled. I moved into the reception area.

I could have asked others—special doctors and nurses, clients at the gym, other CF patients. But if I had invited everyone who loved Angela, no room would remain for the dancers.

At this point, I waited for just one more.

Still unable to reach Marty, I'd taken drastic measures: I'd roused myself from a deep, four-hour sleep at four-thirty that morning and walked over to the foot of the Independence Suites. The city is a dark vacuum at that hour, powering up with a streetlight here and a lone bulb there, readying itself to suck commuters in for another day of business.

Through the bakery window, I saw him before he saw me. His nose and eyes looked puffy. I startled him when I rapped on the front door.

"Looks as if you haven't slept all week," I said.

"Have you?"

"Where've you been?"

"Lost."

I waited. "That's all you're going to say?"

He stretched his arms, one to either side. "God has gone missing." He did not look to the heavens—he directed his words to me. "I've been walking all over this city looking. In the temple, the mosque, every historic church I can find. Even the Cathedral Basilica of Saints Peter and Paul."

I sat him down and went behind the counter to pour him a cup of coffee. "And it didn't help?"

Marty shook his head. "All I saw were walls. Walls of stone, walls of brick, walls of wood. Remnants of God's inspiration. But I felt nothing."

I asked him to visit one last building, tonight, as a special favor to both Angela and me. I knew the facade wouldn't compare in architectural wonder to the other structures he'd visited, but I was hoping to move him with what he might find inside.

Heavy footfalls on the stairs announced his arrival. When he rounded the turn at the top, I saw he was not alone. Holding tight to his arm was Dara Reed. She looked older, as if her steely core had gone spongy.

"I hope it wasn't inappropriate to bring a guest," Marty said.

Leaning forward, I pressed my cheek, for a long moment, to his. I squeezed Dr. Reed's hand and Bebe breezed in.

"Is that everyone?" Bebe said, while handing out more scarves. "You can take a seat through this door. It's time to begin."

I went into the dressing room. The dancers were ready, each in a black leotard and tights accented with one of the vibrant scarves. Vincent had twisted his into a wristband; Jeannie was so tiny she was able to wrap hers all the way around her waist. Luke fashioned his into a headband; Gayle tied hers around her ponytail; Rhonda tied hers at the ankle. Stella spread most of hers flat beneath her leotard, and pulled one corner into view, provocatively, at the hip. The added color was meant to symbolize Angela's enduring spirit, but the air was so somber—so funereal—my walk slowed when I entered. If I'd thought about the grief I'd accumulated in my life, I'd never be able to work my way from under it, but I chose not to engage my thoughts. Angela had changed my heart, and from this source I found the buoyancy for my next words: "Hey, this is a celebration, remember?"

My mother sat on a stool in front of a sink with a mirror above it, dabbing powder onto her face. I stood behind her and rested my chin on top of her head. When I'd extended my mysterious request to come down for the weekend and meet me at Bebe's, I'd asked her to bring along "something nice"—she was now wearing a tailored plum suit that set off her new, slimmer profile. She had one of the bright blue scarves tied jauntily at the throat. She looked great.

"How you doing, kiddo?" my mother asked my reflection.

We smiled at each other in the mirror. My mother had green eyes, just like mine. I had wasted too many years fearing my similarities to her. I kissed the top of her head and squeezed her soft shoulders. "Thanks for being here."

A cell phone rang.

"Good reminder," I said. "Could everyone shut off their cells?"

Stella reached into her bag and flipped open her phone. "It's for you," she said, and handed it to me.

"It's your cell. How could it be for me?"

"Oh Penny, just take it."

I put her phone to my ear. "Hello?"

"Am I speaking with Penelope Sparrow?" It was a woman—
that much I could tell.

"Yes."

"Twyla Tharp here." I looked over at Stella to see if this was a
practical joke, but her face was lit up in a way that would have been
difficult to fake.

"Oh my god," I said. Eloquently.

"Stella told me about your special performance tonight. Your
new endeavor sounds fascinating."

I had to consciously slow my breath; I was close to hyperven-
tilating. "Thank you so much for calling. I can't believe it. This
means so much to me—"

"But I realize this is no time to talk. Best of luck, Penelope."

I handed Stella her phone. "Our new endeavor?"

"I've learned to plan for success," she said.

I could give no thought to future plans. My heart was full
with the moment at hand, and I wanted to give it my entire
focus. But I did give Stella a quick hug before saying, "It's time.
Let's go."

Once out in the reception area, I folded my upper body onto
my thighs for one last stretch. I couldn't remember when I last
performed in such a small space for such a small audience. I felt
vulnerable and exposed, a downy sparrow without its pinfeathers.
Other than Bebe and my mother, none of the assembled guests
knew me as a dancer.

Before we entered the space, I pulled my dancers close
around me. I looked at their faces and their eagerness warmed
me to the point that my joints felt like they were coming

unglued. The dancers looked to me for inspiration; I looked to someone else.

"For Angela."

I went into the studio to address the audience. At my request, Rhonda and Vincent had closed the curtains in front of the mirrors and placed chairs in front of them. I was glad I wouldn't have to watch myself do what I was about to do. I wanted to feel it, fully.

I heard the dancers out in the hall murmuring "*Merde*." One of the odder dance traditions, they were wishing each other luck—"break a leg" being a tad too real for some dancers—by licking their fingers and touching one another's necks while saying the French word for "shit."

I looked at the audience and tried to read their faces. Karen and Haley: impatient. Joey and Suzie: attentive, curious. Bebe beamed.

"I had to do something." These were the only words of introduction I could think of. I looked to Dara, then Marty. Their hollow bodies propped one another up. "Please stay for refreshments after the performance. If you are moved to make a contribution to the Cystic Fibrosis Foundation in Angela's memory, you'll see an envelope marked for that purpose. This is *Air for Angela*."

My mother walked in and took a seat at the piano; my dancers followed. I joined them at the front of their triangle, upstage right.

The group awaited my signal; the first move was mine. But I couldn't budge. Everything about performing suddenly felt unfamiliar. As if I, too, were lost.

My role in this dance was not simply a job I hoped to execute well. Failure could not be made up for in the next town on tour. This was my one and only chance to express fully, in my own language, my love for Angela. The stakes were high, the audience close.

I looked over at my mother. She smiled, nodded.

It was then I noticed the uninvited guests. Standing in the doorway—respectfully outside the room, yet fully in view: Margaret MacArthur, and a taller woman I'd never met.

Anger flashed through my body, but I would not let MacArthur ruin what I hoped to do.

I closed my eyes to clear my mind and create a strong image of Angela. When I reopened them I was ready to begin.

I pursed my lips to accentuate the sound and breathed…in two counts—out, two. Next to me, Stella and Vincent joined in…in, two—out, two. Rhonda and Gayle…in, two—and out, two. By the time Luke and Jeannie added in, we had built a sound big enough that the audience must have been breathing right along with us. With one last inhale and a turn, we gave our bodies to the dance.

We danced big, as an organic unit. Angela's days were not limited to her "expiration date," nor was her spirit bound by her disease, so we refused to let the confines of the room or the length of our limbs constrict our performance. We depended upon one another to sustain our counterbalances, in all their improbable asymmetry. Passes across the studio floor were powered by winds of fate we could almost feel. Above skittering feet, our hands sought to create something controlled and beautiful with fingers that tasted the air. My mother's improvised score was sparse and stark and served to define the periods of silence. At the climax of the piece, our spirited swirls must have churned air all the way to the corner of Tenth and Lombard. Then we pulled it back in, making our way out of the piece by reversing the way it had begun—with fewer and fewer of us breathing audibly—until it was my lone, extended exhale that feathered into stillness.

Stillness, yes. But within it every single part of me—body, mind, and soul—thrummed with life. This celebration for Angela had produced within me a joy unlike any I'd never known.

We were still holding these final positions when a lone pair of clapping hands broke the spell we'd cast. Audience and performers turned their heads as one.

The hands belonged to Margaret MacArthur, watching from the doorway. "Brava, Penelope. Lovely." Following her example, others joined her applause.

It occurred to me she might be drunk—what else would explain her nerve? I crossed the room, took her hand, and pulled her through the reception area to the top of the stairs.

"What are you doing here? This is a private gathering."

Her eyes were clear when she spoke. "Why does it matter, Penelope? You make dance, I watch dance. Just because your motivations were private doesn't mean the work should be."

The woman with MacArthur distracted me. Her feet were still planted by the door to the studio, but she rocked back and forth, small movements becoming larger, as if powering up her body for the tour de force of putting one foot in front of the other. Her slow yet captivating movements mocked my urgency to get rid of MacArthur. Once the woman's steps gained momentum, she walked to MacArthur's side.

"Penelope Sparrow, I'd like you to meet my sister, Laura."

I took Laura's limp hand from her side and shook it. "I'm glad we had a chance to meet," I said. She was tall like me and overweight, with thin, lifeless hair. I recalled MacArthur saying how difficult it was for her to be seen in public and wondered if in all the years since she had stopped dancing, Laura had ever once sat in an audience beside her sister.

Laura's face was damp. She said, "It was good."

"Forgive me, Penelope," MacArthur said. "But when I heard you'd be dancing, I thought I'd better come. Who knows if I'll ever get the opportunity again?" She turned to go and slipped a palm-sized notebook into her purse.

I called after her. "You aren't writing about this."

She guided Laura down the stairs. "You can't control that."

When I turned around, Bebe and Stella were coming out of the studio.

"Damn it, Bebe. I can't believe you told her about this."

"But I didn't—"

"Don't blame her." Stella stepped forward. "It was me."

This revelation struck me momentarily mute.

"And I won't apologize. You got applause from Margaret MacArthur! I hear she never applauds. Just leaves her aisle seat as soon as the music stops."

"And you deserve the attention," Bebe said. "You always have. Get right back in the studio and make another piece." She pressed something into my hand—my key.

"But I'm not a choreographer." I remembered those painful days trying to create for Dance DeLaval, and how I came up empty. If only this key could unlock my creativity.

"What do you call what you just did?"

"I had special motivation. This was a tribute to a friend."

"It was so much more. You allowed your feelings to spill onto the stage in a way everyone in that room could relate to. Angela inspired it, perhaps, but the specifics you chose made a universal statement. That is the art of choreography."

The female dancers had moved into the dressing room, and I joined them to change. I pulled off Debe's dress, now damp with sweat. I hung it on a hanger.

"I wonder if Angela liked it," Rhonda said. She threw a glance toward Stella. "And what Twyla would have thought?"

"I feel certain she'd say that if you had that much fun, you should do it again."

"Okay, Stella, I hear you."

When I turned to get my clothes, Rhonda pointed toward me and said, "Would you look at that."

The other dancers paused and looked at my nakedness. Was it the darkened skin left behind by my bruising that had grabbed their attention? I looked over my shoulder and into the mirror— for the first time in a long time—and was surprised to see that I no longer wore the stain of my fall. Over the course of the past year, new pale skin had grown in its place. "What, Rhonda? What is it?"

They weren't staring at my back—it was my front. I looked down—the damp paint from my costume had transferred to my skin a river of blue and green that spilled from my heart to my right hip, as if Angela had painted it.

In that moment, I loved her even more.

"Tell us, were you happy with the performance?" Jeannie said.

I shook off the bad taste MacArthur's presence always left in my mouth. "Very. Thank you so much. How do you guys feel?"

They threw out words: *Energized. Open. Light. Whole.* I felt them all. I washed my face and ran a washcloth over the rest of my body, careful not to disturb the unintentional artwork transferred to my skin.

By the time I came back out, my coworkers from the Fitness Evolution were ready to leave. "Sorry we can't stay longer," Joey said when I approached. "It was…really something. Thanks for inviting us."

I searched his face. "You had no idea what to make of the piece, did you?"

"The piece." He straightened up as if to align his thoughts. "Well, actually, I, uh—no. Not a clue. But I'm glad we got the chance to pay our respects to Mrs. Reed."

"If that's the type of dancing you're used to, it explains your weird music," Haley said. "Looks like you could show us a few moves."

"I liked that one part where you tipped your upper body over and bent your knee up to the side," said Karen. "I couldn't have come up with anything like that."

"Really?" I wasn't being facetious—when I was immersed in the images that Angela's life presented to me, the movement came so naturally it didn't seem like any special talent. "But you knew Angela, and how much effort it took her to get through the day. It was all based on that."

"What can I say?" Karen said. "My brain doesn't work that way. If it had been up to me, those dancers would have been doing a kick line to 'Staying Alive.'"

"Watching dance isn't about picking up moves," I said. "It's about noting the relationships between motion and space and rhythm to absorb a greater concept."

"I liked your dress," Karen said. "It made you look less hippy."

It was then Haley said, "It was like life. It began with the breath, and ended with the breath."

She turned to leave, but I caught her arm. "Hey—you really understood."

Haley shrugged her size-two shoulders. "I was sitting by the woman in the doorway. The one in the red hat? She comes into the gym sometimes? She said that to the woman standing next to her."

The dancers and some guests had gathered at the table where Bebe had set out juice, vegetables, and dip. Only Luke, Vincent, and Stella were eating. I hugged the dancers and offered each their colorful scarf as a memento of the evening, wishing I could pay them more.

My mother scooted over and threw her arms around me and said, "That's my girl."

"Thanks for being here for me. Here, and there. You know, always."

"How long do you think you'll be? We've got a long drive."

I hated to tell her this now, with others around. "I'm staying down here, Mom. I'm taking on Angela's lease. I can't explain how, but I'll figure something out."

She touched my cheek, and smiled.

"I'll call you," I said. "Soon."

"It was a lovely piece. Don't stop taking class, though. Some of your articulations were rusty—"

"Mo-om."

She opened her arms. "Come here. I mean, don't stop." She gave me an extra squeeze. "Don't ever stop."

I joined Mrs. Pope, Dara Reed, and Marty, who stood near the refreshment table talking quietly. "You're not eating," I said awkwardly, not willing to admit—even to myself—how very much their opinions of the performance mattered to me.

"We're not here for that kind of sustenance," Marty said. He had an emerald scarf tucked in the pocket of his white short-sleeved shirt.

Dara, in an uncharacteristically demonstrative gesture, took both my hands in hers. "I came to see you and Marty and Mrs. Pope, because when Angela arrived…when I saw the body, which shouldn't faze me, I'm a doctor…but she's my daughter…it was like I finally woke up and realized she was gone. I don't know anything about dance, but tonight you honored the little girl I raised, and the extraordinary effort it took for her to grow into a woman. A tribute made with your body—it was just the right thing." She started to tremble. I put my arms around her to hold her together. She whispered, "Angela tried so hard to wait for me. I just ran out of time."

"Come now, Dara, a cup of soup and some rest will do you good," said Mrs. Pope. Dara would be staying the night with her. "Let's go, dear."

Bebe said she'd see me on Monday, asked me to lock up, and headed up to her apartment.

That left only Marty and me.

# CHAPTER THIRTY-SIX

*W*e laughed when we both started to speak at the same time. Always the gentleman, Marty backed off first. "After you."

"Shall we sit?" I motioned to the chairs by Bebe's desk.

"Not here," Marty said. "May we go into the studio?"

We sat in two of the audience chairs. Marty looked around the room—at the barres, the high windows, the curtains hiding the mirrors, the floor, the empty space. "So this is where you came from."

I nodded. When his eyes at last rested upon me, they were moist.

"Penny. You look so beautiful tonight." His voice sounded different. Softer, fuller. "That's not the most important thing I have to say, but it was at the front of my head so I had to move it out of the way."

He wrapped both of my hands in his, but said nothing. The silence became unbearable. I buckled.

"You didn't like it?"

He looked down at our entwined hands and cleared his throat to speak.

Oh no. If he hadn't liked the performance, I would fall all over again, and this time I might not survive. Angela and Marty were so precious to me; I didn't want to let either of them down. A tear thinned on its path down Marty's face, regrouped at his jawline, then dropped to the scarf in his breast pocket. It spread a jagged stain.

After a moment, he said, "I suppose if there were words to express it, we wouldn't need movement."

I let out the breath I was holding. He looked at each of the walls, then closed his eyes and took a deep breath. "She's here, Penny. In this room. Now. I can feel her."

I looked around, too, for evidence. "Angela?" I whispered.

"No." He opened his eyes, his usual peaceful expression restored. "God."

A good night's sleep remained elusive. Margaret MacArthur seemed to have come to bed with me. I tried to focus on the more rewarding aspects of the evening. Like Dara Reed showing up. My mother's restrained and stunning score. Laura MacArthur's damp face. What Marty said, and didn't say. Yet I couldn't drown out MacArthur's slow, arrogant clapping. Somehow, this woman always made me feel as if I hadn't done quite enough.

At least the dancers enjoyed themselves. And I did get a chance to say good-bye to Angela on my own terms. And we raised money for CF—wait.

What had I done with that fundraising envelope? I prayed Bebe had taken it. I didn't remember seeing it on my way out of the studio.

I climbed down from bed, turned on the light, and rummaged through my dance bag. Good thing I did, too, because the damp towel wadded inside would have stunk up everything by morning. As I pushed aside the makeup kit, everything fell out of it. I pawed around through lipstick, eyeliner, and foundation. Beneath my huge jar of cold cream, I found two envelopes.

The one on top was the invitation to MacArthur's luncheon. Why would I care to celebrate her career? "Penelope and Guest"— she was probably hoping I'd coax Dmitri back to the country. I tore it in two and deposited the scraps where they belonged—in the trashcan beneath the deolu.

I turned my attention to the second envelope. "Donations for the Cystic Fibrosis Foundation." Bebe must have put it in my bag.

It was disappointingly thin. What had I expected to find— fistfuls of cash? Nine checks don't take up very much room.

The first, from the account of Vincent Mattei, was for $600. The memo line said "from your dancers." They must have chipped in—how unexpected, and kind, considering they'd volunteered their time. The second, a corporate check from the Fitness Evolution, was made out for $2,500. I flipped through the checks, tallying as I went—our little gathering had raised close to $5,000.

It was the last check in the pile, which at $500 matched my own mother's, that surprised me the most. The memo: In memory of Angela Reed. The signature: Margaret MacArthur.

I lit the votives and sat before them until the sun rose. I sat still, simply feeling what it was like to be alone in the apartment. A deep ache grew within me.

Around five a.m., I heard the flop of a newspaper hitting the floor in the hallway. Another day without Angela. I knew Mrs. Pope felt the loss deeply. But I didn't rush to the door. I was sure I looked like hell and didn't want to scare her. Or Angela's mother, should she already be up. It was no added comfort to have Dara in the building—it made me think of all the times Angela would have appreciated having her here.

In time I did retrieve the paper, and placed it on the new stack growing beside Angela's bed. Since her death, I'd been unable to cancel her subscription or toss any of them away.

A teaser over the headline caught my eye: "A Dancer's Struggle with Body Image: Inside on E1."

My breath caught. No—it must be the lack of sleep. Or the way the candlelight was playing across the page.

I flipped on the light and opened to the Arts & Entertainment section, and there it was: the article MacArthur had been threatening to write for a year now. Beneath a large photo of a thin girl in leotard and tights considering her reflection in a funhouse mirror was the title, "The Body and Its Image: A Dancer's Silent Struggle." Underneath, MacArthur's byline. Adrenaline shot through me. How could she air my problems this way, when she knew how I felt about it? And now, of all times?

The article began:

*The mirror is prominent in every studio, front and center, like a reflective altar. The supplicant moves before it, checking every line of her body against an unattainable standard of perfection. She seeks beauty, forgiveness for her flaws, and redemption through the movement she offers. Whatever encouraging feedback a teacher or choreographer might give will matter less than what the mirror tells her. It sees what others cannot.*

*Each year, all across a nation obsessed with thinness, the mirror's relentless criticism will drive some seven million impressionable young women to the brink of life-threatening eating disorders. Among those at highest risk are dancers.*

*Few professional dancers agreed to be quoted on this topic. Yet I've been following one brave woman for about a year now, and she has finally agreed to speak. Her story began right here, at a studio on Philadelphia's South Tenth Street.*

That's it, I thought. I'm suing. I had never been diagnosed with an eating disorder. I'd been so careful never to push it that far. Anything I'd ever said to her was off the record.

*We stood in the school's front studio, whose vaulted ceiling and high windows funneled in a heavenly light that belied her inner demons. The dancer offered her comments not to me, but to her reflection in the mirror: "The turnout isn't complete, the foot won't fully point, there isn't enough height to the arabesque or sleekness to the thigh or flatness to the belly."*

That lying bitch! I did not say that. As to the heavenly light, the only time I ever saw her at Bebe's was at Angela's tribute. On a moonless night.

*As she spoke, she stretched her bare foot along the floor until it reached a full point, then looked down at it and studied it as if she'd never seen it before. The cracks in her heel calluses were parched rivulets of white. "We reach for a perfection that is unobtainable and then damn ourselves for falling short. We try our best then push harder and then again harder—and when the results don't material-ize, we unleash our anger at our own bodies." She closed the open leg and looked back to the mirror. "The pursuit of perfection is daunting and exhausting with no end in sight. Yet in spite of ourselves, we get up each day and try, while the joy of movement drains from our lives."*

Wow. MacArthur did capture my experience. Rather eloquently. But you can't go around making up quotes.

I'd only wanted to be light enough that my inadequacies wouldn't weigh me down. To finally see beauty when I looked in the mirror.

*The dancer turned to me and said, "Those are the words of a bulimic."*

*She has kept up a façade for years, she says, but her broken body now betrays its secret. More importantly, she says, her secret nearly cost her a relationship with a former protégé that was dear to her. This inspired her, finally, to go public with a disease most often kept hidden. She hopes to stop girls from trying to squeeze themselves into a prescribed and unforgiving mold, where pain—both psychic and physical—is the only possible result.*

Oh my god…

*Her name is Bebe Browning.*

I dropped the paper and tried to absorb what I'd read. My whole life, I'd taken as gospel the nutritional advice of a bulimic. How had I missed this? Then I thought of that bad tooth. The unknown contours of her body, disguised by caftans roomy enough to hide a back brace.

Her suspicions about me.

How hard it must have been for Bebe to share her story. I would not have been so brave.

*Years of psychotherapy have helped Browning address her eating disorder, but the calcium leached from her bones when she was young created a poor foundation for the hormonal changes of late middle age. Her soul still yearns to dance even as her body now struggles to climb to her third floor walk-up. A recent trip to South America on a study grant will probably be her last. At this point, medication can do only so much. Spinal fracture is a constant threat.*

*Browning says if she can keep one young woman from hating her own body the way she did hers, it will be worth speaking out.*

*"A dancer must work with her body, not against it," she says. "One cannot evoke the symphony of life with only one kind of instrument. We need the tubas just as much as we need the piccolos."*

I scanned the rest of the article. Nowhere did MacArthur mention either my name or "Fall of a Sparrow"—she got her story while avoiding all reference to me. Relief washed through me and I laughed. Who did I think I was? I was certainly not the center of the Philadelphia arts world. I was one of millions of women attempting to reconcile their bodies with societal ideals.

I saw it, then: by writing this article, MacArthur hadn't ruined my return to the dance world at all. If anything, she had rolled out the red carpet for the concept of nonconformist dancers.

I was done fighting my body—that war could have no victor. I yearned for the fullness of expression a range of body types could offer, and had so many ideas I couldn't wait to get working on them. I laughed again. One day I'd have to thank MacArthur.

I went back and dug her invitation out of the trash, pieced it together, and read it again.

The Bellevue—my mother would love this sort of shindig. That would be her idea of the high society life, rubbing elbows with the prominent dance personalities whose careers she had followed so closely. "Penelope and Guest"—what would MacArthur think if I had my mother in tow?

Of course, Stella would love it, too. Her waylaid career had cut short opportunities to connect with like-minded artists. Vincent, Luke, Jeannie, Gayle, Rhonda—they had all proved their artistry last night; MacArthur had implied as much with her applause.

Hell, all of these dancers deserved a place at that luncheon, sitting in a fancy ballroom, sipping wine and eating food no doubt paid for by funds our own Commonwealth had allocated to support the arts. Each of the colleagues I danced with tonight had something unique to offer, and as much heart and raw expressive power as the long and leggy clones from the Balanchine factory.

I went to Angela's desk, found some Scotch tape, and repaired the RSVP card. Next to "Name," I wrote "Penelope Sparrow."

On the line below, next to "Number attending," I filled in the number eight and the name of my new company.

# CHAPTER THIRTY-SEVEN

*T*hree months later. Ten minutes before curtain. The premiere of Real People Dance would soon begin, at a venue right on Philadelphia's Avenue of the Arts. For safety's sake, I pushed against the large prop we'd secured to the floor behind the first wing. It felt sturdy.

The union stage manager waved me over. "Listen to this," he said, removing his headset.

"You deal with it," I snapped. "That's why I hired you."

He reached over and plopped the headset over my ears.

"Penny? Is that you? I don't know if she's there, I don't know how to use this thing."

I heard tapping. "Marty? Where are you?"

"Oh good, it's Penny. I'm in the lighting booth."

This is the type of problem you have when working with volunteers. He was supposed to be manning the *ticket* booth.

I couldn't fault his enthusiasm, though. He may have known nothing about putting on a performance, but he had been selling program ads for us at recent Chamber of Commerce meetings, throwing in a free raisin brioche for each business that took out a $50 ad in our program.

I fiddled with the headset. Marty was having trouble hearing me, so I spoke more loudly into the mouthpiece. "If you're in the lighting booth, who's manning the ticket window?"

"That's what I wanted to tell you, Penny. We're sold out."

I had to take a deep breath and hold it—my makeup job was at stake. As recently as noon the day before, I'd panicked when hearing we were less than half sold. What kind of philanthropic foundation would cut us a check if the theater ended up half empty? We would look like idiots.

"Do you hear the coughing?" he said.

I was inured to the muffled sounds of coughing and throat clearing on the other side of the curtain as people took their seats. Audiences always do that, knowing that soon the lights will go down and they must be silent. But now that he mentioned it, there was more coughing than one might expect.

"I sent a letter to Dara Reed, who forwarded it to a colleague at Children's. I didn't want to mention it in case nothing came of it. But he looped his e-mail with it or something and contacted people with CF. In my letter, I told them about the piece you did for Angela and quite a few have responded. I'm looking down on an audience dotted with portable oxygen tanks as we speak."

In light of such wonderful news, I dared to ask. "Did any critics show up?"

"Only one, Penny. I'm sorry."

"Which one?"

"Margaret MacArthur is sitting in L-101. She wants you to know she brought her sister—it's the first performance Laura has agreed to attend in thirty years. I'm sorry we didn't get more critics. Maybe next time."

I let out the breath I was holding. "No problem. How about our other guests?" I had reserved two half-rows for representatives of the organizations Stella had approached for funding.

"Of course I gave up their seats to paying customers."

"Kandelbaum—"

"Just kidding. All present—your friend Bebe ushered them in herself. Dance well, Penny."

Two minutes to curtain. I began to climb the prop—a tall stepladder.

Choreographing material for the show had been the most fun I'd ever had. I created four pieces, two for each half. Jeannie, Gayle, and I had a blast putting together *Triplets*. Who would have thought somebody as depressed as I'd been in the past year might have a flair for comedy? Only an audience would be able to tell us whether it was really funny, but we cracked ourselves up. We had played with the physics of our partnering so I could lift Gayle, Gayle could lift Jeannie, and little Jeannie could lift me. The unison sections, with women of such different sizes, intrigued us.

The larger work took longer to come together, but it ended up being such a good introduction to the individual attributes of the full company that I placed it first on the program. We had been generating movement material on a couple of different themes—balance, risk-taking, and stepping into the unknown—but it wasn't until it came together that I became aware of its autobiographical elements.

It would start with a splash—a spectacular mosh pit dive from the top of this ladder. The audience wouldn't see me until I fell through the proscenium frame and into the arms of my dancers onstage, who would not visibly prepare to receive me. A dramatic, carefully orchestrated, yet random-seeming event that, if pulled off without a hitch, should have people talking for some time to come.

I reached the top and tested my balance. The dancers worked off their jitters by marking the opening pattern one more time. The overhead lights cut out, leaving only a work light that bounced off their body parts while they moved. Disembodied curves and angles skidded through the space. Beautiful, gold-tinged night spirits.

My perception shifted. I no longer stood on a ladder, but on the balcony at the Independence Suites. The darkness toyed with my vision, and instead of the stage, eight feet below, I faced a distant street as I had just over a year before. I remembered feeling nothing when I looked down through the blackness.

Yes. I remembered.

I watched as one of my hands turned off the lights in the apartment I'd shared with Dmitri, and the other shut the sliding glass door that would separate me from the double bed I could no longer bear to use.

Something dug into my thigh—the aluminum straps on the balcony's lone redwood chair where I sat, long ago stripped for winter. I found this increasingly satisfying as my nose and chin grew numb. Beside me, the breeze rattled an empty drying rack.

The sky pressed down with the threat of snow. Clouds blew in overhead, but I couldn't see them; it was too dark. The stars simply went out, one by one.

A rustle. The breeze scooted a piece of paper across the balcony's floor and slapped it against the wall. I picked it up. I knew from its texture it was a handbill from my last performance with Dance DeLaval, less than two months earlier.

I couldn't see—it was too dark—but I knew Dmitri was pictured on it. I ran my hand over it, searching for him, but felt only the gloss of its cold surface. I tried to call up the exhilaration of working beside him, and could not. I tried to remember the way my pores would tighten when he'd move his hand across my skin, but could not. The storehouse of images I relied upon to sustain me as a performing artist was empty. Love, hate, anger, betrayal— they were simple accumulations of letters now, as devoid of meaning as my life.

I had relinquished too much, and when Dmitri left the country, he had taken with him whatever was left of me.

I stood and looked down. A half-block away was the Avenue of the Arts. The backbone of my life. Most of its theaters were dark that Monday. The frigid streets looked vacant.

And then—my breath caught when I remembered this—I sat on the wall and swung my legs to the other side. I told myself not to look down, and when I did, a wave of dizziness threatened. I was awed by the height and afraid to feel anything, especially the dizziness, so I shifted my focus to a narrow ledge below me. I almost lost my grip when I eased my body toward it—my sweater rode up, and the way I'd rolled down the waist of my knit pants caused them to catch on the balcony's concrete lip. My elbow smacked into the wall and I had to struggle to hang on. I did struggle to hang on.

I reached the ledge and planted my feet upon it, perfectly turned out. I fit icy fingers over the top of the wall behind me, arched forward, and awaited one last chance for…something.

One by one my knuckles gave way, and when the first snow-flakes drifted from the sky, so did I.

There was no jump. I didn't fall. I just let go.

And then, the miracle: instead of a downward rush, I felt a force push upward against me. As if the space itself partnered me and slowed my descent. I no longer felt afraid. I felt loved.

The stage manager snapped me back into the moment when he knocked three times at the bottom of my ladder and held up all his fingers.

⸎

Ten seconds to curtain.

I once told Angela I'd never be able to climb up high again, but here I was, boldly perched a whole level higher than the warning sticker that said "Danger: Do not stand on or above this step—you can lose your balance." I pictured her on the ladder at our apartment, painting the sky.

I looked down at the dancers as they took their places. They were the heart of what I wanted to say and the distinctive arms and legs capable of its expression. They looked up, now, and awaited my cue. I raised my arm to set them in motion.

The audience hushed, the curtain rose. My musical director was seated at the piano. With a nod from me, my mother began to play. The dancers swarmed beneath me; I felt the tension as they forced themselves not to catch my eye. They were counting on me to make this happen, and I desperately wanted to. I wanted to make good dances. I wanted to move people. I wanted to inspire Margaret MacArthur to leap from her seat and rush to the *Sentinel* to write about it. I wanted to touch that place, deep within Laura MacArthur, where movement begins. I wanted the philanthropists to consider us a worthy investment. I wanted to inspire the CF kids to lead full, productive lives. I wanted to prove to myself, in Dmitri's absence, that my creativity was sacred and worth protecting.

All that wanting. I started to shake, deep down in my center of gravity. But my hips created a solid foundation that would not crumble. My thighs were strong and would not collapse.

I took a breath so deep that the air tickled my lungs. I let it out on a slow count—Angela. Mom. Dad. Bebe. Marty. My dancers. Dmitri. Yes, even Dmitri, dancing right now for a different audience in another country, who for all his faults, once told me that I was more than just another body. My heart filled and pounded, my soul hungered for life.

Invoking the god within all of them to sustain me, I jumped.

# READING GROUP GUIDE

1. Do you think a person could survive a fourteen-story fall? Discuss cases covered by the media about miraculous survival. How do you think such a thing would affect your own life?

2. What is your perception of Penny as a dancer? Do you think she has what it takes to make it in a performance career? Why or why not?

3. Evelyn clearly believed in her daughter from a young age and provided Penny with the special training she needed to succeed in her field. What other endeavors require a similar focus? Compare and contrast the risks of focused training and generalized education in today's society.

4. After Angela's previous roommate dies, she tells Penny that the woman "just couldn't hold on any longer." How much power do you believe we can have over our own deaths? Discuss experiences you might have with dying people who may have seemed to "let go."

5. Penny thinks she has walked a safe line between "low calorie" and "nutritionally healthy." Do you think Penny has an

eating disorder? Why or why not? How would you define "eating disorder"?

6. Penny says, "Restricting was the closest feeling I'd ever had to self-love." What do you think she meant by that? How is restricting also like self-hate?

7. Each of the novel's characters has a different notion about the relationship between eating and body image. In this regard, compare and contrast Penny, Bebe, Evelyn, Margaret MacArthur, Angela, and Kandelbaum. As you became more aware of the limitations of your body, with which of these characters did your thoughts and/or influences align? Did those thoughts help or hinder you? Have your thoughts changed as an adult?

8. Discuss the influence on Penny's developing body image provided by her mother, her father, Miss Judith, and Bebe.

9. Laura MacArthur was told outright that she had to lose weight to be in the company. In Penny's case, was the pressure to be thin from the dance world, or from within Penny? In what way does our society at large send signals to all women about the ideal body image? Have you ever felt pressure—at work, at school, or at home—to have a body that was different in a significant way than yours? How did you deal with it?

10. Penny describes the scale as "my partner in crime, my lover, and my nemesis." What does this mean? Do you have a relationship with the scale? If yes, what is it, and does it influence your day-to-day lifestyle?

11. Angela and Kandelbaum are Penny's first friends outside the dance world. Why is this significant? What drew the three

of them into such a fast friendship? What were they able to give to one another?

12. Discuss the structure of the novel. How did the author use the opening situation to raise the two questions that drive the novel's interweaving storylines? Was the technique effective in drawing the novel to a satisfactory conclusion?

13. While reading, when did you first suspect Penny might have tried to kill herself? Now that you've finished the book, do you still think Penny tried to commit suicide? Why or why not?

14. In the psych ward, Penny says, "Just because I suffered traumatic memory loss didn't mean I was out of my mind. If anything, I was out of my body." What do you think she means by this?

15. Is Dmitri a villain? In what ways did he support Penny's dream, and in what ways did he hinder her? And when he put his own interests first—was that a bad thing? Whose fault was it that she had to part ways with the company?

16. Penny says, "My passion for dance and my passion for Dmitri could no longer be separated; I didn't know where one ended and the other began." Explain what that means and how this issue is related to her relationships with her mother and her own body.

17. Discuss the role that muscle memory plays in Penny's healing. Have you ever experienced a time when your muscles seemingly remembered something your brain had forgotten?

18. Discuss the concept of space as a dancer's partner. What role does "space" play in other arts: Visual? Architecture? Music? Literature?

19. How was Evelyn's weight a metaphor in her relationship with Penny? Why was their relationship so strained, and when did it start to heal?

20. Compare and contrast Kandelbaum and Penny where it concerns faith and other kinds of support. Do you think Kandelbaum would have considered suicide if he was left on his own after losing Angela? Was Penny able to set a foundation of faith that she could rely upon in the future?

21. Penny and Angela discuss a wrestling match between body and soul at death's doorstep. Compare Angela's death with what Penny remembers of her actions before the fall. Are body and soul separate entities, or are they inextricably interwoven?

22. Compare the Penelope Sparrow who moved to New York to start auditioning to the same character at the end. How has she changed? Name a few of the major turning points that stick out to you.

23. What is Penny hoping to accomplish with Real People Dance? Do you think the world will accept them? In what ways is America's tolerance for individual body differences and intolerance for unhealthy lifestyles becoming more apparent?

24. Were you surprised that Penny hires her mother as musical director for the new company? Do you think they'll be able to work together? What has changed about their relationship?

25. What do you think Penny's life will be like after the close of the book? In what ways will it be different from the career she envisioned as a child, and in what ways will it differ from her experience with Dance DeLaval? If she and Dmitri meet again, what do you think that would be like?

# A CONVERSATION
# WITH THE AUTHOR

1. *The Art of Falling* **is set in the world of modern dance. Do you have a background in dance?**

    Yes. I came to it late—when I was sixteen—but realized at once I'd been looking for it my whole life. While working toward a bachelor's in biology education and a master's in health and physical education at Miami University (Ohio), modern dance became an important part of my life. Freshman year, I went along with a nervous but eminently more qualified classmate to the dance company auditions—she didn't make it, and I did! (Would have loved to be a fly on the wall when that decision was made!) I began to choreograph my sophomore year and continued through my early thirties to create some twenty-five major works, several of them commissions. I gave up dance in my midthirties due to some ongoing back problems and never returned.

2. **Were you a writer all that time as well?**

    I came to writing through dance. I was in a performance in Allentown, Pennsylvania, that our company publicist was trying to get reviewed by the local daily paper. Turns out they didn't have a dance critic. I applied for the position and ended up reviewing dance and writing arts features for nineteen years. I always thought of my role as translating movement into words so that people would have a way to talk about what they'd seen. But I was also filling my mind with oodles of creative images and inspiration from the amazing people I interviewed, and when I decided to nurture my fledgling attempts at writing fiction, criticizing other artists no longer felt right. That, and I couldn't take one more *Nutcracker*.

3.  **Why the switch to fiction?**

I got caught up in the kind of real-life drama that demands close attention. In 1997, after fifteen years of marriage, my first husband committed suicide. Once the shock abated, I thought, what does a writer do to make sense of that kind of event? I had no interest in writing nonfiction pieces about suicide. I wrote some memoir. Ultimately, I decided fiction best fulfilled my lingering need to create, from the chaos of these events, a better story.

4.  **How did you get the idea to write Penelope Sparrow's story?**

Her story sprung from my need to try to relate to what my husband had done. Anyone familiar with the stages of grief knows of its anger, and I felt plenty of that after the suicide. How could he do this to our sons, who were only eight and ten at the time? How could he do this to me? I sensed that the only path to forgiveness lay in empathy. Yet

I'd always been an optimist, looking for the silver lining in every situation. I had no way to relate to someone getting so low that they'd consider self-destruction.

What would that take? I began with a dancer at war with her body so that an ongoing inner conflict underscored all else. I dismantled her support system. Took away the father she adored and left her with the burden of a mother who lived through her. I put her in a competitive world with harsh expectations about a woman's body and where true friendships can be hard to come by. Took away her mentor. I gave her natural talent and exclusive training, then whittled away at her faith and resolve with years of rejection. Then I gave her a taste of success, a taste of love, then yanked both away at the same time. Finally, at that point, I thought, *maybe*.

Then an odd thing happened. When I made Penny's loss of movement physical, she started to fight back. I knew then that I could not only bring her back from the edge, but from the depths of her fall.

5. **That fourteen-story fall! How did you come up with that?**

That part is based on an actual newspaper account. The story didn't name the woman or how she survived, only that she walked away with only a broken arm. And it was the second time she had tried to kill herself! And fourteen stories— she was not messing around. I wondered what it would take for her to get the message that it might not be her time. That led to all sorts of questions that I wove into the story.

6. **How long did it take you to write this book?**

Eight years. One reason I think it took me so long is that Penelope and I were sharing our journey of healing. At times we boosted each other forward, but I'm sure there were times we held each other back. In earlier drafts, she was a much angrier woman. I knew I'd be finished when her story became one I admired.

Never in question, though, was giving up. I deeply love each of these characters (yes, even Dmitri!) and was determined to see their story told.

Like Penelope, I now give myself credit for something I used to take for granted—every day, I choose life. This notion is empowering.

7. **In *The Art of Falling*, which character do you feel most closely connected to?**

I'd be curious what readers might guess about this one! Of course each character carries a spark from me. I wouldn't be who I am today without Penelope's courage, the nurturing of a mentor like Bebe, or the unconditional love from a best friend like Angela. I understand Margaret MacArthur all too well, whose arts advocacy is underappreciated because of her search for excellence. My heart swells when I think of Evelyn Sparrow, content to watch her daughter from the wings just to know she's happy. But my absolute favorite is…Marty Kandelbaum. I love life's hidden philosophers, and my idea of a perfect afternoon would be hanging out with him to gain his perspective on things I struggle with. Okay, and maybe to taste some of his baked goodies.

8. **What do you love most about writing?**

Writing fiction challenges me on every single level that I value. I love to research and gain new knowledge. I love to ask questions until I find answers. I love to tell stories. I love to figure out why people do what they do. I'm a voracious problem solver. As much as I love interacting with other people, I also enjoy long stretches of time alone. I am hopelessly enamored with words, and I love the way good writing communicates on multiple levels. I love that fresh burst of creativity that becomes the first draft, but even more, I love the conscious application of craft during revision. I love the complexity a novel allows. I love the inherent paradox of writing tight while writing long.

For me, writing is not an escape. It's the opposite. It demands that I dive headfirst into puddles of conflict others might choose to sidestep. I must scratch and dig until I unearth emotional truths and then find a way to convey them so that a reader I've never met can share the same journey. Some days, I crank out several new pages, and some days, I sit and steam over one paragraph because I'm just not sure that I've yet found or communicated the truth I sought.

But my writing is absolutely a celebration of life. I am not the type of person who will flit through her days partying. I need to figure some things out. I need to leave a footprint. I need meaning, and my writing is how I create it. And, because writing offers me so much of what I seek in life, I think it's fun!

9. **Who are some of your favorite authors and why?**

I'm glad this question isn't about my favorite novels because there are too many of them! I sample widely from bestselling literature to keep my finger on the pulse of what is selling. I love talking about the books I read with others so I'd call all of it "book club fiction"—if all that's left to discuss when I turn the last page is "whodunit," the book isn't for me.

Although I've only read select authors deeply, if you told me that any of the following had a new book out, I'd purchase it today without bothering to read the jacket cover: Ann Patchett, Anna Quindlen, Barbara Kingsolver, Kelly Simmons, Amy Tan, Janet Fitch, Regina McBride, Roland Merullo, Wally Lamb, and Margot Livesey.

10. **What advice would you give to aspiring writers?**

Anyone who is already writing knows that long stretches will require that you keep your hopes aloft by whatever means possible. For that reason, many will give up. So hanging in there while constantly improving is a prerequisite to success.

But while you're powering up your career, and honoring that nagging voice to write every day, don't completely wall yourself off in your writing nook. Steep yourself in life experience. Your imagination will need that springboard.

# ACKNOWLEDGMENTS

This novel required countless hours of studio rehearsal, production planning, and backstage help before it was ready for its premiere. I had a stubborn love for these characters and wanted to see their story told, it's true, but I also persevered for my children Jackson and Marty, my selflessly supportive husband, Dave, and my entire extended family: in memory of Ron, I needed to share with you a more hopeful story, and wouldn't have wanted to let a single one of you down.

To my crew of advance readers, thank you for your generous input. Certain readers need special recognition because their early enthusiasm sustained me, and because their contributions improved and shaped this novel. Linda Beltz Glaser, you have been my wise adviser and stalwart supporter almost from the start. Thank you for your keen sensitivity and devotion to this story. Cindie Feldman, you now know what your early cheerleading meant to me. Sandra Graham, passing your admirable standards helped embolden me to go the distance. For key developmental guidance, I must thank Ellen Gallow, Jackson Williams, Anne Dumville, Barbara Haines Howett, Fern J. Hill, Jack Althouse,

V. Z. Byram, Juilene Osbourne-McKnight, Patricia McAndrew, Anne Dubuisson Anderson, D. L. Wilson, and Emily Rapoport. Janice Gable Bashman's incisive pen saw me through the end game—thanks, Janice.

For meeting all my writing needs through the years, I must thank my colleagues at the Greater Lehigh Valley Writers Group, as well as my colleagues at Pennwriters, the Sewanee Writers' Conference, and the Writers Coffeehouse run by the Philly Liar's Club. I am indebted to Lana Kay Rosenberg for the whacky moment in which she approved my addition to the ranks of Miami University Dance Theatre: it changed my life. Ironically, it was in the wordless medium of dance that I discovered my voice. Lana Kay, this book would not exist without your nurturing.

For help with research, I'd like to thank Chas Byram, EMT-P; Amanda Craft, RN, BSN; Megan Mercurio, MS; and Doug Gallow, AIA, NCARB. Maureen Chrest generously shared her experience of mothering children with CF, and the nursing staff at the Penn Lung Center at Penn Presbyterian Medical Center answered many questions. I also made use of the following resources: the Cystic Fibrosis Foundation website, www.cff.org; the Avenue of the Arts website, www.avenueofthearts.org; *How We Die: Reflections on Life's Final Chapter* by Sherwin B. Nuland; and *Breathing for a Living: A Memoir* by Laura Rothenburg. Any misapplication of the information provided is my burden to bear.

My gratitude to all of the Philadelphia mural artists whose inspired contributions beautify the city, but specifically those whose works made their way into this novel: Meg Saligman for "Philadelphia Muses," and Isaiah Zagar, whose Magic Gardens includes the mosaic, "Art Is the Center of the Real World." Another artist to whom I am indebted is Eileen Carey, for designing this dramatic, breathtaking cover.

My final *révérence* is in deepest thanks to the team that put this novel on stage and focused the spotlight: my agent, Katie Shea, my editors Shana Drehs and Anna Klenke, and the rest of the hardworking team at Sourcebooks. Because of you, the curtain rises, and I wait in the wings with breathless anticipation.

# ABOUT THE AUTHOR

Kathryn Craft, a former dance teacher and choreographer, wrote dance criticism for nineteen years for *The Morning Call* daily newspaper in Allentown, Pennsylvania. She has a bachelor's in biology education and a master's in health and physical education with a dance concentration from Miami University (Ohio). Long a leader in the dance and literary scenes in southeastern

Photo Credit: Jackson Williams

Pennsylvania, she mentors other writers through workshops and writing retreats. She has lived in New York, Maryland, Ohio, New Jersey, and Pennsylvania, and now lives with her husband in Doylestown, Pennsylvania. *The Art of Falling* is her first novel. You can contact her through her website, www.kathryncraft.com.